Arguing

with the

Dead

Alex Nye

Arguing with the Dead

© Alex Nye 2019

Cover: Graeme Clarke
Published by:

Fledgling Press Ltd.
1 Milton Rd West
Edinburgh
EH15 1LA

www.fledglingpress.co.uk

ISBN 9781912280261

Printed and bound by:

MBM Print SCS Ltd, Glasgow

MIX
Paper from
responsible sources
FSC
www.fsc.org
FSC® C117931

For Micah and Martha, Liz, Nick and my husband Joe...
With much love.

Acknowledgements

I finished writing *Arguing with the Dead* in 2017, so there are many biographies of Mary Shelley published since then that I was not able to take advantage of. However, I would like to acknowledge the debt I owe Charlotte Gordon and her fabulous book, *Romantic Outlaws*, which gave me tremendous insight into the life of Mary Shelley and her mother, Mary Wollstonecraft, and whose incredible research I inevitably benefited from.

Also, to editors Tonne Brekke and Jon Mee who put together *Mary Wollstonecraft's Letters Written in Sweden, Norway and Denmark*. I would also like to mention Lesley McDowell's insightful and beautifully-written novel, *Unfashioned Creatures*, published by Saraband in 2013.

A huge thank you again to Clare Cain at Fledgling Press for her encouragement, enthusiasm and continual support: to friends throughout Scotland's writing community (I won't name them in case anyone is left out); also to friends and family who make positive noises about my ongoing struggle at the creative rock face, always cheering me on. A writer needs other people to believe in what they are doing, and I have been extremely lucky in my family: beginning with the memory of my parents, Barbara and Ken Gollaglee, who encouraged my love of writing when I was young, and never questioned it as a life choice later; my aunt, Beryl Foreman, (tireless reader of every novel I have written), my brother, Nick Gollaglee and my sister, Liz Kumar.

Last but by no means least are those who have lived with me during the writing process: my husband Joe, and my children, Micah and Martha, who always show such understanding and support.

INTRODUCTION

I've always been fascinated by three historical and literary figures who might seem unconnected but in my mind are linked: Emily Brontë, Mary Shelley and Mary Queen of Scots. All three are female poets and writers (Mary Stuart also merits this description) whose closeness to Nature and the landscapes they inhabited fills my imagination.

Mary Shelley, the narrator of *Arguing with the Dead*, has a strong literary and historical connection with wild Scotland. What fascinates me most about Mary Shelley is how Nature is a huge source of inspiration for her. Mary loved wild landscapes, mountains, rivers and bleak snowy heights, places which were still seen as hostile and unappealing in the early nineteenth century when Mary was imagining the scenes of her famous novel, *Frankenstein: The Modern Prometheus*. She used wild landscapes – a Hebridean island at one point, and also the Mer de Glace at the foot of Mont Blanc - as a backdrop for her Monster and his terrible tragedy.

People have often misunderstood the idea behind Frankenstein, in part due to the clichéd Hollywood portrayal. Mary feels deep empathy for her Monster, who is rejected by his Creator, the scientist. Having created a being out of cobbled-together body parts, Dr Frankenstein is utterly repelled by what he has made, while the Creature himself struggles to acquire language, culture and education. The Creature is, however, doomed to eternal isolation, rejected not only by his Creator but by everyone he comes across. The only person in the novel who accepts the Monster and welcomes him into the fold of human intercourse is a blind man who cannot see what the Creature looks like. The novel poses the question (echoed in a poem called *Basking Shark* by Norman MacCaig): *Who is the Monster now?* Without knowing it, Mary Shelley used poignant symbolism which still rings true to this day. Her Gothic tale can be used in schools and colleges to offer profound understanding on issues like equality, inclusion, respect, the importance of education, science and belief, and of course medical and scientific ethics. From that point of view alone, it is an amazing text.

But it wasn't just the novel itself which inspired me to write *Arguing with the Dead*. It was Mary's turbulent and difficult life, full of contradiction and conflict, hope and despair.

It was no surprise that Mary came to write a ground-breaking novel. Her mother was Mary Wollstonecraft who wrote *A Vindication of The Rights of Woman* (a hugely significant text, which was neglected by successive generations until being eventually re-embraced in the 1970s).

Mary's life was filled with losses and bereavement. She travelled extensively, and witnessed the aftermath of the Napoleonic Wars first-hand. She was a woman of profound ideas influenced by everything she saw and felt. To some extent, she was more fortunate than most. Mary found a voice at a time when most women were silent.

Little did she realise that her novel would find its way into the global imagination in the way that it has. Her novel came from a deep place, and that is why it resonates today.

Arguing with the Dead bears some similarities to *For My Sins*. Both have a strong and sensitive female protagonist who is also the narrator, and suffers much in the course of her life. Both have a colourful and eventful history. Both have links with the Scottish landscape which I love, and both are haunted by their past losses. But that is where the similarity stops.

The seeds for my first historical novel, *For My Sins*, about Mary Queen of Scots, were first planted a long time ago, in the fallow soil of childhood when I read the novel *A Traveller in Time* by

Alison Uttley, and I suppose I could date my passion for Gothic literature back to this early encounter with a traditional children's book. It is a fascinating novel set in an ancient farmhouse, where the heroine opens doors and slips back into the sixteenth century, and to the time of Anthony Babington, who saw the imprisoned queen as a tragic heroine to be rescued. He was executed for his efforts. The tragic and romantic appeal of this story planted the first seeds of my love for Scottish history, particularly the tragic queen, when I came to write my own novel, *For My Sins*, where Mary is imprisoned at the end of her life, stitching her tapestries while being haunted by the ghosts of her past.

What I hope to do, both in *Arguing with the DeadD* and *For My Sins*, is to inhabit the mind and heart of a significant woman of the past. I hope I have done my two Marys – one a queen, the other a great novelist – justice.

PART ONE: THE CURTAIN RISES

Putney, February 1839

Four o'clock in the afternoon: the sun has already set. My tiny cottage in Putney overlooks a broad stretch of the Thames which has been frozen all winter long. It is quiet here. Percy is away at Cambridge, and no sound of life intrudes on my solitude.

I rest my palm on my portable writing desk which is scoured and marked by its own journey through life. It has crossed continents, traversed borders and boundaries. Close by me are familiar quill and paper, pot of ink. A small fire spits and crackles in the hearth. I no longer require many material possessions. Everything I own is dedicated to making sure my son, Percy, has a good life when I am gone.

One bird hops onto the window ledge, puts its head on one side, peers through the distorted glass. I observe his antics with quiet amusement. There is no one to remark on this little incident, to share the pleasure of it. It does not worry me, for I am used to my own company, keeping my own counsel. It was a habit forced on us from early childhood when Father required strict obedience from my sister and me.

Those words sting. "My sister and me…"

This is a melancholy time of day. Outside the world is frozen and raw, yielding little in the way of nourishment. Birds starve in search of one bright berry that is not to be had.

My thoughts catch at me. It is the early years that come back to me now, those first years at the Polygon with the big wide empty rooms and the grand piano and the first-floor balcony overlooking the bright square… Our walks to the cemetery, to sit on my mother's grave where Father patiently taught us to trace our letters. My little fingers probed the channels carved and chiselled into the surface of the stone: the visceral feeling of mossy exploration, fingernails grating slightly as they found their way. The place was like a flowering meadow, one of the best places on earth. Mary-Jane – my replacement mother – could never understand that. Why would she?

It grows dark, and I get up to light another lantern. The little room swells with candlelight. Firewood is not always easy to come by nowadays, but I manage better than most. There are many poor souls in the city and countryside beyond who suffer in these harsh winter months.

Putney is a pleasant place to stay, and I love my cottage for all its quiet simplicity. It is small and compact with a garden which can be pretty with flowers in the summer months, although it is fairly barren at the moment. I have visitors who make their way here – when the weather permits. I have lived long enough to make plenty of enemies, but also friends.

Life would be bearable were it not for the headaches which trouble me, and the worry over Percy's future. My father-in-law, Sir Timothy, is a bitter and resentful man, and withholds what he can while he is alive. I have no doubt that the old man has stored up a few unwelcome surprises for Percy and I. No doubt there will be certain caveats attached – as ever – to make our lives as difficult as possible when he finally meets his Maker. I try not to be pessimistic but I am afraid I do suspect the worst of both Shelley and his father. It is sixteen years now since Shelley's death, and I suspect he will have left most of his wealth to other women, even Claire probably – my own sister – putting our son Percy low on his list of priorities.

I am a survivor. I have survived my husband, most of my children, and I will survive whatever else Sir Timothy chooses to throw at me.

I am living a life of careful penury now in order to protect what little is left, and maybe one day my son will enjoy the benefit of that. I can do without luxuries. God knows, I had enough of those once. Shelley used to put everything on account, and hoped to pay for it once Sir Timothy expired. But as it happened, my husband died first, leaving me with a mountain of debt to manage which Sir Timothy could have lifted, but refused to. For myself, it would not matter, but for my son…

The only pleasure I miss is having the means to travel again – as we did in my younger days.

Perhaps I will travel again soon, if this perpetual winter ends. It seems there will never be a thaw, and the Thames will never again flow freely between its wide banks. But of course it will, for life continues no matter what afflictions we bear. I have learned this the hard way. Even when the endless dark of winter descends, there is life underground, biding its time, the curled bud, the broken bough waiting to regenerate, to unfurl, even when we are reluctant to acknowledge it.

A white tide of snow ebbs at my window. All of England is in the grip of this big freeze. The moonlight reflects off it at night in a visible and radiant glow, and there are violet-blue shadows between the drifts by day. I have a task which keeps me tied to my desk most days. I am busily occupied reinstating Shelley's name for posterity.

Last year I was approached by Tennyson's publisher, Edward Moxon, who offered me the grand sum of £500 in total to edit a four-volume set of Shelley's works. This I agreed to do, with some reluctance, but also with true diligence and purpose. My own novels do not sell so well, so why not begin on a task which will feed us and occupy my mind? I am proud to support my son and earn my living by my pen, even if it is only a meagre income, barely enough to live on. I am proud to be an independent single woman, fighting as my mother did in a world of powerful men to maintain the memory of those I loved – my mother, my husband, trying to ensure the future of my son. This is the story I tell myself.

While Percy is at Cambridge I work alone on these volumes, carefully pruning, weeding, slicing. I walk into the garden of Shelley's poetry and attempt to tame the wilderness I find there, without sacrificing any of its magic.

I have been forbidden by Sir Timothy to write a biography of his son. He accuses me of having ruined his son's prospects, and dragging him to the devil. When we ran away to Europe together all those years ago, we left a trail of disaster in our wake, I admit that. But Sir Timothy is no angel, and at least we lived openly and honestly by our principles. How many mistresses and illegal liaisons did the baronet hide from everyone's view?

However, Sir Timothy grudgingly agreed at last to give Percy (being his grandson) a yearly income of £200.

"However," his lawyer told me at the time "if you insist on writing your novels, he has intimated that he will cut that income by half with each new publication. Sir Timothy does not consider it a fit occupation for a woman, especially given the subject matter you choose to write about."

"I see."

"In addition," his lawyer went on, "if Sir Timothy was ever to hear that you have fallen into debt, if he gets wind of the fact that you are struggling financially in any wise that you cannot support his grandson…"

"My son, you mean?"

" - then he will seize Percy, and raise him at Field Place which – by all intents and purposes – would be a more fitting home for the poor lad than anything a woman like yourself can offer him. By law, he has the right to do that," the lawyer reminds me. I do not need reminding.

I live with that threat hanging over me. But I have continued to defy Sir Timothy on both counts. I continue to write, I support my son, I avoid debt – with or without his help.

The headaches are blinding when they come. I am certain that extremes of emotion bring them on. I had to lay aside my pen yesterday evening and rest. I sat by the fire and held my brow, unable even to read.

This morning I rose with the dawn, put on a warm cloak with a shawl wrapped about my head, covering my face from the chill wind, and took a short walk by the frozen edges of the river. There was no one about, not even a cart rolling by. The artisans' tools were silent. There was a wonderful pure stillness in the air. The sky was such a beautiful hue, a strange blend of orange and crimson, a roseate glow making the shadows blue and grey. Soft tonal shades… making me wish I could paint. I did not walk for long as I could not endure the cold, but I was able to collect bread from the baker. He was surprised to see me, and asked after my servant.

"Good white bread today," he announced, handing over a loaf. I brought it home via a narrow path cleared through the drifts.

I have one maid, Lizzie, a young girl who comes in early and lights the fire for me, sweeps and cleans. I like to talk to her. I lend her books and am teaching her to read. Her young hands are already chapped and reddened from her chores. This will be her lot in life, I fear – but she has an enquiring mind, and I like to see her sit with a book and puzzle over the marks on the page, the look of triumph and delight as the words begin to form a pattern, the sentences build into a narrative.

Lizzie had the fire going on my return, and I drank my coffee and ate my bread – soft and not too chalky – by the fireside, while she bustled about me. She refused to eat with me, saying she would end her fast when her chores were done. Then, before she left, we spent a good half-hour reading. I insist upon it, whether she likes it or not. All women are sisters in adversity, did we but know it, and should support one another to overcome the barriers we face.

My mother's spirit lives on in me; her example ever before me. She has done for women what must never be undone, though it is hard to keep her example alive.

How many women like Lizzie might have written books instead of washing pots and scrubbing floors, if the world were a different place?

Behind me the fire spits in the dark. Outside the Thames lies still and unmoving beneath the ice.

I wish I had enough money for Percy to have his own yacht, but there are no funds to be had for this, not until I have managed our mountain of debt. He has not inherited his father's skill as a poet, but what he has inherited is a passionate and irrepressible love of sailing.

A curse, more like…

Nothing can quench that desire of his, to be messing about in boats, sailing free on the tide, managing the currents, embracing the wind. What I have ensured is that someone taught him to swim. Percy swims well, and he sails well. When he owns his own yacht, it will be a seaworthy one, well-made. There will be no half-measures or cutting corners on cost. No risk-taking, as his father was wont to do.

I lift my head and gaze across those frozen waters to the far bank – vanishing now behind a thick veil of darkness - and I think of another view in Italy, of a wide bay from a grim square villa where the wind did howl and set up a gloomy cadence. I never did like that house; I thought it a melancholy abode with dismal connotations and I was right to think so. For it was here Shelley lost his life. He set sail across the Gulf and never returned. He stayed with his friends for several days, merrily partying, drinking and entertaining everyone, in good spirits I was later told. The morning they set out to return, the sea was deceptively blue and calm. They did not heed the darker skies piling up behind them from the south.

In the darkened villa I sat and waited, and when the storm hit I comforted myself by thinking they would surely have not set sail in this. I waited, and I waited, Claire and I, like captive birds, nervous, edgy. The path down to the shore was a perilous one, almost inaccessible, and the house stood high above the bay like an exposed stage set where some Greek tragedy was about to be enacted. This is what it felt like to me. There were no comforts in that villa, no sense of calm or peace, nowhere to rest. It was just huge and bare and echoing, with the sea stretching before it, dark and boiling as the storm came on.

And my husband never came home. The sea claimed him. The boat he had built with his friend was not fit for such a journey, and with its top-heavy sails was easily capsized by the ferocity and strength of the waves.

We were not on good terms when he died. We had quarrelled.

Lizzie tells me not to mind my memories. She is a good girl. I often wonder what it is like to be her, to walk the river-path every morning to my cottage, to light the fire, to sweep and dust, and set the pot to boil on the stove?

This is such a small space – too small to contain my many memories – and yet I feel a certain peace here, in the presence of Lizzie.

Her view of it is that she is grateful to have such a mistress as I.

"You have books, Mrs Shelley, you have things just nice, and you teach me to read and write. There aren't many employers who'd be so kind."

When she leaves my cottage, I notice that her shawl is looking worn and in much need of mending. I resolve to purchase a new one for her the next time I visit the dressmaker. I don't have any call to have new dresses made for myself. Two new gowns a year will suffice, but I shall make a point of visiting Mrs Sweeney to see if she has any good warm woollen shawls she can spare.

Will Lizzie be offended if I offer her such a gift?

Life was different once. For a time we lived in grand villas and castles, magnificent apartment rooms above foreign cities like Florence and Pisa and Livorno, gazing down at the Arno or the Tiber. But it was all built on sand, a palace of dreams with no material substance behind it. Shelley lived in the future, and he lived on credit.

Lizzie once asked me if I miss all of those luxuries I used to enjoy, and I told her honestly. I value this independence, despite its many hardships. In the past I was not required to eke out trifles as I am compelled to now, but I always had a skill at parsimony. I knew how to make do, even then, even if Shelley did not.

Oh, *the past*… many things were different in the past…

Lizzie left some time ago, and I am alone now with my memories. I raise my eyes to an embroidery hanging on the distempered wall with the words 'The pen is mightier than the sword' stitched in bright green silk – my favourite colour. My stepsister Claire laboured over it when she was carrying poor little Allegra, and I have kept it by my side ever since, hanging it on the wall of whatever bedroom I find myself in. It travels with me. Another remnant from a former life, one that no longer exists. Remnants and relics are all I have left, the scattered leavings of a life lived too intensely.

I was never one for sewing, although like many women I mend our clothes to make do with what we have, to save on the tailor's bill. Thrift has become a lifelong habit, and I do it well.

I look around this room where I have settled myself with my few transportable goods, all of them useful, most of them bearing cherished memories.

I am a veritable nomad. I have had many homes over the years, rented rooms and hired houses and villas here and there, across London, Germany, Italy, France, the Alps. I have been fortunate to see so much, but the losses have been legion.

I am haunted by ghosts…

There are some losses we live with every day of our lives and never recover from. I will never be done grieving for them.

Even this cottage does not belong to me. It is just another halfway house. I have had many writing rooms, many desks in many cities where I have sat with my pot of ink and begun work on a new manuscript. The tools of my trade travel with me. My memories, and my papers… so many papers, locked up in a chest, waiting to be sifted and sorted through.

Shelley left his papers in complete disarray. Jottings, scribblings, doodles, half-finished verses on torn bits of parchment, water-damaged, faded and smudged: I fight my way through the tide of paper, drowning in a sea of parchment, clinging to the raft of an incomplete stanza. Edward Moxon assures me that Shelley's poetry would be lost and forgotten were it not for my labours. He has charged me with the onerous task of rescuing his work. I am a good editor, and I am sifting my way through his texts with a keen and incisive eye. Of myself, however, there will be no trace. This is the mark of a good editor. I will leave nothing of myself behind.

I will be a ghost, a mist on the ether.

No one will ever know how much of those towers and building-blocks of manufactured stanzas and heroic compositions will be mine. I will ensure the best survives and that the bright gems and pearls are thread through with an invisible narrative holding all together. No one will ever know. But I will receive my payment in due course, and with it, I shall feed myself and my son, and ensure he continues to study at Cambridge. (That is, after all, one condition Sir Timothy has met. He pays Percy's tuition fees.)

It has been a long night. My neck is stiff – an occupational hazard. I stretch my arms and wince as I hear a bone crack.

The desk is scattered with a snowstorm of papers. All night long memories came flooding in. In the course of this work I have found out most of Shelley's secrets, even those he kept from me: the ghosts of other women, his many misdemeanours, some of which I knew about, some I did not.

All night long they rose before me in the darkness, all those lost souls. Little Clara and William, Allegra, Byron. Flashes of memory… A torn scrap of paper took me back there, as if no time at all had elapsed.

I stare out at the snow-filled path in front of the river where a solitary figure walks in the early dawn. If I half-close my eyes I can fancy that young girl is my sister, returned from the dead.

But the shawled figure turns her head, and a stranger meets my gaze. I raise a hand in greeting. She walks on. The scandal of her death is brushed away, like a speck of dust on a coat collar.

Phantoms surround me.

When Percy is with me the ghosts recede. His good nature and mild company put all such gloomy thoughts to rest.

But when I am alone and my desk makes its demands, then the ghosts crowd in; the ones I left behind in Italy, my little ones.

As everyone was fond of telling me, it is a mistake to live in the past…

I am left only with the leavings, scattered about my desk, falling gently in my heart like leaves from a tree that is slowly dying.

The Polygon, London 1800

I hear our distant voices, two children, Fanny and myself, walking beside Father through a flowering meadow. Except it is not a meadow. Not really. It is August. The sun is shining, and we have a posy of flowers to give to Mother. I am two or three years old, barely big enough to walk this far; Fanny is three years older, but already she is serious and sad. She remembers mother clearly, and still longs for her.

Godwin (Father) walks beside us, talking to us as if we are adults.

"And this is not a sad place to be, is it, Mary?" He turns to me first, and I nod obediently.

Fanny's eyes light up. "It is the best place to be, because Mother is here. And although she is sorry to be dead, I know she loves it here…"

Godwin fights a measure of impatience, as if swatting at a fly. He ignores Fanny and turns to me.

"And how indeed could you know that, Fanny dear?" He laughs a little dismissively.

Fanny's face falls.

"… because she tells me so…" she adds, on a whisper.

At first, she is not sure if anyone has heard her, but Godwin's head whips round. She has Father's attention at last.

"The dead cannot speak, Fanny. Your mother loved you both dearly, and it is right we should have her memory before us, but it would be a pity for you to become irrational, child."

Fanny – who is only six – stares back at him.

"… but she does…" her small voice pipes up.

"Fanny, dear," Father says. "You are not quite able to grasp this yet. Your father was not a man of ideas. He was a man of passions, yes, but he did not have your mother's – nor my – erudition. He was not a sophisticated man. Just an avaricious one…" he adds.

I have no idea what he is talking about.

"Imlay was not a bad man," he goes on, as if talking to himself. "But he was not a good one, either. He certainly did not deserve such love as she gave him, nor the sacrifices she made for him, and let us hope, Fanny, that you will not inherit any of those Imlay traits, but show yourself worthy of your Wollstonecraft heritage. Guard against it, Fanny, dear. Be more like your Mother, less like your Father."

"Less like you, Father?" she cries, puzzled.

"Dear God..." he exclaims impatiently. "Less like your natural Father, dear. Keep up."

"Natural?" she asks.

Still we are none the wiser.

The memory of us skipping through that flowering meadow with our little posy to visit Mother's grave is one of many I can recall, for we visited her every day, Father, Fanny and I, until Godwin began to exclude Fanny, and took only myself…

"I see in you something your Mother would approve of… something she would encourage and nurture."

"And not Fanny?"

Fanny is no longer beside us. She has vanished from this memory.

"Oh, Fanny is all very well. A good, kind girl, but she has not your *heritage*, Mary. She lacks spirit. Perhaps throwing my blood-line into the melting pot has helped, after all..." he chortled.

It was best when Father let Fanny come too, then we three would wade through the long grasses like mariners braving the sea, myself up to my neck in it. And when we reached Mother's grave at last, we sat against the tomb and read books, or else we traced the letters in the worn stone, spelling out the words of our mother's name until we knew them by heart. *Mary Wollstonecraft Godwin*.

Our voices twitter on through the flowering meadow. We are still too young to realise this is a cemetery, and that the stones around us are the markers above dead people, to anchor them to the earth. To us it is a place of happiness and peace.

Number 29, The Polygon was a haven of peace to Fanny and I. I can still remember the library with its smooth sea of parquet flooring, shelves of books towering to the ceiling, surrounding us like a high fortress. It always seemed to be summer in Somers Town...

In most of my memories I can feel the sunlight pouring through the tall windows, bathing us like a baptism. But then something shifts. A shadow passes the window. I feel it darkening our world.

Is this the moment it all changed?

I remember Father bursting into the room, his cheeks flushed and inflamed in an unaccustomed way. He was not normally given to sudden, jerky movements, but that afternoon he looked oddly agitated.

"Ah, my dears," he cried, with a touch of melodrama. "We are going on a little jaunt today. How would you like that?"

Trips usually meant a walk to the stationer's or the bookstore or through the fields to St. Pancras churchyard where the flowers grew tall between the familiar grey stones.

"A trip to the theatre with our neighbours, the Clairmonts!"

Fanny looked up.

"Is she the lady you were speaking with the other day, when you were out on the balcony?"

Father made an attempt to hide his fluster. "That is the one, my dear. Charming woman. She has always been a great admirer of my work, you know. Her children are…"

"Noisy…" Fanny said boldly. Those were the days when she would still speak her mind, long before she had been crushed by life.

He paused.

"Are they, my dear? I hadn't noticed. I wasn't aware you had met little Jane and Charles."

"We haven't, Father," Fanny murmured. "We can hear them. They're quite loud; their voices echo in the square."

I nodded my head in agreement, although I was not entirely sure of the facts. After all, there were so many different sounds out on the square, the slow rumble of cartwheels or the clip-clop of hooves. Voices, laughter, children too, but none of it usually invaded the quiet interior of our well-appointed house. Not that I knew of.

All of this was about to change.

Time has a way of tricking us, speeding up when we least expect it. The next thing I knew we were squashed inside a hired carriage as it rumbled over the cobbles. Myself, Fanny, Father, Mrs Clairmont and her two unfamiliar children. Two families, cheek by jowl. There were too many feathers and ribbons and pins and brooches which scratched and fluttered at my nose. There were different smells, overpowering and aggressive. These new odours were not the ones I was familiar with: they were sweet and sickly, feminine. Like a small animal, I sensed our territory being invaded: I was not in the least happy about the way Father was conducting himself. Normally sober, calm and collected, he seemed all aflutter, too ready to burst into raucous laughter at a remark made by Mrs Clairmont. He was flushed.

I remember the impression the theatre made on me. It was huge and buzzing with excitement, row upon row of animated faces in the auditorium, eagerly awaiting the rise of the curtain. The footlights burned hotly at the edges of the stage. There were painted 'flats' to suggest hidden and imagined worlds, and there were heroes on stage who faced darkness and distress, but rose victorious at the end.

I sat in rapt silence, completely unaware of Charles and Jane bickering away to the left of me while Fanny regarded them both with barely concealed horror. Father was preoccupied with Mrs Clairmont and seemed to miss quite a bit of the drama.

Then we had to endure the torture of the carriage ride home, where the adults bundled us children together declaring with delight that we were "bound to be friends."

Jane regarded me with a sour look from her corner of the carriage. She was one year younger than me, and although we did not know it yet, we would become firm rivals and have a long history together which would stretch far into the future – with dark repercussions.

The next morning Fanny and I were very quiet.

"Did you enjoy the performance yesterday, girls?" Father asked at the breakfast table, his eyes glittering in a way that didn't seem natural for him.

Fanny bowed her head but would not speak.

"I loved it," I piped up. "We both loved it, didn't we, Fanny?" Fanny did not reply. "Could we visit the theatre again?"

Father laughed. He seemed unusually delighted by life at present... since the Clairmonts moved next door.

"Well, we shall see about that. It's certainly a possibility. Mary-Jane..." he cleared his throat, "Mrs Clairmont, I mean, is very fond of the theatre, and she is in sore need of some companionship. As, I find, are we."

"Are we, Father?"

Fanny remained silent.

When she did speak, it was not what Father wanted to hear. "Could we go alone next time? Without the Clairmonts?"

An ominous hush fell. I could tell – even at that young age – that Father was not pleased.

"You will get used to them in time. It is good to have company – once in a while."

It wasn't long before our quiet household became invaded by the clatter and chaos of the Clairmonts. Mrs Clairmont laughed loudly, and reprimanded her children as they pounded noisily across the gleaming floors of our peaceful home.

Fanny and I watched in silence.

There was nothing to say.

And there was nothing to be done.

At night in our beds we whispered about it under cover of darkness.

"Perhaps they'll move away soon?" I suggested.

"But they have only just arrived," Fanny pointed out.

I blinked at her through the gloom. She seemed to have changed lately. Her boisterousness and candour had gradually faded. She seemed less like herself, more ... absent.

*

"Fanny, Mary, I have some delightful news for you both, and I am sure you will share my happiness and – yes, relief. After these years of difficult solitude, we are to have comfort, at last."

Fanny tried to smile. I could feel the tectonic plates of the earth shifting beneath my feet. The world was about to end.

"I would like you to say how-do-ye-do, very nicely, to…" he paused for effect before turning towards the open door "… your second mamma."

As if on cue, our next-door neighbour appeared in the room, smiling almost apologetically. She had already become a too-frequent visitor to our home as far as Fanny and I were concerned.

It was very unwise of Father to surprise us with this news in front of Mrs Clairmont herself, as there could only be one outcome, and it was embarrassing for us all.

"We do not want a second mamma!" Fanny and I wailed.

Mrs Clairmont reddened while Father stammered and stuttered, at a loss for words.

I wondered if Mrs Clairmont knew about our daily visits to the graveyard. A dead loved-one held dominion over us all, and no one living could replace her. Mrs Clairmont – my poor stepmother – had yet to learn this. You cannot argue with the dead.

How easy it is, to conjure those early memories, to feel what it is to be a child again. I remember brushing my way through a sea of grasses, releasing clouds of pollen into the air, picking at the tiny dusty seed-heads of dead flowers. I remember thinking that the bumblebees looked like fat little soldiers, decked in imperial-looking gold.

Men in aprons and uniforms helped Mrs Clairmont move her wooden boxes and few pieces of furniture into Number 29. Now the house she used to occupy beside our own stood empty, waiting for new tenants, while our own home was full of intruders.

We hid in our rooms, or took to escaping to St. Pancras.

When I leaned against the tombstone, I could feel mamma's secret heart beating beneath the earth.

I told her about Father's plans for a second mamma.

Mary Wollstonecraft Godwin did not reply.

Father was supposed to be strong and resolute; he was supposed to soldier on alongside his daughters, educating us in the ways of liberal independence. Instead he had failed at the first hurdle. He wanted a wife to mother his girls, to order the food and meals, to see about the laundry. He wanted assistance so that he could retreat further into the dusky obscurity of his own study.

And when he emerged from that study, it was not to be with his daughters any longer, but to laugh and cavort with Mrs Clairmont, to blush and stammer and behave in an unrecognisable manner that we were not at all used to.

I tore at one of the stalks and swatted a fly with it.

Fanny and I were accustomed to speaking quietly in our house. We lived among writers and knew how to keep the peace, but the Clairmonts had absolutely no understanding of the rules.

There were some compensations. When we returned home, there was a meal waiting for us. Clean vegetables with our meat, and a pudding. As my spoon carved up the soft deliciousness of that wobbling confection, I watched Mrs Clairmont (Mary-Jane, as we agreed to call her) attending to her son Charles, fussing over his collar.

I decided that this was one of the benefits of living under a new regime: there were more puddings at table whereas before we had none. Fanny and I acknowledged that Mary-Jane was quite good at dealing with the food and laundry. Is that why Father had taken up with her?

When I heard them giggling together behind his study door, I wondered if there might not be another reason.

The Polygon, 1807

Years pass and we gain a little brother, William, five years younger than myself. Father dotes on him. He is the apple of everyone's eye, the fruit of the Godwin/ Clairmont union...

Another memory rises to the surface, one of furtive eavesdropping...

I had crept outside onto the landing, and was listening intently. There were no lights burning. A pale bone-white moon shone in at a high window. In the hall below was a faint flicker of candlelight beneath the study door, and voices raised within. The rest of the house was in darkness.

"I have always respected her memory, like a second presence in this household..."

I leaned over the banister, slid towards the top of the staircase.

I could hear Father's voice, stern like gravel or a bed of stones when the sea hits it.

"... *difficult*, my dear..."

I listened at doors while the adults conducted their lives in sticky disarray.

I was halfway down the staircase when the door opened and Mary-Jane emerged, dabbing her eyes with a handkerchief. It was too late to escape. I stood still, hoping she would not notice me.

She was halfway across the hall before she happened to glance up. I must have appeared as a silent ghost, standing there in my white shift.

She gasped, but recovered herself quickly. We stared at each other.

I can repent of it now, in my wisdom, but as a child I think I must have sent her a look of triumph.

She and Godwin were not getting on so well after all, then? Our replacement Mamma had not succeeded in becoming quite the replacement he had hoped for – as is so often the case with 'second mammas'.

Later, when I climbed back into bed, I warmed my cold toes against my sister's bare legs, and she stirred in her sleep. The bed sheets rustled.

"Where have you been?" she asked.

"Nowhere."

I began to scratch at my rash until my fingernails were bloody.

"Leave it alone!" Fanny scolded.

"I can't help it."

"You will make it worse."

"The chamber pot is full," I murmured, playing at the helpless little sister, in need of my elder.

"I know. I'll empty it in the morning."

Then she rolled over and went back to sleep.

Jane Clairmont, on my other side, lay very still, as if she was listening to us. I lay between them both, trying not to scratch. A human buffer. Soon enough, divided loyalties would come into play.

"Mary, why can you not be a good girl towards your stepmother?"

I hung my head.

"Why do you show her such insolence?"

"I didn't mean to upset her."

"That's not your mother's view of it."

I wanted to cry out, *She is not my mother*, but stifled the words before I spoke them. For that would not do at all.

"Fanny is grateful for the attention we give her," Father said. "She is grateful for all that Mary-Jane tries to do for her, whereas you?"

He broke off.

I stared at the floor, my cheeks burning.

"I would like to see some improvement in your behaviour towards your mamma," he muttered. "Please make an effort to be more accommodating."

Under Clairmont there was a new regime. The portrait of our mother still hung in the study above Father's desk; she could not banish it to a remote corner of the house, much as she would have liked to. She dismissed the nursemaid and the two maids we had been used to, and hired new staff. Strangers. A governess and a tutor.

I was ten years old when Godwin began to voice his worries and anxieties about money. While we children revelled in the freedom of our address at the Polygon, with its wide empty rooms and its first-floor balcony overlooking the bright square below, we had no idea that it was all built on credit. The notion that we could afford to live at such an illustrious address was an illusion. Here we had access to clean air, clean food, clean water, well away from the stench and filth of the city streets. We had space to play and to roam, but I was beginning to sense that it could be taken from us at any moment. It was a precarious palace we lived in. There were invisible cracks in the edifice through which the winds of change were blowing, threatening to transform our fine hopes into a ruin.

I withdrew even further into Godwin's library. I liked to be surrounded by books, quietly reading, the smell of leather and dust scenting the air with its perfume, heavy volumes towering above me, the grand piano in the bay window overlooking the square. It gave me comfort and joy almost as deep as the flowering meadow where our First Mamma lay.

It did not always last long. The door would slam open, and Mary-Jane might appear.

She would stop if she saw me.

"I am looking for your father…"

"I have not seen him," I would reply.

She would prepare to leave then glance back at the piano. "And leave that thing alone, will you? Unless you hope to learn to play it."

Have I imagined such harsh rejoinders, with a child's sense of injustice? Perhaps she was kinder than I remember.

That afternoon, she caught up with Father in his study across the hall.

"*Not again…*" I heard him murmur, before the door swung shut behind them.

"But I am *worried*, William. I have been through the accounts, and it is simply not adding up. Surely, dear, even *you* must see that?" Then her voice became soothing. "I know you have so many great preoccupations of the mind, believe me… I know… and I value that above all else, but… well, we cannot live on credit alone, dear. You know where it will end."

A muffled response from Father.

"Debtors' prison!" Mary-Jane barked. "That is where it will end. Believe me, I know. I have been there. My own *children* have been there."

My ears pricked up, and I found myself leaning forward to listen.

Debtors' prison? This was news to me. Fanny and I had no idea that Mary-Jane had such a colourful past. We always imagined her to be the respectable widow Father told us she was.

"I know you are right, my dear, but what is to be done? I have a status to maintain..."

There was a short silence.

"I know exactly what is to be done. We have to leave this house." I heard Father make a noise of protest, but she added, "You cannot afford to pay the bills."

My heart sank into my stomach. Leave this house? I gazed up at the rows of silent books, the tall windows letting in the bright light, the vast expanse of parquet flooring, stretching away from me like a polished sea of gold.

But what troubled me more was that Mary-Jane had revealed herself to be a person of more good sense than Godwin. She, it appeared, was the practical one, ready with a solution to our problems.

I flinched suddenly as a door was slammed.

Then I heard her heels rapping sharply against the flags. She was sobbing again, in rage.

A carriage drew up outside Number 29.

We had been ordered upstairs to our room.

I cracked the door open an inch, and listened to the quiet commotion far below, the cheerful greetings, Father's obvious delight, Coleridge's familiar voice full of warmth and good humour. We have a visitor.

"Mary," Fanny warned. "Close the door."

"No."

"You will embarrass Father."

"He did not used to mind."

"Mary-Jane will catch you."

"We shall see."

My stepsister Jane was watching me in mute admiration, in awe of my quiet defiance.

I crept to the banister, peered over the side.

Father was greeting our old friend, Coleridge, below.

"Come," Father said, and ushered his guest into the study. The door softly closed behind them, excluding me. Their voices became muffled.

There was no one about.

Mary-Jane was in the nursery with William.

I crept stealthily down the stairs into the hall, Jane trailing me like a shadow.

All was quiet.

The study door opened and a maid emerged, carrying a silver tray. She left the door ajar and sailed across to the back kitchen.

Here was our chance.

We slipped inside, and disappeared behind the couch. Two silent girls in our nightshifts.

The study was warm, and full of crimson light. A cheerful fire was blazing in the hearth, and the reflected flames danced on the hearth-rug. There were candles lit, and a shaded oil lantern burning on a side table. I remember the ruby glint of a bottle of port, and the tinkle of glasses being filled. The smells were rich, wood-scented, exotic almost, for that is what Coleridge was like: he brought with him the essence and dark excitement of his travels. I could hear the roar of the tiger, smell the wild untamed jungle in his presence, as if he conjured them there with his words.

Father and Coleridge continued their conversation. If they

knew we were there, they gave not a hint of it, ignoring our presence completely.

"It does me good to see you again," Father said.

"It has been a long time."

"All is well?"

I heard Father sigh. "Too many creditors knocking at the door. Sometimes I do not know how to stave off disaster."

"Life is hard. Perhaps something will turn up soon…"

"Writers always live in hope."

When Coleridge began to share with Father his poem, *The Rime of the Ancient Mariner*, I fancy he knew fine well that we girls were hiding behind the couch, listening. Maybe that was why he choose to recite it.

The crimson and ruby shadows glowed in the darkened room as he swept us back in time to the horrors and riches of his tragic story

> *"What evil looks had I from old and young! Instead of*
> *the cross, the Albatross, about my neck was hung!"*

The mariner killed an albatross and thereby caused the deaths of his shipmates. Guilt hung about his neck like a noose. I felt a cold, nervous excitement. It chimed with something buried deep in my own experience.

I know what that feels like, I thought to myself. I know what it is to carry a burden of guilt, of blame and responsibility. Was I not responsible, indirectly, for my own mother's death? Child-bed fevers are common, even now. Mothers often give up their lives so their daughters might live… But the realisation that I might be to blame for my own mother's demise arrived in my lap as if it had fallen from above like a great fat bird with bloodied feathers. I am guilty of murder! I thought. Or manslaughter at the very least. I carry my own albatross.

At this point the door burst open and Mary-Jane appeared among us. The spell was broken, the world of the *Ancient*

Mariner shrivelled and died. We were no longer travellers in an inn, listening to foreign tales. We were two errant girls, caught out in the act of eavesdropping.

Mary-Jane was quick to out us from behind the couch, fulsome with apologies. Coleridge made to protest, but Father looked conflicted, as if he did not know whether to insist that we be allowed to stay.

Mary-Jane clasped a shoulder each, and dragged us from the room.

I heard a voice behind murmuring *"… surely… too severe…?"*

We were not given the chance to say goodbye.

There were tears and protests as she noisily marched us back up the staircase, her voice echoing through the household.

To Coleridge we were the two little girls of the great Mary Wollstonecraft, come to eavesdrop. He remembered us listening to his tales with open-mouthed wonder when we were knee-high; I wonder if he even noticed that the girl beside me was not in fact Fanny, but another – an interloper. Children often look the same to adults, and they change so quickly as they grow…

Fanny had decided to remain upstairs, too depressed to join us in eavesdropping. I feel a trace of guilt now when I think about how we excluded her that evening, and on other occasions too.

Fanny Imlay was slowly being usurped.

PART TWO: REBELLION

Skinner Street, 1807

W e were sworn to secrecy by a desperate Mary-Jane, as she hissed at us to hurry and dress.

Creditors had been beating a path to our door all winter, and then turned away, disappointed. Godwin and Mary-Jane had been unable to pay the rent on our beautiful home for the past six months – the visits had been getting more aggressive - and so they plotted an elaborate and farcical escape in the middle of the night.

We gathered our few things, and I held William's hand while we tiptoed down the staircase for the last time. We assembled in hushed tones in the grand elegant hallway under cover of darkness. There was not even time to glance into the library, that space I'd always revered, and whisper a final farewell.

Outside a cart was waiting, already loaded up with Father's books. Another was full of our linen and other household effects, all hastily packed into wooden chests.

Father looked furtive, like a comic figure from the *Merchant of Venice*.

This was our leave-taking of the Polygon, the place where Fanny and I had been so happy – at first, anyway. The houses around the square were all shuttered against the night, no candles or lamps lit, not a light showing: no one observed our departure. Our neighbours were all in their beds, like the good citizens they were. But we – the Godwins/Clairmonts – had already begun to stumble on the wrong side of respectability once more.

It was a strange journey, undertaken at night when no one respectable was abroad. Mary-Jane comforted and cajoled us, declaring that it was "an adventure", that it was "best for everyone" and that our new home was "quite delightful, much more central and therefore interesting…"

On and on she prattled, while we listened to the quiet rolling of the wheels against the cobblestones, and the tramping of the horses' hooves. Poor Mary-Jane. With the hindsight of age I can see she was perhaps doing her best to console us.

When the carts rolled into a dark and narrow street, and then passed the ominous facade of Newgate Prison, we three girls glanced at each other curiously. Not long after this the front cart drew to a halt.

Surely, there must be some mistake?

"London is a city of contrasts," Godwin was saying "where the rich and the poor live cheek by jowl."

"But which are we, Father?" I couldn't help asking. There had always been some confusion over the issue. One moment I was taught that my heritage was of the highest order, the next that we were teetering on the brink of ruin. We must buy our groceries on credit and lie to the landlord about the rent! Is that what rich people did?

"All writers, Mary, come up against the challenges of straitened circumstances. You ought, really, to understand this by now."

I was ten. I was beginning to understand a lot of things…

If you have the *appearance* of being rich and grand, if you live at an illustrious address, you will easily obtain credit from local tradesmen, especially if you happen to be a lord or baronet's son.

But there may come a point when your creditors grow impatient, lose faith in your wealthy status, and expect to be paid. Lord knows, our Father was no lord or titled earl. He owned no lands. He was a man of ideas. And ideas do not necessarily pay the rent.

Our new house was tall and narrow, five stories high with a schoolroom at the very top, from where we could hear a lone bell tolling with a sad cadence.

The first time we heard it Fanny, Jane and I crowded the small high window and stood on tiptoe to watch as a prisoner was led from the ugly maw of Newgate prison. He was kneeling upright in a rough cart, a rope around his neck.

"Where are they taking him?" I asked.

"Tyburn," Charles said, appearing suddenly behind us.

"The gallows!" Fanny added. "Execution day."

I stared, my eyes transfixed by the horror of it. I doubt Mary-Jane had any idea that our schoolroom boasted such a view, if you managed to angle your head in such a way.

I felt suffocated and claustrophobic in our new house. I missed the wide flowering meadows of Somers Town, the country lanes, and I missed the short walk to Mother's grave.

My exploratory forays around the neighbourhood were an education. The sights are painted on my memory forever.

The blood flowed freely onto the steaming cobbles.

I would walk through Smithfield with its slaughterhouses and butcher's market, where I would see a man in a filthy leather apron take a knife and carve yellow slabs of flesh from a great carcase. He slit the belly; organs and guts spilled into the sawdust. In my panic, I stumbled and kicked something: a bucket of entrails. I stared down at it and gagged: fat yellow worms twisting in a pulsing knot.

I came upon a narrow alleyway between tall buildings, and glanced along it. Glimpses of poverty reeled before my eyes. Ragged children sat dirty on a doorstep with puddles of water caught in the cobbles at their feet. I often wandered here by mistake, knowing that Father would not want me to see such sights.

I remember turning away from the rank alleyway where some people – women and children – were forced to live their lives.

I walked all the way back to St. Pancras Churchyard and sat – as before – on Mother's grave. In my lap was a book pilfered from Father's library, its leather-soft covers open like moth wings.

I relaxed my back against the easeful stone. So familiar was this spot, and so undisturbed in its quiet solitude. Father used to come here with us all the time. Not any longer. Bees droned lazily in the nearby grasses, and wildflowers bobbed their heavy heads. There was nothing morbid or macabre here, no filthy smells or glimpses of poverty. I gathered a few flowers and carried them home to put beside my bed, as a reminder of the old days, before Father remarried.

The walk home tired me, and when I arrived back the place was in uproar.

Fanny looked at me, her eyes bulging with dread.

"*Where* have you *been*?" she hissed.

But I didn't have time to answer before Mary-Jane loomed behind her in the narrow corridor.

"Where…" she screeched "… have you been?"

"Nowhere!"

"Such nonsense is this…"

Mary-Jane grabbed my shoulder and propelled me into

Father's cramped new office. He was sitting behind his desk, the portrait of Mother above him, although the picture frame looked too big for the room.

"Mary," Father said. "You have had us all very worried. It is not fitting for you to be wandering the streets alone now that you are reaching a certain age."

"I am ten years old, Father. I do not really see what danger can…"

"Do not answer back," Mary-Jane snapped.

"Do not answer back," Father echoed.

Exactly who is in charge here, my ten-year-old self wondered.

"I will ask you again – where have you been?"

I glanced down at my toes peeping from beneath my petticoats. My rash was beginning to irritate, and I lifted a hand to scratch at it.

I shrugged. "St. Pancras Churchyard… where we always go…"

"No, that's too far. And you should accept your Mamma's guidance in this. What seemed appropriate for you once, is not appropriate now."

She is not my mamma… I knew better now than to give utterance to this thought.

I climbed the stairs, found a small pottery jug and filled it with water from the ewer on my washstand. Then I placed the flowers I'd gathered inside it.

"Where did you get those?" my stepsister Jane asked me.

"The graveyard where we used to go."

"Where your mamma is buried?"

I nodded.

By morning, the flowers had wilted; bruised petals lay on the table like damp tissue paper. I was afraid that my memories would not fare any better.

Once upon a time there was a girl in a fairy-tale. Her name was Mary, and she lived in a dark basement unpacking books under the evil gaze of her wicked stepmother. Every book she unpacked was like a memory, and she held it aloft in her hands before transferring it to the dusty shelves. Like Cinderella, she hoped for something better to happen but she did not know what. She imagined she had an invisible albatross which hung about her neck, weighing her down, and wondered if its weight would ever be removed…

I found this scrap in a notebook recently, from long ago. I was always scribbling the beginnings of dark tales, which never amounted to much or led anywhere.

My thoughts took their own meandering path as I worked away under Mary-Jane's guidance.

Mary-Jane had opened up the ground floor of our tall teetering house as a children's bookshop, where she also sold poetry and essays. I found myself gainfully employed behind the counter, or squatting on a low stool between the high dusty stacks, unpacking wooden chests of books, slowly stacking them on the shelves. The tinkle of the bell would herald the arrival of a new customer. Some were writers themselves, and I listened to their conversation with Mary-Jane. As much as I resented her, she had won my grudging admiration. She appeared to have a head on her shoulders for the business side of things, where Father had been quite unequal to the task. It looked as if she might have saved us from ruin.

The River Fleet was not far away, giving off its noxious humours. Mary-Jane worried for the health of her own children, so she began looking at prospectuses for schools – despite our straitened circumstances.

Fanny and I were not part of these grandiose plans. Charles, being a boy, was entitled to an education.

I argued with Mary-Jane about it, my voice raised to match hers, and a decision was reached. I was to be sent to a boarding school in Ramsgate.

"You want an education," she shrieked. "Then you may have one."

The house in Skinner Street had paper-thin walls. We could hear every noise out on the street, the barking of dogs, coughing, someone hawking and spitting in the gutter, carter's wheels rumbling over the bumping cobblestones.

I remember standing outside their bedroom door while shadows leapt up the walls from the nub-end of a candle I held.

"Something has to change. She has become ill with longing." Father's voice.

"…and with sitting too often on that damp grave of her mother's, no doubt," Mary-Jane said. At first, I wasn't sure if they were speaking about myself or Fanny, but of course I ought to have realised: Fanny was invisible. No one noticed if she was withdrawn or unhappy. The family had allowed her to fade into the background, to expect nothing less

"What about that friend of yours? Baxter?"

"I have made his acquaintance but once, my dear."

"Nevertheless. That will do, surely."

"But Scotland is such a long way from London…"

Scotland?

"It will give her a break," Mary-Jane suggested, then added in an undertone. "It will give me a break too. You know you can be exceedingly precious about your daughter, Godwin…"

I waited for Father to rush to my defence. My stepmother wanted to be rid of me, and this is how she would engineer it. I felt like a forlorn child in a fairy-tale as I carried my feeble candle back up the staircase to bed.

*

"Scotland?" I cried.

I had been summoned to Father's study.

"It's for the best, Mary."

"It is what *she* wants!"

"If by 'she' you mean your mother…"

"She is not my mother!"

"Daughter, you are sowing seeds of discontent between my wife and I. You are the cause of much strife and tension. It is a sad state of affairs."

There. It was said. The ultimate betrayal. She had forced him to choose, and he had chosen her – above his daughters. He had betrayed us, and betrayed the hopes and last wishes of Mary Wollstonecraft.

When my stepmother walked in she shot me a steely glance.

"You must listen to your father, Mary. He knows what is best for you."

I rushed past her into the hall. "Who will look after Fanny when I am gone?"

"Don't be ridiculous," Father shouted. "We all have an eye to Fanny. She muddles along quite nicely."

"I think not, Father."

But no one listened to me. They had made their decision.

Later, when I was sitting in the shop below, quietly shelving books, Mary-Jane found me there. There was no one nearby to overhear our conversation.

"It is not what you think," she surprised me by saying.

I looked away from her, and ran my fingertips along the spines of the books.

"Do you see that desk over there?"

She pointed at the counter-top, where customers made their purchases.

"That is where I have worked tirelessly, ceaselessly, and – yes – where I have raised the funds to pay for Jane's French lessons. I have not only served customers, but have put in hours and hours as a translator. If I should choose to arm Jane with those same skills, then – my dear – what is that to you? Your education is a matter for your own father."

Saying this, she turned on her heel and left me.

Scotland, 1812

My travel chest sat four-square in the hall, ready for the porters to transfer it to the stagecoach. The family were gathered in the narrow hallway to see me off. I was nervous.

Fanny watched from the shadows, and I wondered for a moment what would become of her when I was no longer there to fight her battles. Who would stand up for her?

Our stepsister Jane looked genuinely sorry to see me go. She stepped forward and pushed a thin volume into my hand. I glanced at the cover. It was a copy of Christabel by our friend Coleridge.

"For you," she whispered. "And when you return we shall all be waiting for you."

I smiled. She was given to melodramatic gestures.

My half-brother William was being held back by Mary-Jane.

"I want to go too," he argued.

"No, William, you will stay here with Mamma," she told him firmly.

The rest of us clambered up into the waiting carriage.

"So exciting!" Jane was twittering beside me. "To see Scotland, to travel. Such a romantic country. Maybe you will see the Jacobite rebels and perhaps you will fall in love with one of them."

"Jane," Father scolded.

"You might see fighting. There are garrisons there still, are there not, Godwin?" she crowed. "I read that there are. Pockets of resistance against the English king."

I glanced through the window of the carriage and caught my stepmother's eye. A moment of understanding passed between us. For her this was a victory of sorts. She will have the house to herself, I mused, and then when the others return, she will have only silent Fanny to contend with. She held William's hand tightly, and forced him to wave goodbye although he was peeved at not coming with us.

I gazed out of the window as we manoeuvred through the crowded streets near Smithfield. Jane was still chattering away, but I had stopped listening. I had nothing to say. Nor did Fanny.

"You will find William Baxter to be a capital fellow, I am sure," Father said. "He is eager to make your acquaintance, my dear."

I struggled to find my voice.

"Have you met him before, Father?"

"Once," he coughed into his kerchief. "But enough to know that I was much impressed. A radical Scotsman. Four daughters. Widower. When he heard of our *difficulty*..." I glanced sideways at Father, wondering what he meant to imply by that word, but he studiously avoided my eye "... he was more than happy to help. It was *his* suggestion, after all. Capital fellow. Businessman. Could be of use... in the long run..." Father added, thinking no doubt of his own dwindling finances again – ever a preoccupation of his.

I was bound for Dundee, where I had to hope that William Baxter would indeed prove to be the 'capital fellow' that Father imagined.

That night we stopped at an inn for food and rest. Father was worried about the expense so we boarded somewhere cheap. Fanny did not notice, but Jane was full of observations and comments about the standard of service and the state of the beds, which she inspected and declared they did not seem clean – in this, she reminded me of her mother.

The state of the rooms was the least of my worries.

I was dreading the journey to come. I have never travelled well in a carriage, the jolting of the motion upsets me exceedingly, so I wondered what I would feel like on a boat sailing all the way up the east coast to the far North of Scotland. It was all very well for Jane to be bubbling with excitement, I thought. She did not have to undertake the journey alone, but would return home to the favour of her own mother.

We sat in the dingy front parlour while the inn-keeper brought us food. Another guest sat at a nearby table, eating his meal and drinking a jug of ale. The fire was unlit, being June, but one or two candles fluttered on the chimney breast and there were lamps on the tables to light up the dim interior.

I fell to studying the other guest, wondering about his destination, where he was from, what his business might be. How fine to be able to travel freely like this, as a gentleman? He lifted his gaze, and caught my eye.

I dipped my head, and tried to concentrate on what Father was telling us.

"So, my dears, it will be an experience for us all – to be separated for a while. No doubt you will miss your sister…"

"Indeed, we will Godwin," Jane chimed in. "I wonder if they have syllabub here?"

Father must have been feeling indulgent that day, due to the enormity of the occasion.

"Syllabub?" he enquired, leaning towards the landlord hopefully, who shook his head.

"Oh. Well perhaps white soup then?" she added, barely bothering to conceal her disappointment.

"I think perhaps it would be better if you allowed me to order supper for us all."

Fanny and I exchanged knowing glances in silence.

When will it end? I thought to myself, as I anticipated the farewells to come. *How soon will I have to part from those I love, and carry on alone, braving the sea?* I had never been on a boat before, never set sail across the ocean. It was not safe to travel inland: safer to risk storms than the highwayman. But I hated painful partings; the prospect of them made me anxious and sad.

When four bowls of gruel arrived, Jane looked at hers with distaste, but her sour mood did not last long. She took up her spoon and devoured the lot with an exceedingly good appetite. She was obviously enjoying the chance to be abroad, even if her adventure would only take her as far as Downe's Wharf.

"When you arrive in Scotland, my dear, I want you to take as much benefit from the fresh sea air as you can. A break from Skinner Street can only do you much good – and certainly no harm. It is right that you and your mother should be parted for a while…"

She is not my mother…

"You are an intelligent girl, Mary, much like your dear mother before you. However, it is your stepmother's belief that you think too much for a girl of your age." I stared at him with liquid eyes. "It is imperative that you guard against the Wollstonecraft tendency to melancholia… as I have urged you before. Try to… well, try to enjoy life."

He shrugged his shoulders and spread his palms in a gesture which was not entirely familiar with him – as if he was emphasising how simple was the whole business of living. And yet, I knew this to be a lie. As did he. It was all a façade, put on for my benefit. Life was not simple. Life was not easy to negotiate, dogged as it is by grief and sorrow. Yet here he was, pretending for my sake to be like other people, to take life in his stride when in reality he did no such thing.

The stranger across the room was eavesdropping on our conversation, although he made a great show of concentrating on his own meal.

I wondered about him. Of course, being in a darkened inn set me to thinking about Coleridge's tale, and how secrets are divulged in places such as this.

There was to be no such romantic encounter tonight, however. We clattered up the narrow wooden steps to our room, and lay down all in a heap, my two sisters and I. Half-sister, stepsister, but no full sister. Relationships came in halves and steps.

Father had a room across the corridor, and promised to wake us early in the morning in time for me to catch my berth on the *Osnaburgh*.

"I will miss you, Mary," a voice whispered in my ear, as I tried to sleep. It was Jane, lying to one side of me.

I turned my head towards Fanny. She lay silent, with her eyes open, staring up at the dusty rafters above our heads. She did not look at either of us. She seemed to be staring prophetically into her own stark future.

Downe's Wharf was full of jostling figures and crowds, men loading and unloading wagons, oily ropes, horses standing dolefully in their traces, waiting for the business to be over.

That was exactly how I felt – waiting for the ordeal to be over.

"Come, Mary," Father strode ahead, and we followed.

The ship itself reared up at the quayside, a creaking structure with its name emblazoned on the prow, the lettering faded from the lashing of salt seas against its stern.

Dread clutched at my bowels and knotted my insides.

"Don't be afraid, Mary," Jane chattered. "You are to have such an adventure. How I wish I were lucky enough to come with you. It's favouritism, I am sure."

Then came the embarrassing moment of Father trying to accompany me up the gangplank, in order to settle me in my berth and make sure that all was well, but it was forbidden.

"You do not have a ticket, sir."

"Yes, but surely you will allow…"

Turning away, I left him to it.

"Do you have any idea who I am, young man?"

"I have no care if you be the Queen of Sheba, sir. Rules is rules."

Jane was all ears, leaning in to hear the outcome of this exchange. Fanny and I faded back into the crowd, not wanting to draw attention to ourselves.

"Damn it, man…" Father's equilibrium was disturbed: he did not want this to happen today of all days. It might be a bad omen, to part on such a stressful note.

All Godwin's anxiety bubbled up and transferred itself straight into me. I felt it raging and coursing through my once quiet veins. Now I, too, was all aquiver, full of uncertainties and questions which were too late now to have answered.

Father began to scour the crowds in a final burst of anxiety.

"There, Mary, there is one," he bound forward and practically accosted a single woman travelling alone, with her travel cases by her side waiting to be lifted up the gangplank by the porters.

"Madame, might I be so bold as to…"

She looked faintly alarmed.

"It is my daughter, you see. She is travelling alone. I wonder if I might be so bold as to ask whether you might befriend her on the journey, see that she is safely taken care of? One cannot trust to anyone…"

It occurred to me to wonder why he hadn't considered this earlier, but I was mortified that he should request this of a total stranger.

She gave Father a knowing look which I did not altogether trust, and then smiled sweetly.

"Why, of course. What is her name?"

"Mary Godwin and…" Father fumbled in his purse and brought out a silver coin or two, in the hope this would clinch the matter "…this is for your pains."

Her eyes glittered in a manner faintly reminiscent of a witch in a fairy-tale as she accepted the payment.

"Thank you so much," Godwin was declaring. "… so grateful… There, you see, Mary?" he cried triumphantly, as if all the dreadful business of a week-long solitary voyage was solved in an instant. His conscience was clear, his mind at ease.

He handed me over to a perfect stranger, forgetting to ask her name, and watched us up the gangplank.

I waved goodbye to Fanny and Jane, suddenly realising that in all the commotion on the quayside we forgot to kiss in parting.

I made my way onto the deck of the Osnaburgh, in the wake of the stranger who seemed icily silent once we were on board. She stood beside me on deck, for appearance's sake. I spied Jane waving like mad below, but Fanny looked lost. Father looked a little hysterical, as if he could not quite make up his mind if he should feel reassured or not.

There was much delay before we set sail. Then at last the timbers began to creak and groan as we moved slowly out to sea, and I watched the diminishing figures on the quayside grow smaller and dimmer. Fanny, Jane and Godwin merged with the rest of the crowd until I could no longer pick them out. The banks of the Thames, with its untidy jumble of rooftops, were lost behind the early morning mist.

When I turned to my companion to ask her name, she had gone. I was standing alone, among strangers.

Robert Spinks, the Master and Captain of the vessel became a minor celebrity on our week-long voyage. I found a berth below, and once we were clear of the coast, the sea began to roll. As I predicted, my sense of equilibrium left me in an instant. I lay on the narrow bunk, desperately ill, filling the chamber pot they'd given me. I had to struggle up onto the deck and empty it into the sea if I was to have clean air.

When I returned to my berth and searched for a coin in order to buy myself some fresh water and gruel, I could not find my purse. I searched my bunk frantically but it was no longer there. I stared at the other passengers, but no one met my eye. I lay back down and allowed despair to engulf me. My travelling companion, the icy stranger, never reappeared during the journey but took pains to avoid me. Coins pocketed, she vanished into the crowd.

I thought of Jane, so full of excitement at the prospect of a week-long voyage, as I leant forward to void my breakfast into the basin the next morning. I had had to beg a little bread from the ship's captain, after explaining about my lost purse. The sea was rough for June, the waves piling up against our creaking wooden vessel. Captain Spinks and his men did not seem concerned about the weather, and barely bothered to reassure the passengers.

I lay flat on my bunk, staring up at the straining timbers. After several hours of this, I forced myself to sit upright, and clutching the railings I struggled up on deck, pulling myself against the force of the downward plunge.

A blast of salt sea-air hit me, and grey foaming spume sloshed across the deck. One of the sailors stopped me in my tracks.

"Probably best go down below, miss," he advised. "It's not really a day for taking the sea air."

Another massive wave crashed over the wooden railing. I clutched the rope to stop myself being flung down the oak steps.

The vessel pitched and rolled, at the mercy of the North Sea.

"Land ahoy!"

I sensed a movement of bodies around me. Tangible relief was in the air. It had been a hard voyage as far as I was concerned, my first ever at sea.

I vacated the below-decks misery for the final time, and climbed up on deck to witness my first sight of a foreign land. Low green hills stretched away from the coastline, bare and treeless. The distant port of Dundee looked very small and humble compared with London. Low wooden warehouses nestled against the wharf: a working mill or two stood proud on the hillside above. Something drew me to stare at the eyeless windows of those factory mills as we came closer to land. What would it be like to work inside one of those? I shuddered at the thought.

Aware that I must look a fright, I made an attempt to smooth my hair and frock. I had not been able to bathe or wash properly for more than a week, and my undergarments needed changing. My auburn hair was damp and hung in greasy coils. I tried to twist it back into ringlets. I had no hat, but a travelling cloak fastened over my chemise dress to cover the worst of the damage. I also had no money. I was arriving penniless. The embarrassment of this added to my shyness and insecurity. What would I say to my host? I was completely reliant on the goodwill of these people I had never met before.

The wharf slid closer to us, and I picked out individual details. I could make out a dog barking and wagging its tail. A boy in rags staring up at the ship in awe, waiting for it to strike anchor. Men on the quayside, working. Groups of well-dressed folk who stood around waiting, among them a man accompanied by two young women of about my own age, or slightly older, and a smaller girl whose hand was being held by a nurse. I fixed my gaze on them: these must be the Baxters.

Glancing sideways along the deck rail, I caught sight of the woman Father had accosted back at Downe's Wharf a week ago: she who pocketed his coins, and abandoned me for the rest of the journey. She studiously avoided my eye, and I had not the will to address her. She would probably ignore me, if I did.

"Ah, can this be our own Mary Godwin?" Baxter cried.

The cobbles beneath my feet rocked and swayed as if I was still at sea.

A tall, dark young woman, a little older than myself, stepped forward, her eyes dancing with excitement, then concern.

"But you are not well," she cried, throwing an arm about my shoulders.

I was thin as a rake, and very pale.

"I have been suffering from sea-sickness for most of the journey. I am sorry you should see me in this dreadful state."

"Don't be silly, Miss Godwin. We are here to help you. Everything will be blossoming now, you will see," Isabella said, for that was her name.

Another girl stepped forward, Christy, and declared softly, "It shan't take us long to get back to the Cottage, and then we can make you comfortable and dry."

There was some uncertainty about recovering my travel chest, but William Baxter was known in Dundee, a respectable manufacturer who employed people here at the wharfside and elsewhere, so he quickly established the whereabouts of my luggage – such as it was.

I stammered my gratitude, and began to explain how my purse was stolen.

"Poor Miss Godwin," Isabella cried. "You have had such a time of it."

A smaller girl called Kathleen, who was watching all of this in silence, turned to her father and said, "Miss Godwin is lovely. Can she stay with us forever?"

Mr Baxter laughed. "We shall see, Kathleen. We shall see."

The countryside rolled past, endless green hills, squat white cottages, a sky of scudding clouds. A bracing east wind swept in from the sea. This was my first sight of Scotland, land of intrigue, romance and rebellion, where Jacobite rebels disappeared into the mist and took refuge in the mountains. It was a place of danger and excitement, where kilted men were accustomed to walking for days and lying down in the heather to sleep. I was already falling under its spell, fed by the tales I'd read.

The Cottage was not quite what I was expecting. It lay in a tiny village called Broughty Ferry, on the north bank of the Tay. A beautiful fourteenth century house came into view as we turned at the bend in the lane.

"The Cottage," they announced.

It rose before me, grand and well-proportioned and utterly beautiful.

I was in heaven. It was far superior to anything I had imagined. Lawns swept down to the banks of the river, with a view of the Firth and the hills beyond. A grand backdrop against which romance or drama might unfold. My fourteen-year-old self was transported with delight.

Once my damp clothing was exchanged for warm, dry garments I felt almost human enough to eat the scones, oatcakes and tea which were served in the dining-room under the cheerful supervision of Mr Baxter and his daughters. A soft gauzy dress replaced the one I wore throughout the voyage.

"So soft," I could not help remarking, to which Isabella added, "courtesy of Baxter's cotton manufacturing mill." I touched the smooth fabric with interest.

"*This* comes from your own working mills?"

She nodded.

Then we were seated at the dining-room table, surrounded by glinting silver and chinaware, but there was no formality. Everyone chattered away to Mr Baxter, completely uninhibited and comfortable in his presence – not at all like Fanny and I when in Godwin's company. The tea was served in good china, that sparkled yellow and gold, and somehow made the tea hotter.

"So," he was saying as he liberally buttered a scone. "I shall leave you girls to become acquainted. I hope you will not think me rude, Miss Godwin, but I have some business to attend to this afternoon. What are your plans for the rest of the day?" he asked Isabella and Christy, as if they were entirely used to making their own arrangements, unchaperoned.

"I thought I might show Miss Godwin the grounds, Father."

"Explore at your leisure," he smiled generously.

"Please, do call me Mary," I murmured, but to my embarrassment and horror, my voice came out as a high-pitched squeak. It was mortifying to suffer a sudden attack of shyness in front of these lively individuals with their healthy gleaming curls and generous open smiles. It was all so different from the claustrophobic atmosphere of Skinner Street.

Isabella's eyes danced. "Mary, it is!" she cried.

A blue-patterned wallpaper lined the walls of this dining-room, decorated with tiny blue flowers. It was such a contrast to the distempered walls of Skinner Street.

I sat in silence and listened to the conversation of this family who all appeared to live in absolute peace and tranquillity with one another, without divided loyalties or lingering resentments. It was an eye-opener, and made me glimpse the possibility of a life beyond Skinner Street.

Isabella and Christy saw me sensibly installed in a room of my own on the first floor, which overlooked a grassy lawn sweeping down to the banks of the Tay. I could tell Isabella was watching me closely for signs of approval, but she needn't have worried: I was transported with delight at my new surroundings. As she chattered on, I longed to break through the wall of shyness that surrounded me and kept me apart from others.

The room itself was small and square with a narrow fireplace, a comfortable bed full of pillows and quilts, a dressing table and an easy chair in the corner by the window. A private space all of my own. I had been used to sharing with my sisters, Fanny and Jane, sharing all of our woes and anxieties and competitive desire for attention. But here the air was bracing, not stuffy or overcrowded. I could breathe. There were no fetid smells, no reek of blood and entrails, no tolling of the bell to remind us of execution day at Newgate. I was also miles away from St. Pancras Churchyard.

Perhaps that was what my stepmother wanted all along, to break the habit of a lifetime. In my youth I was harsh in my judgement, and assumed that she found the dead threatening because she could not argue with them. I believed that it threatened her to think that my attachment to Mary Wollstonecraft could be deeper and richer than the thin thread which bound me to her.

"What is that?" I asked Isabella pointing towards a high fortress standing guard at the mouth of the Tay.

"That? Just a ruin."

I stared out at the wild view before me.

We were side by side, about to become firm friends, facing the future. The future was out there somewhere, on that grey tide, with the hills and mountains in the distance.

"We have no castles like that down in London," I said. "Nothing so dramatic. Just Newgate Prison," I added on a sigh.

She glanced at me.

"A prison? You live near a prison?"

I nodded.

"We hear the bell tolling when there is to be an execution. I always feel sorry for the convicts. I can't help thinking about their families…"

"And what they must have done?" she added gleefully.

"We are all guilty of some crime, I suppose."

She gave me a strange sideways look.

"But not enough to hang, surely? Mary, you need cheering up, taking out of yourself. And I am just the person to do it."

She turned on her heel and headed towards a distant jetty.

"Where are you going?" I called after her.

"To see my sister," she shouted back. Her voice was lost on the wind.

I stood still and stared at her. "Your sister?"

"Our other sister. Come on."

Reaching the jetty, she had hitched up her skirts into her waistband, bent down and was pushing on the stern of a small rowing boat.

"Can you give me a wee hand, Mary?"

I did as I was told, and together we dragged the boat off the shingle into the shallows. Isabella untied the rope, and grabbed the oars, pointing one down against the bank and pushing with all her might. The small skiff moved out into the water, with us on board.

The current took her, and Isabella began to row with practised skill.

"I thought I'd had enough of boats to last a lifetime, but this is…"

I stared down at the rippling surface of the Tay, shimmering like silver scales in the sunlight.

"She lives just over there."

Isabella pointed with her chin toward the far bank. I could just make out the façade and chimneys of a white house behind the trees.

"This is how you visit your sister?"

Isabella smiled.

"She does not always keep well, and she needs our company."

There was something in Isabella's expression which made me study her and wonder at her motives.

"Should we let someone at the Cottage know where we are?" I murmured, glancing back over my shoulder.

Isabella shrugged. "Why? Father does not mind. We do this all the time. It is a kindness to Margaret."

The wind picked up, but Isabella seemed not in the least bit worried. She pulled on the oars with ease and grace. As the skiff began to bob and rock from side to side, she noticed the look of panic in my eyes and deftly turned the direction of the boat slightly to use the tide.

"Have no fears. I know how to do this," she shouted above the wind. "I will teach you."

"I will teach you."

These words filled me with excitement. It was as if I had arrived home, away from the filthy city streets to a landscape where I could breathe. Everything was wide and majestic: the wind, the sea, the sky, the air.

At last, I felt truly alive.

The boat bumped against the pebbles of the far shore. Isabella leapt out and I watched her tie the rope to a wooden stake driven into the bank. She demonstrated the best way: a sailor's knot, to stop it drifting away. Above us was a soft bank gradually sloping upwards towards a beautiful white cottage. A gentleman in a short fashionable jacket came out to greet us. He was small and dark with lively eyes. I had the impression he was used to expecting this visit.

"Isabella, my dear," he cried.

She allowed herself to be kissed.

"Margaret will be delighted."

His eyes travelled over me. "And who is this? Can this be?"

"Yes, it is," Isabella told him.

"Ah, to meet the daughter of Mary Wollstonecraft and William Godwin. This is indeed an honour," he smiled a little playfully and put a hand to his breast in a mock gesture, as if greeting royalty.

I smiled awkwardly.

I am used to my name going before me in certain circles because of my 'illustrious forebears'. I wondered what it would be like to be recognised for myself only – rather than as an appendage to others.

"This is David," Isabella said. "My sister's husband. David Booth."

I was vaguely familiar with the name.

"My father has spoken of you."

"I am – was – an admirer of your parents," Mr Booth informed me. Before long it appeared I too was allowed to call him David, as if we were all part of one big, happy family, but there was something here which struck a discordant note, even though I couldn't quite work out what it might be.

"How is Margaret?" Isabella asked.

Her brother-in-law hesitated. "She is not quite so well today, but no doubt your visit will cheer her up."

There was a soft cry from the door of the house above us:

a young woman who looked remarkably like Isabella appeared there.

"Again?" she cried. "To what do we owe the pleasure this time?"

"Do I need an excuse? I have brought Miss Godwin to see you. Or should I say, Mary?"

Introductions were made. Margaret was ordered back to her chair by her husband, where she sat for the rest of our visit, looking pale and languid. I could already see there was cause for concern here, but no one else seemed to mind. They chattered on regardless, as I suppose people must in the face of illness. What else is to be done, after all?

We sat in the front parlour and looked out at the river, watching the clouds race across a changeable sky. After a while a servant brought tea.

"We have one servant only," Margaret told me. "Jean, but she works so hard. I do not know how I would manage otherwise."

"You manage beautifully, my dear," David assured her, his hand resting on hers.

I noticed Isabella watching this exchange intensely, as if she could not help herself. Ah, I thought, there is a story here between these supposedly quiet lives, and I will be the one to find it.

Throughout that afternoon, I found myself shyly watching everyone else. Isabella talked more to her brother-in-law than to her sister: David Booth himself was quite happy to play the part of a man of the world. He liked us to hang on his every word. A touch of grey on his sideburns revealed him to be older than I at first suspected. He noticed me watching him, and I glanced quickly away. I could see that it disconcerted him.

Such an embarrassing habit, to be caught out staring.

"More tea anyone?" Margaret murmured.

"I'll pour," Isabella offered. She grabbed hold of the silver pot and almost knocked it over in her clumsy haste.

"Steady, Isabella," Margaret reprimanded her quietly.

But Isabella would not be told what to do, and shot her sister a warning glance in return. Illness or no illness, there was a tiny hint of tension here, and our man – David Booth – sat in the midst of it, proud owner of one sister, adored by both.

I had worked it all out, in an inkling.

I caught his eye again… and David Booth flinched. He had seen through me the way I had seen through him. He knew that I knew. What should we do now? Continue as if nothing had happened, I supposed, as I sipped my tea and accepted another wedge of cake.

"Will you stay the night, Isabella?" Margaret asked her sister.

Isabella shrugged. "We have not brought anything with us. Only ourselves."

"And that is all you need to bring," his voice chimed in, smooth as butter.

Ah, Mr Booth, I have your measure…

"Will your father not wonder where we are?"

"He will know," Margaret assured me. "He always knows."

"I see."

"And as for clothes and things, you can borrow some of mine."

"Oh, very well," Isabella cried as if reluctantly persuaded to give in. So we were not to return to the Cottage after all, but would stay the night here, across the Tay, where no one apparently knew where we were. I thought briefly of my stepmother shrieking when I'd stolen away in the afternoons to St. Pancras' Churchyard, to sit on the graves and pick flowers. This first taste of true freedom felt delicious by comparison.

David Booth glanced out of the window. "Anyway, the tide is running high. It would not be wise to risk a return journey. Wait until the morning."

"And we can talk philosophy all night," Isabella declared. She clapped her hands on her knees for emphasis.

"We can air a few ideas, if that is what pleases you. We must entertain our guests, after all."

Margaret paled slightly: a wave of tiredness swept over her. "I do not think I…"

"Of course not. You must rest, my dear."

"I am always resting," I heard her say.

"It cannot be helped."

"No one blames you for it," Isabella added.

Margaret had gone to bed. I was sitting before a crackling fire, listening to the rain patter against the window-pane. Isabella and her brother-in-law exchanged ideas like bright shuttlecocks in the candlelight. They were full of radical notions. I confess I had heard it all before. Instead of politics, I wanted someone to tell a story, the way Coleridge used to, when he told us the tale of the Ancient Mariner.

Politics did not set me ablaze the way stories could.

The evening extended itself, and we sat there in the shadows, two young girls. Isabella was older than I by two years. At sixteen, she was ready to taste life, to launch herself at it. David seemed oddly proprietorial towards her, and I was not entirely sure that I liked him. Or trusted him. His eyes lingered too long in places they should not, and he enjoyed Isabella's adulation too much: in fact, he encouraged it. He eyed me discreetly while Isabella was chatting, and again, his eyes rested a fraction too long on me until I was forced to look away. There was something bold in his gaze, something I did not understand.

It was gone midnight before we finally went to our beds. Isabella and I were compelled to share a small chamber upstairs.

Before she blew out the candle Isabella whispered to me, "Mary, what do you think of my brother-in-law, David?"

I turned my head on the bolster: the linen rustled. "What do you mean?"

"I mean," she added, smiling "what do you really think of him?"

I was quiet at first. "He seems very nice."

"I watched you watching him," Isabella said. This caused me to blush. "You are very astute, Miss Godwin. I think you can read people like a book."

I shrugged. I did not like the way the conversation was leading and was keen to divert her attention from the subject.

"I like him, Mary," she confessed in a girlish whisper.

"What?"

"You heard me." She rolled onto her back and stared up at the ceiling above us.

I waited for her to say more.

The confession I had feared and yet partly hoped for – it was coming – but I was not completely sure I wanted to hear it. What would I do with such a confession? A love triangle, between two sisters? What could be more complicated? It was obscene, it was hurtful, it was … dreadfully exciting.

"Tell me a bit more."

"Well," Isabella said, tucking her hand under her head. "It is all in my head, of course, but I fancy that David Booth really does enjoy my visits rather well, and it gives him some hope in a life which might otherwise be tinged with regret and sadness. Is it wicked to think so?"

She looked at me for confirmation.

"It is a bit," I said.

"Yes, I thought you might say that. So perhaps I should not have told you after all."

"No, really," I burst out. "You can tell me anything."

I rolled onto my stomach and stared out at the sky through the window close by. So much sky. No Newgate Prison. No Smithfield Market with its smells of butchery and raw flesh. No tall teetering buildings blocking out the daylight. No basement bookshop with its stacks and stacks of dusty books to be shelved, and customers to serve.

Just this. A sky full of starkly visible stars and a view of the sea.

"I could imagine living in Scotland forever, and being happy here."

"You can if you like."

"Look." I raised myself on my elbows, and used the ring on my finger to scratch my initials on the glass.

"What are you doing?"

"Leaving an imprint. M. G."

Isabella giggled and began to do the same.

"But you have no need to," I told her. "This place will never forget you. It is your home."

Little did either of us know that one day this house would become her prison.

If I close my eyes to the Putney dawn, I can still hear our smothered laughter, heads bent together in conspiracy, whispering secrets in the dark. I should have warned her; I should have told her about the lingering looks, the dark glances.

"Careful," I should have said, that night when we lay there.

A knowing moon looks in through the window. We are there still. No matter what happens in the future, that moment remains. I am a time traveller. The moon observes us as if she knows everything about us that others cannot.

Isabella and I lost touch eventually, when we were older. I would write to her, and she would refuse to reply. I had fallen out of favour by then. I was in disgrace according to polite society, and Isabella – who had never cared about polite society before – chose to ostracise me the same as everyone else.

Her sister Margaret continued to fade. As I had suspected, she was not long for this world, and soon after her sister's death

Isabella saw her wish fulfilled. Her secret passion for David was allowed to flourish, and after some initial disapproval, her father allowed the match to go ahead. Such was her fate. So David Booth exchanged one Baxter bride for another, and once she was his, there was no more need to row across the Tay to visit him. She had to stay there in the little white house forever...

But of course, back then, we did not know any of this. I could only guess and surmise.

It was clear that Isabella and her brother-in-law loved to argue and clash swords: they fought a continual duel of words which to them was exciting. Margaret and I were mere bystanders, watching the state of play. It was interesting, in a way, and sometimes I was tempted to join in – to disagree and challenge just for the sake of it.

I was sitting in the stern of the little boat the following afternoon, watching Isabella row us back across the estuary. She concentrated and pulled hard on the oars. The tide was less frisky than the day before. I loved the effortless glide across the silky surface, ripples parting the way. I turned my head to watch David Booth standing on the lawn. He raised his hand in farewell and turned toward the shadows of the house where his sick wife was still resting indoors, too tired to see us off. She was used to these comings and goings. It was not such a huge event for Isabella to drop by in this manner.

I lowered my hand into the water and my fingers were dragged backwards by the current. Droplets fell when I lifted them again, a shower of pearls in the bright sunlight.

Isabella laughed. "That's all very well, while some of us do the work."

When we arrived back at the far shore beneath the grounds of the Cottage I was expecting questions to be asked, some sort of commotion caused by our absence, but it was not even remarked upon. Mr Baxter was not at home.

I retreated to my room, slipped into the chair beside the window, took out my notebooks and began to write. This was a luxury I could never enjoy in Skinner Street, where every room was bursting to the seams, and unwelcome intrusions frequent.

I wanted a grand story, an unfolding drama of spectacular proportions.

I waited, and I waited.

"One day something original will arrive in your head," Isabella told me later. "What you need to do in the meantime is *live*."

A squawking of seagulls rose up around the ruin on the opposite bank of the Tay, black specks swirling in the sky. Its dark turrets stood stark against the skyline.

"Have you ever broken any rules, Mary?" Isabella asked me.

It was perhaps a week later, and we were lying side by side in the upstairs bedchamber of Margaret and David's cottage again, after another night of discussion in the downstairs drawing-room under David Booth's fraternal supervision.

"What rules do you mean?"

"Oh, some rule that society insists is terribly important and must never be broken."

I thought for a moment.

"No, I don't think so. But I think I would quite like to."

She giggled. "Me too."

In the end, it will not be Isabella who breaks the biggest taboos of polite society. It will be me, and I will be punished for it. Isabella herself – once she has become a respectable lady – will join in the general approbation against me. She will ignore my letters, withhold her friendship, refuse to have anything to do with me again.

"It would be so magnificent to break all the most important rules of polite society," she declared dreamily. "Or at least, one of them, at any rate. A tiny one."

"And which tiny one would that be?"

"I don't yet know," she laughed. "I haven't decided."

The moon was still looking in at us.

"Do you believe in marriage, Mary?"

"Of course not. Marriage is a trap for women, whereby they lose all their rights. That's what my parents believed. But then my father married again, without another thought. He reneged on all of his earlier promises to my mother. That's what makes him a hypocrite, I suppose." I spoke with all the harshness of the very young.

"Mm…" Isabella murmured. "A grand romance is the thing. A romance that would take us far away from the tiredness of all this…"

I yawned, and blinked my eyes slowly.

This small room, where my initials are now scratched into the window glass, witnesses many a whispered discussion like this. Gradually, over time, Isabella continues to elaborate on her feelings for her brother-in-law, and although we both know it is wrong, I encourage her. And I fail to warn her about the strange looks he gives me, where his eyes linger too long even when I look away. I never admit to her that I do not actually *like* David Booth at all.

Or perhaps I did? Perhaps I warned her to be careful, and she accused me of jealousy, because she did not want to hear the truth. I do not remember.

Do we think about Margaret's feelings in all of this?

Margaret is sick and ailing. She is also kind and gentle. She is a loving presence, but an invisible one, and David Booth seems to prefer it that way.

During the long carefree days and the lingering evenings

when the twilight is gloaming across the Tay, Isabella and I entertain romantic notions about her brother-in-law, and whisper our secrets into the dark.

"Is that not a kind of incest?" I asked her.

"How can it be? And even if it is, what then? You have heard of the poet Byron, of course? He is said to have an intense relationship with his own *sister*, Augusta."

My eyes widen. "His own sister?"

"So they say."

When I sail back to London in November, it is with promises on both sides that I will return again in the spring.

"A winter in London will not be such a hardship," Mr Baxter reassures me. "You have yet to experience our winters."

"I would not mind the winters," I tell him.

"Let us hope you have a smooth passage home, my dear. In more ways than one."

I am sad to part with Isabella and Christy, and sad too that we will not be taking any more boat trips across the Tay to visit David Booth – and Margaret, of course.

There is a swell out on the North Sea, and I take to my bunk, dreading that I have not been in time to avoid a winter storm.

Skinner Street, 1814

Back in Skinner Street that winter, the atmosphere was worse than I imagined. I was thrown in at the deep end, and forced to forget all the pleasures and freedoms of my life in Scotland. This was my reality now.

Mary-Jane was continually harping and bickering; Father was more remote than ever. He hardly spoke to me, other than to stare at me with a desolate expression on his face while he explained the reality of our situation.

"I am in debt, Mary. I cannot manage to stay afloat. We are inches away from ruin."

There was no need now to listen at doors. He stated the truth openly, unable to hide or prevaricate. Indeed, it had become his one lament, his constant refrain.

"We will be taken away – all of us: you will see your father ruined. And all I ever strived to do was to write, and to tell the truth. But who cares about that, now? No one cares."

My stepmother, impatient with these laments, threw herself into the industry of the bookshop.

"There is no point," Father told her. "We are a sinking ship, and you cannot breach the flood that way."

I was beginning to feel impatient with Father's melodrama. Reluctantly, Mary-Jane and I shared a sneaking moment of complicity and understanding. Neither of us wanted to give in to his melancholy; both of us preferred to seek solace in industry. I worked hard in the bookshop, and tried to think of other ways I might earn money.

Then one evening Father was all astir and excited with news of a new acquaintance he had made, one which might change his fortunes.

"He has been an admirer of mine for some years although I did not know it. And of your mother's too," Godwin added, at which I noticed my stepmother bridle for an instant. Another painful reminder of her deceased rival. Father ignored this and carried on. "He is keen to pay us a visit."

"What is his name, Father?"

"Shelley. Percy Bysshe Shelley. The son of a baronet, no less."

I was a little disillusioned to hear him speak like this, placing such store on a title. It struck me as hypocrisy, and I couldn't help contrasting this with the sanguine and stoical behaviour of William Baxter. If a comparison was to be made, Father did not come out of it very well.

"He was recently expelled from Oxford along with his best friend, Thomas Hogg."

"Expelled?" Mary-Jane cried, shocked. "Whatever for?"

"Atheism," Father announced proudly, as if this highly recommended him to us. "He wrote some diatribe against religion, and then distributed it as a leaflet in the quadrangle amongst the undergraduates. The staff were furious."

Father sounded absolutely delighted.

"The son of a baronet, you say?" Mary-Jane asked.

"That's right." He nodded, then turned to me. "Mary, you are to please him as much as you can. Let him think well of us. Put us in a good light. We rely on this connection: it could be the saving of us."

Godwin, my father, was convinced that the twenty-one-year old Shelley, who described himself as a poet, and a devotee of Wollstonecraft, was rich beyond our wildest dreams; he had promised to help secure a loan for my father and save him from debtors' prison. Indeed, Percy Shelley will promise many things in his life.

When our guest arrived at the house in Skinner Street, I was washed, dressed and combed, the younger children were in bed, the house was relatively tidy. No one would guess at the chaos that normally reigned during the day.

A fire was lit in the study, and rather than be excluded, Fanny, Jane and myself were all allowed to stay, but cautioned to be on our best behaviour. We were to present the front of a united family, full of interest and witty banter. Our duty was to charm Shelley, and make him believe in our myth. The great myth and legend of the Wollstonecraft/Godwin alliance.

When Percy Shelley was first shown into the room, I watched him discreetly from my obscure corner in the shadows. A tall, young man, very slight of build, with messy hair, a deliberately-loosened cravat, as if he could not quite be bothered to straighten it: nankeen trousers, fashionable short jacket. His eyes were lively and full of good humour. He looked about him quickly, trying to work out which one of us was the daughter of Mary Wollstonecraft. His gaze swept briefly over Fanny, lingered longest on Jane, and then came to rest on me.

Was he disappointed when he saw a quiet reserved creature who preferred to remain outside the limelight? My stepsister Jane took centre-stage, as was her way. She offered to play the piano, so we trooped through to the drawing-room to watch her perform. With very little encouragement she began to sing, showing off her skills to their best advantage. She was lively and voluble and quick to charm. Her chatter made up for my silence, but I fancy it was not the chatter he was interested in.

When I observed Father struggling to please Shelley, I winced. Fanny was even quieter than myself, but she watched this newcomer shyly, and her eyes lit up and smiled in a way she had not done in years. He was very funny – comical, even. He had a child-like sense of mischief.

He explained to us that as a boy he had once harboured dreams of becoming a scientist, and was interested in conducting experiments.

"And was that the time you set fire to the butler?" my father asked him, in all seriousness, without realising how absurd he sounded.

"Yes, I am afraid it was. But it was all in the interests of science, you understand."

The unfamiliar warmth of laughter filled the room.

"However, I do not think Sir Timothy appreciated it."

"Sir Timothy?" Father asked.

"My father."

"Ah, the baronet!" and I felt myself cringing at Godwin's transparency. Surely this young man had not failed to notice it? He could not be impressed with what he saw.

But, of course, what I failed to appreciate was that it was not my father – or even, perhaps, the legacy of Mary Wollstonecraft that Shelley was interested in. It was the three daughters of the household, with the multitude of romantic possibilities that presented themselves.

Percy was an advocate of free love, as I learnt to my cost. He dreamed of rescuing young women from their slavery and servitude and releasing them into the wild, as if we were animals instead of people. He wanted us wild and unchained instead of tame and domestic. At least, that was his theory. I remembered this in years to come, when I stood at the basin, my hands chilblained from the water, my belly swollen with another pregnancy.

So, this was how the curtain rose on our drama…

Skinner Street, London 1814

The next time Shelley came to visit, Father engineered it
so that I must sit next to the young poet when supper was
served. We did not have many servants in the house, so
the task of cooking and serving food fell to Mary-Jane.

"Mary, pass Mr Shelley the salt, will you?"

"Really, there is no need to feed me as well as entertain me,"
Shelley cried, "although I have to say it is comforting to be here.
I find such a welcome here that it melts my heart."

"We do our humble best," my stepmother declaimed, and I
wordlessly begged her to be silent.

Shelley shot me a look and winked at me.

"Has he spoken yet about any kind of loan?"

"Not in so many words, my dear, but I know that it cannot be
far from his mind. He is fully aware of our predicament. I have
apprised him of the facts. He knows that debtors' prison is a very
real possibility."

"Then why does he not act?"

"Be patient, my dear. He is the son of a baronet, accustomed to having things his own way. He perhaps sees no very real urgency in the matter."

"Then acquaint him better with the facts," my stepmother snapped. "It is no use hoping and postulating. One of us needs to take action."

"And so I have, my dear. You know that."

"I know nothing of the kind, Godwin. All I know is that you have invited an aristocrat to dinner, and hope to be rescued by him. Experience has taught me that it is always better to be independent if one can help it."

"Mary-Jane," I heard my father's tone become imploring. "If I could pay off all of our debts, I would."

"Perhaps we should live within our means, then," she declared.

"You mean live like paupers?"

"Is that all we can hope for?" she added. "Then what is the point of all your great learning?"

Father paused for a moment before replying, and I imagined him to be shaking his great head from side to side. "In truth, I have no idea."

And there it was. The stark truth of it.

It would be better to be the owner of a cotton mill like William Baxter, anything rather than a thinker and intellectual, a man who wrote books.

Who needs books?

"We do," my stepmother told me later that morning, when she caught me on the stairwell. "I need you to serve in the shop again, Mary."

This was our livelihood now. Not great works of learning which explored the rights and wrongs of humankind, shining a light into the darkness... Instead it was this. Serving at the counter, keeping the accounts, making sure the shop remained open and customers were enticed to buy, while my stepmother translated works from French into English in her spare time.

I was loath to admit it, but during these lean years I realised it was my stepmother who kept the wolf from the door, not Godwin. And one further thing became clear to me. My future was not the one I imagined when I lived with the Baxters and enjoyed the freedoms of that wild Scottish landscape. Instead, the best I could hope for was to become a governess or lady's companion, or – in the immediate future – a life spent working in the bookshop, keeping it open to customers, bringing in a small revenue. And it was not even an income which could support us in Skinner Street, with Newgate prison nearby and the stink of Smithfield butcheries never far from our nostrils. It was a far cry from the Cottage and the banks of the river Tay, and it was a far cry from Number 29, The Polygon.

I wonder what Isabella's life is like now, I thought, in the little white house surrounded by trees, married to her former brother-in-law, despite the disapproval of their Presbyterian neighbours? Could I have enjoyed that life? Might David Booth have chosen me when poor Margaret died? And if he had, would I have been content with that?

I do not think so.

It was not long before Percy Shelley began to visit me in the bookshop when he knew my stepmother might be absent.

The first time, I was surprised to see him. I shyly asked him what he was interested in. He smiled with amusement. "That's very funny, Miss Godwin."

"Excuse me?"

"What I am interested in?"

"Well?"

He ran a finger along the spine of a hefty edition of *Tales*

Collected by Perrault. "I don't see the necessity of rushing a purchase. Do you?"

"I suppose not."

"Let us talk instead."

Percy listened to me; he wanted to know my views on every subject. Those stolen hours spent together in the quiet bookshop were the beginning of something.

Customers became used to seeing the young Percy Shelley lurking behind the shelves, as if he was part of the furniture.

My stepmother, however, had other ideas.

She ordered Jane to keep an eye on us. This was no inconvenience to Jane at all, who was eager to be part of the drama so that she might have her own opportunity of beguiling Mr Shelley.

"I have always had so much respect for your mother's views," Percy told me.

In my confusion, I assumed at first that he was speaking about my stepmother, but he was referring, of course, to my own mother, Mary Wollstonecraft. She held sway over her followers from beyond the grave.

"She was a great critic of the institution of marriage," he said.

"Yes."

"And yet she married your father in the end." He waited out a pause. "Why was that?"

I hesitated. "I don't know."

"Of course you don't!" Shelley said. "You were not even born, so why should you know the answer?"

He grew suddenly gloomy and added, "We all succumb in the end. Even when we know marriage to be a cage. You must not judge your parents too harshly, Mary."

A darkness had descended on him.

"What do you mean?" but he would not answer.

I sensed he had his secrets.

*

Most often these days it was my stepmother and I who were left alone in the shop together. My stepsister Jane was busy with her French and music lessons. I would hear her voice spiralling upwards through the core of the house like an invisible staircase of sound while I sat, Cinderella-like, in the basement with the books.

Mary-Jane found me here, attending to the latest customer – a widow who had brought in her three young children to buy books. I watched them choose *Swiss Family Robinson*.

"A good choice," I told her, although I did not add that it was translated by my stepmother. I did not want to give her any credit, so grudging was I in my youth. I wrapped the package while the three children stared at me.

After they had gone, Mary-Jane swept in and I sensed she had something preying on her mind. She slammed a newly-arrived box of books on the counter, and caught her breath.

"Well," she said, "I think it best that you hear it from me before your father finds out."

I waited.

"Our young Percy Shelley? Whom your father thinks the answer to all of our prayers? I would not fix your heart on him if I were you."

I felt my cheeks flush.

"I have no idea what you mean."

Mary-Jane smiled. "Oh, you know perfectly well what I mean. I shall warn Jane of the same. He might well give your father a loan, but if you should find yourself falling in love with him, it would not be a wise choice."

She paused. I felt the air crackle.

"He is already married."

Percy Shelley, the man who had been finding his way into my

heart, drawing me to him like a moth to a flame, was a married man. Respectable... well, no, not exactly that...

I felt my face grow hot.

"Percy and I are nothing more than friends."

"A young woman called Harriet Westbrook. You know the name?"

I shook my head.

"A young woman of *good* family, nineteen years of age. She bore him a child."

I listened in silence.

"So, the next time Percy Shelley comes a-visiting the shop, lingering down here instead of visiting your father upstairs in his study, send him on his way, would you? Send him up to your father, so that he can discuss the terms of the loan he promised. That, after all, is the purpose of his visit."

"You are a man with secrets."

Percy's face fell. We were alone in the shop. He had found me here, and despite my stepmother's warning, I did not send him on his way. I decided to challenge him instead.

"There is nothing between us. No promises have been made, so I suppose I have no right to feel betrayed."

He did not speak.

"You have a daughter."

He did not bother to deny it.

"What is her name?"

He looked up. "Ianthe." A small smile lit up his face as he spoke her name. "She is six months old." I was surprised to feel a knife twisting in my gut.

"I thought you did not believe in marriage?"

I would not allow him to walk away without first shedding a little blood.

"I don't, but Harriet had other ideas! She and I were very

much in love at first. I liked her. And we were happy. But she worried too much about what people would say. I assured her we were happier as we were, but she talked me into marrying her. She wanted the badge of respectability, some outward sign of security, I suppose." I held my breath while he talked. "That was when it all changed. She became... someone else. Needy, insecure. She stopped being free-spirited and had her mind set on other things, trivial things. It was not a good idea to get married. I warned her, but she wouldn't have it any other way." And so he absolves himself of responsibility – as people do.

"Why did you leave her?"

He seemed lost in thought for a moment. "I was not in love with her anymore. The magic, the spell," he shrugged. "It was over."

The sound of the bell over the door brought me sharply to my senses. I hurried to attend to the next customer. Shelley turned away and pretended to browse the shelves.

My mother, Mary Wollstonecraft, had a lot to say about the institution of marriage. She said it was a death sentence to the freedom and independence of women. Once you are married, she wrote, women have no legal rights over their own property or even their own children.

She was keen to show up the legal institution of marriage for the travesty that it was. And my father, Godwin, had agreed with her. And yet he had since married twice. First my mother, in order to protect her from the world's prurience, and secondly – Mary-Jane Clairmont – for reasons best known to himself.

Shelley did not leave the shop. He waited for the customer to leave.

"Why should you apologise to me?" I told him. "You have made no promises. There is nothing at all between us."

At this, he was nonplussed.

"What does your family think of your marriage?" I asked him.

An expression of sadness flitted across his features for a moment. "I am not allowed to see my mother or my sisters. I miss them. Sir Timothy did not approve of the marriage, but he disapproves even more of the fact that I left her."

"I think I agree with him."

"It makes no difference. He stopped speaking to me when I was expelled from Oxford."

I stared at him. "My father thinks you will secure him a loan which will save him from ruin."

Shelley looked sheepish. "And so I will – if I possibly can."

"I can't help thinking that's highly unlikely. Nevertheless, he continues to believe it to be the case. I am ashamed that my father should think like that. It is most embarrassing."

"Why?" Shelley asked. "It's no fault of your father's if the world does not value the work of its great thinkers and radicals."

"My mother was poor, but *she* still managed to write. No one helped her. She always had to help herself." I felt a little disloyal as if I was betraying my father. "She asked favours of no one."

"You should not compare the two," Shelley said. "One is alive, the other is…"

"Dead?"

"Immortalised in memory." He studied me then. "You are very caustic, Miss Godwin."

"Would you not expect me to be?"

"You are so quiet, so reserved, and yet – one-to-one – you are more than capable of speaking your mind."

"… for one of my frail sex? I should hope so."

"I apologise, Miss Godwin. I think I have offended you."

He gave a quick bow as if we were suddenly strangers.

All that springtime, as the city streets retained the heat, and the stench of rotten waste grew high on the air, my father continued to believe that Shelley was a rich man, with thousands upon thousands of pounds at his disposal, money and lands a-plenty. He had no idea that Shelley had been disowned by the baronet.

Neither I nor Shelley enlightened him, for I could not see that it was relevant. If Father wished to befriend Percy Shelley for whatever reason, that was his business, and I would not interfere.

However, my stepsister Jane seemed to have acquired information for herself, which led me to believe she was having private conversations of her own with Shelley.

"I wonder what Harriet Westbrook is like?" she mused out loud on one occasion.

I looked at her.

"Excuse me?"

"Harriet, his wife. I can't believe you don't know, Mary?" she teased.

"Of course I know. I am just surprised that you do. How on earth…? Never mind that now, but you must say nothing of this to Godwin."

"Why?"

"It will upset him. And there is enough upset in this household to last a lifetime."

There was a short pause. "I do wonder though," she persisted. "So tragic that they should fall out of love again." She leaned closer. "Apparently, I heard a rumour she was pregnant again when he left her. She only found out afterwards."

I stared at Jane.

"Oh – did you not know? I expect he'll have to agree to look after her. What do *you* think will happen?"

Father called meeting after family meeting to warn us of his imminent ruin.

"Shelley is my only hope." He looked at me pointedly. "The son of a baronet. With connections like these, we can possibly save ourselves from a fate worse than death."

My stepmother, Mary-Jane, interrupted him. "I will not see that happen again. I cannot go back there."

"You are very strong, my dear," Godwin murmured. "Very strong. And I feel wretched, utterly wretched, that I have brought you to this juncture again."

"Perhaps if we stopped paying Charles's tuition fees and brought him home from the school he is attending?" I suggested.

It was out before I knew it.

My stepmother fixed me with a steely gaze. Poor Mary-Jane: no amount of nurturing and care on her part would ever endear her to me at that point. The portrait above Father's desk divided us, reminding me of what I had lost, and reminding *her* of what she could not possibly hope to replace.

"And have another useless mouth to feed?" she barked. "I am teaching my children to be independent, Mary. You too. One day you will need to stand on your own two feet."

"There is no need for such drastic measures," Father declared peaceably. "Let us first of all see what comes of my connection with Shelley. He is a capital fellow, full of admiration for the philosophy and ideas we espouse, and with good intentions, no doubt."

Jane and I exchanged glances. My stepmother had obviously not yet dared to enlighten him.

While Father continued to hope, I continued to entertain and encourage a secret passion for Percy Shelley. I knew his faults, and yet I forgave him. I could change him, I told myself. He would be different once he and I became lovers. I would transform him into the man he might become. We talked for long hours together. We shared poetry, debated serious topics.

"There are so many people I would like you to meet, Miss Godwin. Political reformers, those who push for change and equality. Why do you smirk?" he asked me.

"You are the son of a baronet. Some might say you know very little of equality."

He held up a hand to his chest in mock agony. "That wounds me. But you are right and I am wrong – in all things, I see. That great brow of yours contains more wisdom than my little pinkie…" he held up his finger to demonstrate and waggled it.

"Great brow? You make me sound like a deformed monster."

"Not at all. I admire your brow very much."

I glanced at him and a spark of mischief darted between us.

"I do not think you should be speaking to me like that. What would Harriet say?"

"It is not Harriet I am thinking about."

In June we met in secret away from the bookshop. Jane donned a feather-light shawl and accompanied me into the summer twilight: no one suspected whom we might be meeting.

Percy was already waiting at my mother's graveside when we arrived. A large white moon hung low in the trees, and an owl hooted. To me this was not a morbid location, despite the graves which clustered close, the solid tombs and monuments to the dead. So many voices clamoured here, their lives so busy and full of words and ideas and whispered conversations, yet now they lay silent beneath us, all conversation stilled.

Percy told me how much he missed his little sisters and his mother. "My father forbids me to see them. He tells them I'm insane. He threatens to have me locked up if I show my face at Field Place again."

"Perhaps it's just an idle threat."

Percy shook his head. "You do not know my father."

Jane hovered nearby and joined in our whispered dialogue at times. She was younger than me by less than a year, and to both of us, Shelley – at twenty-one – seemed to carry the air and authority of a much older man.

He put an arm around me, pushed me back against my mother's grave, and gently stroked me in places I did not yet know existed. Jane turned her back. She was standing far off among the trees. Oddly, Percy did not seem to mind her presence there. As I felt him move on top of me, I looked up into his face, but he was staring straight ahead, into the trees, where I am almost sure my stepsister lingered.

When we were done, he smoothed my dress down, kissed me on the lips. He had taken possession of me. I knew what I was risking by doing this, but it filled me with excitement and tremulous joy. At last, something was happening to relieve the dreary monotony of life at Skinner Street.

On the way home Jane was sulky and cross. "Your eyes look different," she remarked.

I walked ahead of her, to hide my blushes.

My body felt soft and languid, and at the same time, a new wolfish hunger was awake inside me, like a slumbering monster uncurling from its long sleep. I would do anything, go to any lengths, to secure another meeting with him.

I did not expect my father to disapprove. After all, he'd encouraged me to captivate the rich young baronet's son, to impress upon him the value of our acquaintance. On top of which, Godwin had always been very open with us about our mother's values and ideals before she died (even if others thought those views eccentric), that she saw the institution of marriage as a poor deal for women. So Godwin's outrage and anger came as a shock.

When Father found out, Shelley and I were forbidden to see each other. Skinner Street became a prison, a cage, just as Percy predicted it would, and he longed to release me from it and set me free – like a bird.

I felt cheated, misinformed. I remembered Father urging me to make Percy welcome, to do my best to please him, but apparently this did not include a romantic liaison. Why were the unspoken rules of life so baffling? I wondered. The differences between what people said, and what they meant to say, seemed to create an unfathomable gulf which I failed, completely, to negotiate. I clung to the cliff-face of one, while gazing across at the other, not knowing how or where I had gone wrong.

I gazed out of the narrow window of our schoolroom at Newgate Prison – now a prisoner myself, forbidden to leave the house – and listened for the ominous tolling of the bell.

"I will help you," Jane promised me, arriving in the schoolroom on her light feet and with a finger to her lips. She loved a conspiracy, a bit of drama. As she was still allowed to leave the house, she contrived to meet up with Percy in secret, and carried letters back and forth. I considered for a moment why she was so quick to agree to this, and wondered what her own private conversations with Percy were like in my absence – but it was only for a moment, brief as a butterfly's wing – before I continued headlong down my path of destruction or redemption.

Then came the dark night we took flight from Father's house. In my own case, never to return. It was an irrevocable step, and even now, I cannot truly say if it was the right decision, but it was the only one offered to me – a young girl without opportunities for freedom, or to see the world in my own right. No matter what happened along the way, I could not have reached full maturity under that claustrophobic roof. Father could not afford to send me abroad, and I was not allowed – as a young woman – to travel alone. But I did regret that I caused pain to my own dear father. Whatever his faults, I did not wittingly choose to hurt him.

So one dark night, I lay fully clothed on my bed, a travelling bag hastily packed at my side. The house took a while to settle. I heard Father's footsteps on the stairs for the last time, Mary-Jane's lighter tread: coughing, beds creaking with their weight.

There were few secrets in this household; every noise carried through the inferior paper-thin walls.

My travelling-bag was hidden beneath the thin blanket. I kept our imminent departure a secret from Fanny, knowing that she might beg me to stay, or alert Father. When the clock struck three, my stepsister and I crept from the room. Fanny stirred in her sleep, but did not wake. Did I stop to think what it might be like for her in our absence, left all alone at Skinner Street without an ally to defend her?

We stealthily made our way down the staircase, our pumps in our hand, avoiding the creaky stair. The door made barely a noise as I pulled it open onto the London night.

We hurried through the dark streets. What if we should reach Hatton Garden too early, and Shelley was not there? What if he failed to keep his promise?

But the carriage was waiting. I could see the gleam of its lanterns up ahead. Percy was about to lift me into the seat, but I stopped him.

"Wait!"

"What is it?" They both looked at me in alarm.

My heart was in my mouth. I could not swallow for the sudden dread I felt. Jane seemed to have no such misgivings. She was ready for an adventure, and did not rightly care where it led her, as long as it was away from our parents.

"We have to leave a note for Father."

"What?"

"I have to go back and leave a note for him. I cannot leave without a single word. I must let him know that I love him, and am doing what makes me happy."

The other two looked at me in astonishment. Percy rubbed his forehead. Jane looked impatient, as if she would like to slap me.

"Could you not have thought about that before we left the house?"

I ignored her.

"Mary, you can't go back there now. What if they see you?" Percy implored.

"I don't care. I have to."

I left them both standing there by the waiting carriage, and ran home to the tall, lean, hungry-looking house in Skinner Street. Its darkened windows reproached me, but I paid no heed. I flung open the door, crept to Godwin's study, and penned a quick note to him. I suddenly could not bear the thought this might be a permanent parting…

I heard a movement upstairs at one point, lifted my head to listen, half-hoping, perhaps, to be caught in the act. But no one appeared. The other occupants of the house lay sleeping, unaware of what the morning would bring. It would be poor Fanny who would wake to our empty beds, and know immediately what had happened. Perhaps she already knew… Perhaps the sight of her sleeping had been a ruse and she had heard every quiet movement we made?

When I hastened back to the other two I could see their heads bent together in the darkness. A sudden pang of jealousy hit me. What could they be discussing?

"We thought you were taken prisoner again," Jane cried, her voice high with excitement.

I sighed at her tone of melodrama. Percy handed Jane into the carriage first, then myself: the driver raised his whip, the horses moved forward as one, and the carriage lurched away across the cobblestones. Glancing out the window, I watched the darkened streets of our rundown neighbourhood roll slowly by.

When would Father find my note? Would he give chase?

What would the future hold?

PART THREE: AN EXPERIMENT IN LOVE

France, 1814

We were not the only refugees on the road. Hundreds of people seemed to be on the move. The war with France not long over, few people had ventured across the Channel since it began. I felt like an adventurer or an intrepid explorer, treading where few had gone before into a region scarred by battle and warfare. But the idea of glamour did not last long...

"Perhaps we did not choose our time well, Percy, my dear," I murmured, observing the hungry refugees, among them soldiers with horrific injuries, their uniform in rags.

"Once we reach Paris, I will be able to secure a loan from my father and then we can continue in relative comfort. All will be well. You will see."

But I did not want him to protect me from these sights. They were the reality, and I couldn't help feeling it would be wrong to allow his father's money to shield us from it.

It was becoming harder to place any trust or faith in Percy's confident assurances. The voyage to Calais was terrifying. A storm hit just before dawn, and I did not think we would survive.

Now the air was hot and the ground dusty beneath our feet. As we trudged on, the sun climbed higher in the sky, baking the dirt road before us.

Jane begged for a rest, so we left the path, and took shelter in a field where the crop stood ready to be harvested, but it was a damaged crop, much of it already stolen by hungry soldiers on the road, or decimated by battle. Percy spread his coat on the ground and we sat upon it like three peasants having a picnic. Percy leaned back against a boulder and I leaned against him, and in this way the three of us drifted off to sleep.

I was woken by huge drops of rain, splashing onto the cracked dry earth around us.

We took shelter in a nearby cabin where a woman eked out an existence with her five children. Eyes peered at us out of the gloom, and when she offered us a cup of watery broth I refused. I did not want to deprive them of their next meal. Percy left a coin with her. She would not take it at first, so he left it on the chair by the door.

An hour later, when the rain had stopped, we were on our way again, the dirt track steaming up ahead. Our clothes dried on our backs.

That night we slept in a hayloft, the next night in a barn, sharing two loaves of dry bread that we managed to buy in a village along the way.

"Once we get to Paris," Percy kept saying, glancing nervously at the expressions on our faces. Both of us were weary and travel-worn, and even Jane was half-tempted to flee back to London and to our 'prison' in Skinner Street, the schoolroom with the view of Newgate Prison, and the dusty bookshop in the basement. Is this what we left home for? To be hungry and homeless? I could see that even Jane was beginning to doubt the wisdom of our venture.

In Paris, Percy visited the bank, while Jane and I sat in a small square of flowering trees, watching the neighbourhood go about its business.

"Are you worried about the future, Mary?" Jane asked me.

"Why do you ask?"

"You look so unhappy. If I had been whisked away by the man I am in love with, I should not look so long in the face. Perhaps Sir Timothy will have relented and Percy will come back with heaps of gold coins," Jane said after a while.

I turned to her in disbelief. "This is not some fairy-tale, Jane. What we have done changes everything."

"But I thought you were the one brave enough to fling aside convention?"

"I am. I was."

"And now you are regretting it."

"I do not regret it," I snapped back.

We sat in the sunshine and listened to the birds in the trees above. A man on sticks shuffled by and stopped when he saw us. He was dressed in rags and one of his hands had been mutilated, while both of his legs were twisted at odd angles – another casualty, perhaps, of Napoleon's war. He held out a grimy paw for money or food, but we had neither.

We stared back at him and I felt suddenly helpless. Jane shook her head sternly and he moved on, but I couldn't take my eyes away from the poor wretch and I gazed at his back as he dragged himself on his way. It took him an age to cross the square and I wondered if he did it on purpose, to deliberately wring the last dreg of guilt from us. Jane nudged me and murmured, "Stop looking."

A little while later Percy emerged from a building across the square, waved and headed towards us looking triumphant. I could tell he was making a valiant effort to hide the evident stress he was under.

"I managed to secure sixty pounds," he cried.

Jane and I gazed at him. How far would sixty pounds stretch? Enough to set up home somewhere? How many miles would it carry us, across how many borders?

He threw an arm around each of us in a comradely fashion, which delighted Jane, but left me feeling slightly uneasy.

"And, my fair beauties, there is more where that came from," but his smile was strained and there was a shadow of doubt behind his eyes. He did not believe he had the wherewithal to support two fleeing maidens, despite his title. His legacy was useless to him: he was forbidden access to it and had to beg and borrow just to secure a single ha'penny.

We travelled across Europe as an uneasy threesome until the money ran out. I remember little of our stay in Switzerland, other than the fact I was irritated by the closeness which seemed to grow up between Percy and my stepsister. I would hear them laughing together, or catch a rapid exchange between them, a little duplicitous eye contact. Jane, for her part, seemed jealous and preoccupied, even sulky at times.

When we tired of Switzerland we travelled home via the Rhineland on a canal boat, propped against the gunwale in the sunshine, dirty as paupers, scribbling in my notebook. There was something about that trip which inspired me.

One day Percy and I managed to evade Jane by leaving her with the boat hands, and we took a trip into the hills to inspect the ruins of a castle I could see peeping through the trees.

"What's that up there?" I asked, immediately intrigued.

A walker on the towpath told us it was called Frankenstein Castle, and that an alchemist named Johann Dippel, born there in 1673, conducted experiments on corpses that he stole from a nearby graveyard. According to the man, he made a formula known as Dippel's Oil which was the equivalent of the 'elixir of life.'

"Those who take it would live forever, without even the aid of a sorcerer's stone. If you believe in that stuff," he added. I stared up at the ruined castle. "We have to go there," I told Percy. The elixir of life. What kind of man would dare? The rest of our return journey is a blur, but that one afternoon climbing the hill to the ruined Castle Frankenstein sticks in my memory. It was indeed the only time we managed to escape the cloying presence of my stepsister, who seemed always to be an unhappy third in our trio.

None of us relished the prospect of an ignominious return to England after our two-month absence. Percy urged on us the need to be cautious if we were to have enough funds to last us. He knew that, like it or not, he had to face up to his father's family solicitor, and arrive at some arrangement if we were to continue to feed ourselves or maintain a roof over our heads.

Eventually, after a long boat trip along the Rhine and through the dreary flats of Holland, we found ourselves stranded at the port of Maassluis, while a storm raged out at sea. No one was leaving today. Or the next day. Percy expressed his relief that we had saved enough money by sharing a little room, and now we had just enough to eke out another three nights in an inn.

I was slow to rise in the mornings, complaining of sickness, a vague miasma which hung over me until midday.

On our final day in Europe, just as we were about to board the boat, Jane watched me turn green and vomit into the chamber pot.

"You have such a weak stomach, Mary," she boasted happily. "How will you manage the sea voyage home?"

I met her gaze, and lifted a hand to my belly.

Realisation dawned and she slowly put her hand to her mouth, speechless at last.

London, Winter 1814

We arrived at the coast on a misty morning and gazed at the boats drawn up against the mud. Percy found one to convey us up the Thames to London, but there was a slight hitch. He had discovered that Harriet – his legal wife – had emptied his bank account. There was nothing in it. Not a bean, not a sovereign.

Percy was distraught at first, but I urged him to calm down.

"I have friends, Percy, don't forget. When we get to London we'll go to the Voyseys for a loan and a place to stay overnight. They'll help us," I reassured him.

Old family friends of my mother's before she died, I felt I could rely on them.

"But how are we to pay for our passage up the Thames?" Jane pointed out.

Percy had gone very pale. He looked across at the boatman, patiently waiting our custom.

"I'll reassure the man he'll be paid at the other end."

The boatman was silent as he took us up the river, and Jane

and I sat in the stern, gazing out disconsolately at the briny mudflats as we passed, and the marshes extending beyond into the mist. It was a gloomy sight. I began to wonder if it had been wise to return to England where we were surely not wanted.

I could see Percy struggling with his resolve, and wondering how to inform our boatman that he did not have any money to pay the fare.

Then the familiar bridges and docksides of London began to appear on either side and we gazed once more on the shores of home. The Thames became busy with river traffic, and our man negotiated his way through it all, taking us as close as he could to the centre of town, where an embarrassing discussion took place.

Jane and I stood apart on the quayside, feeling awkward.

The boatman was shaking his head.

"What is it?" I asked, as Percy leant towards me.

"He refuses to trust me. He says if we disappear into the town, he'll never see us again, and he wants payment for our passage."

"So what are we to do?"

Percy shrugged.

So it was that we became a party of four, trooping through the dusty streets of London to the Voyseys' house, the boatman refusing to let us out of his sight.

I found the house of my mother's old friends easily enough. The others stood apart while I knocked at the door, conscious of my dishevelled state.

A servant answered, and when I explained who I was, she looked at me oddly, and asked me to wait.

The door closed again in my face.

It did not open again for some time. When it did, the servant greeted me once more but with a changed expression, less polite, more guarded.

"I am afraid Mrs Voysey is not available at the moment…"

"Oh, but I can wait. It is very urgent, you see…"

Her eyes grew cold.

"I'm afraid I'm not at liberty to let you in, miss," was all she said.

I stared at her for a long life-changing moment, because I was beginning to realise what this meant. I was in disgrace, a pariah. Word had gone before me. My flight to Europe with a married man had rendered me an outcast. Nothing could be clearer.

The boatman was watching all of this in part-dismay at the inconvenience, and part-amusement. There was a sneering realisation in his expression, as if he was beginning to understand who he was dealing with, and did not feel quite so inclined to be respectful.

When I was near tears, Percy comforted me.

"And what now?" the boatman asked, a furious gleam in his eye.

Percy, ignoring him, took me aside.

"We'll go to the Westbrooks. I'll speak to Harriet."

"Harriet?" I asked.

He nodded.

"Your wife?"

He nodded again.

Sometime later, I found myself standing beside Jane on the doorstep of a house in Chapel Street, near Grosvenor Square, feeling utterly abject. The boatman stood below us at the bottom of the steps, having been forced to accompany us along the way. He was not pleased. Jane seemed amused, the boatman was angry because he had been inconvenienced, and I was mortified, but too tired to care.

I stared at the grain of the wood, wondering what was going on behind that closed door. This time I could not eavesdrop the way I used to outside my father's study. Whatever was taking place inside there was invisible to me. We had been forbidden admittance. Only Percy was allowed beyond the threshold of his wife's home. If anything was calculated to make me feel disgraced, it was this, standing outside the Westbrooks' family home while Percy was inside, talking to Harriet. What was worse, he was attempting to beg for his own money in order to pay our furious boatman.

We made an odd trio standing there, waiting for Percy to emerge. Half an hour turned into an hour and one hour turned into two.

There was nowhere to sit, but I was fatigued, so I finally sat down on the step. One or two pedestrians stared at us in passing, wondering at the motley crew gathered there on the doorstep. Jane seemed not at all homesick, nor discouraged by our current disaster. Her spirits were still fairly high. She seemed glad to be taking part in this adventure even if she was not the leading lady. I did not share her optimism.

"Nothing ever turns out quite how you expect it."

Realising I had spoken out loud, I glanced at the boatman, who glanced back.

"What *did* you expect?" Jane said.

"Certainly not this." I did not expect to be sleeping in barns and haylofts, without a penny to pay the boatman, who was growing increasingly impatient.

"This is costing me," he muttered. "I'm losing fares. Time is money."

"My husband will pay you for your time as soon as he…"

"Husband?" Jane could not resist saying.

I shrugged. "It is merely a detail."

The boatman raised his eyebrows and his expression changed. What little respect he had remaining crumbled away.

"Maybe we should knock again," Jane said, "and see what is happening?"

"No!" I jumped up to stop her. The thought of being denied

admittance again, and asked to wait by that footman of theirs was too much to bear.

The disgrace of sitting there slumped on the step like a pauper was bad enough.

The boatman shook his head and glanced at the rows of windows above us, as if he could not fathom any of it, or the strange behaviours of the middle classes.

"You look faint, Mary," Jane observed. "You need to eat."

"I shall eat when Percy returns."

The situation began to seem impossible. I was half-inclined to apologise to the boatman, and abandon him there on the doorstep; make our way back to the shadows of Skinner Street where Father and Stepmother would be waiting for us. Where Fanny would be wondering what had happened to us… except that we could not. We were not welcome. So where could we go? I had no choice but to sit and wait.

At last, when all seemed lost and I had given up hoping, the door opened, and Percy burst out, looking exhausted but triumphant.

He was profuse with apologies and charm, paid the boatman more than his fare, but also for the bother of his time as well. I watched him count out coins from his purse into the man's outstretched hand.

"There, my dears," he said, putting a hand on each of our shoulders. "I have enough for us to rent a place for a month."

"And what then?" I asked.

"Then we shall see."

I watched our companion, the boatman, disappear along the street, shaking his head. I wondered what he thought of us? Of Jane and I?

"Who did you speak to inside the house?" I asked Percy, as we left Grosvenor Square behind.

"Harriet, of course. And her parents."

I eyed him carefully. "How long were you alone with Harriet?"

"I don't know. A few minutes, perhaps. I cannot say."

"Did you promise her anything?"

He stopped suddenly and turned to stare at me. "Mary, what is all this questioning?"

I continued walking, and bit my lip. "I am just curious as to how you persuaded Harriet to part with some of her money."

"*My* money," he corrected me.

"Did her parents accuse you of abandoning her?"

He sighed. "They accused me of a lot of things, Mary, but I do not wish to repeat it all. Let us just be happy."

"I am trying, Percy. I really am. But it is hard when—"

"When?"

"When I do not know what you were talking about inside that house."

"Well, I could hardly invite you in. You would not have been welcome, my dear. You know that."

"Of course, I know that."

"So, let us not wonder anymore," and he coaxed me – Shelley-like – out of my reverie.

"You are becoming gloomy, Mary, and that will not do," he reprimanded me. "Where is my free-spirited girl? The one who cares not a jot for the good opinion of the world?"

She is right here, I wanted to tell him, *but she has just lost her freedom and her wings.*

Jane was never far away, listening hungrily to every exchange between us.

Margaret Street was a narrow, dark and brooding kind of place, just off Oxford Street. It was not too far from the Westbrooks' house, where Harriet lived with her wealthy parents, waiting to give birth to Percy's son. She was there – still loved by her parents – and I was here. Orphaned and alone. My only surviving parent had effectively cast me off. That was the stark truth of it.

The buildings were tall and red brick, and one of them was a church with a beautiful interior. I ventured inside there sometimes and admired the candles glowing in the gloom, and the gleam of gold at the altar. I gained some comfort from those shadows, although I did not believe in God. I wished it was a myth I could take refuge in, as so many others did, but – like Shelley – I knew it to be nothing but a tissue of lies, a comforting construction to keep us from recognising the difficult and harsh truths about the world and our place in it.

We rented two rooms here, but Shelley was often absent, 'negotiating' with Harriet in order to regain access to his own bank account. He visited the bank and his father's solicitor, and became involved in all kinds of complex dealings which left him exhausted and frustrated. I do not know how often he met up with Harriet in private, or what he said to her, or promised her. She was carrying his child, after all, but so was I. I tried not to think of it, for I refused to believe evil of my Percy.

Jane and I remained in the tall narrow house, waiting for events to unfold. I felt passive. Too passive, aware of the burden inside me, unable to shake off my lethargy. We could not afford a servant, so I fetched and carried water from the outside pump, and coal for the fire. When I wiped my forehead I left smears of soot behind. I dabbed at it with a corner of my apron, and tried to wipe it away, and told myself that it was a wonder I did not lose this baby. I wondered if Harriet was having to fetch and carry, or did someone light the fire for her, fill the pitcher with water for washing? Womankind will never be free of her shackles. Unless she be rich and entitled to a fortune of her own to relieve the burden of work. And even then, she must conform and behave according to the expectations of the society she lives amongst, and in particular the man who comes to own her fortune when she is married – for she is not allowed to own it for herself.

I leaned heavily against the mantlepiece, and held my belly. My dress was soiled. Why would Percy's father not relent and give him access to his own fortune? It would ease my burden and give me some relief from drudgery, for then we could employ a maid to help. How many great works of literature fail to be written because women are busy fetching and carrying, and must sweep floors and continually meet the demands of a household?

And why would my own father not give in to his feelings and reach out a hand of friendship? I would not say 'forgive', for I had done nothing to forgive, only acted on the values and principles I was reared on.

I could not bear the silence, and after a few weeks I wrote to my father and stepmother, begging for forgiveness – not that I felt I had done anything wrong – but more because I did not wish to lose my father's love.

The letter was sent, but there was no reply.

Then there came a moment when I felt sure Percy's love had cooled.

I heard feet on the stairs and the click of the door latch.

Percy was home.

"Where is Jane?" he asked.

"Am I my sister's keeper? She is free to come and go as she pleases."

"You are exhausted."

"What did you expect?"

His face and demeanour changed. "Do not complain, Mary."

"Why? Because Harriet used to complain?"

He turned away from me with a dark expression. Was that a trace of disgust I saw in his face? Had I begun to disappoint him, as he had begun to disappoint me?

Life is never what we expect.

The freedom I was promised as I rode out of town in that hired carriage with Percy by my side? And Jane, of course. That freedom had evaporated, and I was left – like every other woman – in chains.

As my pregnancy advanced Percy hired one housemaid, although we could ill afford it, and for a while I felt the workload shift.

Then one afternoon when Percy was absent, the maid knocked on the door and told us that two ladies were below and requested to see Jane.

"Did they give their names?" I asked.

"Mary-Jane Clairmont!"

Jane was through the door in an instant, and rushed down the staircase, taking the stairs so fast I feared she would fall.

I waited and stared at the housemaid. "Please, go and invite them in, Annie."

Annie bobbed a curtsey, but was back within a minute.

"They refuse to step inside, Miss Godwin."

It was as if someone had flung a bucket of ice-water over me. I stood, and took it.

"Then what are they doing?"

"They are talking with Miss Clairmont on the doorstep."

Annie left me alone, and I dashed to the window and flung open the casement. There, on the street far below me was my stepmother, deep in conversation with Jane, and beside her was my sister, Fanny.

I could not help myself, I cried out Fanny's name into the street below, regardless of what passers-by might think. Her little white face looked up at me for a moment, but Mary-Jane pulled her aside and she bent her head so that her face was obscured by her hat.

I continued to lean out of the window, but my stepmother ignored me, and forced Fanny to do the same.

They talked for some minutes, and not once did they look up at me. Then I watched in dismay as they retreated to a waiting carriage further along the street without troubling to look back or lift a hand in greeting. It was months since I had set eyes on either of them. Of my stepmother, I had expected nothing else, but as Fanny's skirts disappeared inside the carriage I felt my heart give a lurch. I thought of us walking as little girls through the flowering meadow, Mother's grey stone up ahead. The carriage set off and Fanny was gone.

I heard the rustle of Jane's skirts on the stairs, and the door opened.

I turned to look at her, but she avoided my eye.

"They would not speak to me," I murmured.

"I am sorry, Mary. I did try, but Mother would not hear of it."

"What did she say?"

"She tried to persuade me to return."

"Why do you not? You could escape from this." I indicated the dark room where we all lived cramped together.

Jane gave me a sharp glance. "Is that what you want?"

I did not answer.

"I am not done with our adventures yet. And besides, what is there to return to? No, I have hitched my destiny to yours, Mary, for better or worse."

I was silent for a moment. "What about Fanny? What did she say?"

"You know Fanny. Very little."

"She has probably been forbidden to communicate with me. Did she have any message from Father?"

Jane studiously avoided my gaze and I waited for what she was about to say next.

"I am sorry, Mary. It is not good news." I looked up hopefully, my heart in my mouth. "He has warned all our friends and family that they must never communicate with you again. Mamma says he wants nothing more to do with you, Mary."

I did not bother to reply. I sat down on the hard bed by the window and waited for Percy to come home, holding a hand to my belly where that secret and uncelebrated little burden lay curled like a bud.

London in the autumn is a time of mists as fires begin to be lit in all of the houses. A haze of smoke drifts on the damp air. Percy took us to the Serpentine pond and set fire to paper boats he had made and pushed them away from the bank. We watched them briefly burn, before turning to fine powdery black ash and cinders. The effect of the burning light against the rippling water was starkly beautiful. He said it was poetry in motion. Life is fleeting, and we must grasp what we have, before it fades and dies. This is the message of those burning boats, he said. We are all made of paper, which can turn to ash and be borne on the wind...

He and Jane both knew I was carrying a child, and we three clung together as if the rest of the world was against us.

I tried not to mind as news of Harriet reached us in November. She had delivered a healthy baby boy and Percy was delighted.

"She is calling the little man, Charles," he declared. "A capital name, do you not think, my sweet?"

"Capital..." I murmured.

"And what about you, Jane? What do you think? Or am I to call you Claire now, my dear sister?"

She smiled a little languidly, and her eyes sparked mischief, which I knew was the response Percy preferred. He would rather I had been as full of sparkle and vivacity as she, instead of care-worn. Worry is not a very attractive quality.

My stepsister had changed her name to Claire, as she felt it reflected the atmosphere of the Revolution. She told me that in French it meant *sincere, authentic*. I found this hard to credit. She also changed the date of her birthday. She now declared it to be 27th April.

"That was my mother's birthday! Why would you want to do that?" I asked her.

"To show my allegiance to the memory of Mary Wollstonecraft, of course."

"But she was *my* mother."

"And why is that relevant?" Jane snapped. "It is not about whose mother she was. I want to emulate her beliefs. You, of all people, ought to understand that, Mary."

Percy laughed, and I fell silent.

Jane had become Claire. She declared she was a new person, with a new identity, sloughing off the old, shedding layers like a snake.

"It is like a rebirth," she explained.

I watched her transform into a butterfly that winter as she tried to steal Percy from beneath my nose. I knew what was happening, despite their protests and denials, their claims that I was mad to think so, and that it was the pregnancy talking, giving me strange ideas and gloomy thoughts.

I ignored them and withdrew to the silence of my bed. I longed now for Fanny's stoical silence. I remembered those two little girls walking through the flowering meadow to their mother's grave, their giant of a father beside them. Godwin no longer seemed like a giant. He had toppled on his plinth.

London, 1815

In those days I was mostly hungry, I remember that. Percy spent a lot of time at the bankers' offices in town, and at the Westbrooks' house, visiting Harriet. Sometimes Jane (whom we were now compelled to address as Claire) went with him, although not when he visited Harriet, of course. I sat alone at the window of our dark little room in the tall house, and waited for callers, hoping still that Father might change his mind. My burden grew heavier, and I dared not leave the house for fear that all of London would see me and gossip.

The only face I saw was Annie, who lit the fire for me, and urged me to rest. Percy and Claire seemed always to be engaged elsewhere. I knew what they were about.

In February a severe frost settled on London and our darkened rooms became chillier than ever. The baby arrived early when no one else was there. Annie helped me to give birth in that desolate room where no one came to see me. A tiny girl, born too soon, so frail that her skin was almost transparent. But yet she lived. She breathed in and out, and I watched her delicate ribcage rise and fall as if it was a tiny miracle, and could not tear my eyes away.

When Percy and Claire returned, they were astounded to find me bedridden, a mite of a child in my arms.

Annie told me to rest, but I could not. For twelve days, I lay in that dark room and fed my daughter every day, while the Angel of Death hovered above the bed with his flaming sword. I did not look up at this vision, but I felt him hanging there, although I did not believe in God. I told myself that if there was a God, then he was not merciful and kind.

On the thirteenth day, I woke early, leaned across the crib and looked at my daughter. She did not move. I tried to wake her for a feed, but she would not stir. Her little ribcage, which used to flutter like a bird's wing, lay still. Not a single breath escaped her. I spent an hour trying to feed her, pulling at my own breast and lifting her onto it and holding her there, before I would accept that she had gone. It was dawn, the sun had not yet risen, and Percy was not at home. I was alone in the tall narrow house in Margaret Street, where my stepmother and my sister refused to see me. And my daughter, my first born, lay dead in my arms.

Annie left me alone to grieve.

"I have suffered much for loving you."

"I am sorry, Mary."

"I do not want your pity, Percy."

"You must not be bitter, my dear."

"Must I not?" I looked up at him, I wanted my words to scourge him, to cut like the swipe of a knife, slashing this way and that. I had learnt so much about life and the world in recent months: about whom to trust, whom to forgive, and how hard it was to believe in any goodness in the world.

Throughout that long winter I had listened at doors, while my body grew big with child, and I heard things. I heard whispered conversations, laughter. I saw secretive, furtive looks exchanged.

"I have never made any secret of my affection for Claire," Percy said when I accused him. "She is like a sister to me."

"A strange way to be with your *sister*?"

"Your imagination is running wild with grief, Mary. I swear that you have nothing to fear."

"I do not believe you."

He sighed.

"Those evenings when I went to bed early, you and Jane were always left alone together. What did you talk about?" (At this point I still refused to call her Claire.)

Percy shrugged. "I don't know. I can't remember everything we said."

"You became close. Closer than a brother ought to be with his sister. For she is not your sister, is she? Whatever you say. We are a strange trio. It is no wonder people avoid us."

"Mary, you should not speak like this. You need time to grieve."

"Oh, I have all the time in the world to grieve."

He stared at me. "Do you regret running away with me? You have almost admitted as much."

I hesitated. "I don't say regret. But… nothing is as I expected it to be, or hoped for."

"I have disappointed you. I promise, I will do my best to change things. Remember our plans? How we wanted to begin a literary journal, and write, and change the world?"

"You cannot change a world that does not want to be changed."

"But you can still write!"

"I am tired, Percy."

"Then let me come to bed with you. I will hold you in my arms and make up for all that has gone wrong between us. I promise, all will be well again soon."

"Can you bring our daughter back?"

He was silent.

"… and make my father forgive me?"

Percy's face turned stormy. "Godwin is a hypocrite. He does not deserve a daughter like you."

"I think if my mother had lived, she would have understood. Don't you think so? She would not have acted like a hypocrite. Nor would she have abandoned me. She would have been there for me, no matter what Godwin said to her."

I closed my eyes and saw the wildflowers gently swaying, brushing against the graceful grey stone, the lime-coloured lichen beginning to grow.

"Our little girl has joined her, Percy. She will be with her now. Safe in her arms."

Percy did not say what I knew he was thinking – that there is no God, that I would never see my mother or our little daughter again.

The harsh winter moved forward into spring. When I caught Jane (whom we must now call Claire) vomiting into the basin, I stared at her in disbelief. It was then I noticed the changes. Her waist was thicker than it ought to be and she was pale. She stared back and neither of us dared speak.

I was closeted in two dark rooms of a crowded house with a girl who had always tried to compete with me. The child Jane had become the woman Claire, reborn and even more dangerous.

Claire watched Percy and I grow close again, and she was jealous. When Percy suggested that she should spend some time in the country – a wonderful euphemism – we all knew what he meant to imply.

At the beginning of May, Claire set off on a solitary journey, to a cottage in Devon where she would spend some time 'resting'. No one need ever know, except we three. And strangely, we barely spoke of it. It is odd how people who live so closely together can avoid talking about the one thing which stares them all in the face, the one thing that really matters. In this way, families create their own subterfuge, live in denial and hypocrisy throughout the long years of a lifetime.

Once Claire was gone, I felt a sense of relief. The house was empty. In it were the shadows and regret of the terrible winter I had lived through. Annie took care of me, fetched me hot drinks even when I had not asked for them. My mood darkened. A monster was born and lay curled inside my thoughts, biding its time. I scribbled away in my notebook. Percy urged me to write, and so I would write. I did not yet know what might emerge, but eventually something would creep forth from the darkness, like a blind creature seeking the light.

Percy's mood had improved, helped no doubt by the fact his father had agreed to give him a thousand pounds a year, more than enough to keep us from starving. We would be able to afford servants and a cook. Our lifestyle would improve. No more sleeping in haylofts on the continent, should we decide to return there. But I could tell he felt there was something missing from the house in Margaret Street. He missed the easy laughter and light conversation of my stepsister. He missed Claire. My stoical silence was a poor substitute. I am a listener, I always have been. I like to observe other people and take note, rather than offer opinions of my own at first. Perhaps this made me poor company in his eyes.

I was haunted by a genuine fear that Percy would abandon me, or decide to join Claire in Devon. And yet, no mention would be made of the swelling waistline, the symptoms of nausea, which sent her off to 'rest' in the first place.

The parks and squares in London began to blossom. This hint of colour reminded me of my old home at the Polygon, before the Skinner Street days. I longed for the country air.

When I realised I was with child again, I hesitated to share my news with Percy. Instead I guarded it close, and lit a candle in the church in Margaret Street, even though I had no belief in God, and no time for organised religion. Yet it comforted me, this one little flame. I watched it waver and grow tall in the shadows. Would my candle stay alight? How long would it burn this time before being extinguished?

When I felt the child quicken in my womb, I knew it was time to tell Percy. He did not hesitate, but swept me up in his arms, and declared we must celebrate.

"You must be happy, Mary. You must not be afraid," he assured me, noticing my downcast face.

I pretended to be delighted for his sake, but I knew he had become bored by the routine of our household drudgery.

"I do not know what I feel."

He looked perplexed, as if he could not possibly fathom the extraordinarily complex workings of the female mind. It puzzled him, so I kept my fears and doubts to myself.

"We will move to the countryside," he announced. "Yes, we must. I can afford to now. What is to stop us?"

"To join Claire in Devon?"

Percy brushed off the comment. "No, no. Not that. We will move to Bishopsgate, and you shall have a cook and servants and will not trouble yourself to do anything but write, my dear."

He glanced at my notebooks.

I did not tell him I had a monster lurking there. Monstrous thoughts, but nothing at all that would cohere into a sensible whole.

"Once we leave London your mind will be clear, and you will be free to write as you please."

"I am free to write as I please now."

"But this is such a dark street…"

"I thought you found it convenient for taking care of your business?"

"Yes," he sighed. "Perhaps. But there is no need to be quite so on top of everything. I can do very well from Bishopsgate, and I will come through to London if the need arises."

Come through to London and leave me alone in the country? Is that what you mean? I had the sense, however, not to voice my accusation out loud, for fear of alienating him still further, or even pushing him into the arms of another woman.

Bishopsgate, Spring 1816

I lay on the sofa in our red brick mansion near Eton, looking across the lawn. The French windows stood open to the garden, and the sunlight slanted onto the russet shades of the rug at my feet. I could hear the tick of the clock, slow but resolute, and the tinkle of tea-cups and saucers from the hallway. Annie had come with us. I knew that she would enter soon, bearing a tray of tea.

There was a beautiful stillness on the air. The trees were thick and lush, and the child in my womb made me feel heavy and ponderous. Claire remained in Devon, so I had Percy all to myself: no distractions to make me fretful and anxious. Percy seemed so… light and airborne at times, as if he would float away on a whim.

Annie placed the tray on a nearby table and asked me if I was feeling quite well.

"Yes, thank you, Annie." I smiled. She was one of the kindest people I had come across since leaving Skinner Street.

I poured tea, and listened to Percy walking in the garden – for we had a garden now. I could see him through the late afternoon shadows, pacing the lawn, staring at the flowers and the trees. He sighed. I knew I had caught him out in the act of pining for someone other than myself.

"You miss Claire," I told him, when he came in for tea.

He was quiet. "What do you want me to say? Do you want me to deny it?"

"I want you to tell me the truth at last."

"The truth? I love *you*, Mary. Why can you not be content with that?" The endearments poured so easily from his lips, but the criticisms also.

"Yes, I miss Claire," he admitted. "She is a chatterer, and fills the house with her nonsense, but it brightens the place up, cheers us both – you admit it. And it gives you a confidante and companion."

"I can do quite happily without Claire. I hope she might stay in Devon forever."

"Mary!" he teased, shocked. "Your own sister!"

"Stepsister," I reminded him. "We share no blood in common. And she is more like her own mother than I care to remember. I find her company irksome at times, and that's the truth of it."

"But then you forgive her and you like her again."

I pursed my lips and said nothing. This was the myth he preferred to believe in. It seemed strange to me that Father was not angry with her: it was me he blamed, and so he refused to speak to me, while for Claire, there would always be a warm welcome at Skinner Street.

"They think I led her astray, that she is the innocent victim in all of this."

"Godwin does not deserve a daughter like you, Mary. None of them deserve you. And you should set no store by what they think."

It was very easy for him to say, but how could I not feel injured by my own father's rejection? It would be a strange thing if I did not feel it.

The autumn mists gathered, and before too long it was necessary to have a fire in the evenings.

Percy invited a gentleman called Leigh Hunt to supper. Mr Hunt, a radical thinker, wanted to start up a journal to shake the foundations of the pompous British establishment to its core. He was a good-looking man, confident, amiable, and I imagined he had a great many friends. He did not seem especially interested in meeting me, but was far more taken with Shelley.

"Do you write at all, Miss Godwin?" he asked me, more out of politeness than genuine curiosity.

"Not really."

"She is lying," Percy said. "Tell Mr Hunt the truth, Mary."

"I have written nothing that anyone would care to read."

He asked when the baby was due.

"January. It will be a winter baby," I replied. I felt a flutter of dark anxiety at the thought – I recalled my little girl and her feather-light ribcage, her grey face in the early London dawn. The men exchanged a glance. Leigh Hunt had many children, I was told. His wife was a sculptor and painter, and yet she had a house "full of brats." Percy's words, not mine!

"It will not be a severe winter," Mr Hunt said, and I was grateful for his reassuring words. "The countryside is the perfect place for a new-born. No humid airs from the city."

"Exactly, my love," Percy uttered in relief, delighted that his new friend should be so positive.

"What does your father think of it all?" Mr Hunt asked him.

Percy hesitated, and an awkward silence fell. "Sir Timothy has cut me off from my inheritance with barely a penny. Although he has recently relented a little."

"And Godwin?" he asked, glancing from me to Percy.

"My father also does not approve," I answered quietly. "I am no longer welcome in my old home. Claire may visit Skinner Street, but not I."

"Claire?"

"My stepsister!"

"Claire accompanied us on our journey to Europe," Percy explained. "She was a godsend to Mary when times were difficult."

"She no longer lives with us," I interrupted.

"She is staying temporarily in Devon for the time being," Percy went on. "But doubtless she will join us again soon. Mary cannot bear to be parted from her sister."

"Stepsister!" I corrected him.

"They are so close."

"I can endure a separation from her better than you think."

"They have their differences, but in the final resort, they cannot be without each other."

Throughout this exchange Mr Hunt watched the shuttlecocks fly, his head moving comically from left to right.

"Claire?" he mused, "she sounds very…"

"Vulnerable," Percy added.

Inside me I felt the baby kick. Glancing down, I could see my gown ripple with the faintest of movements: it was an unnerving sight.

"Am I your sweetheart, Percy?" I asked him later, when we were alone again. Leigh Hunt had returned to Hampstead and the house lay still all about us.

"You are indeed, my dear!"

"Then what is Claire?"

"She is family," he added.

"Yours or mine?"

He gave me a rueful smile.

"Don't be mischievous and tiresome, my dear."

The house was quiet and Percy and I sat either side of a crackling fire, reading. Sometimes Percy read to me – his poems and discourses – and as I listened my mind became calm and tranquil again. But always the fear lurked, dark anxiety about what the future might hold. I thought of my mother and what happened to her…

Percy had stopped reading and was watching me. "What is it?" he asked me. "Something troubles you."

I attempted to deny it at first, but he would not have it.

"I know you better than that, Mary. What is it?"

"I am afraid," I admitted at last.

"We are all afraid."

"Childbirth is dangerous."

"You will be perfectly safe."

"You cannot promise that. My mother died of childbed fever."

"You are not your mother. You will have better luck."

"Is it luck then, whether we live or die?"

Percy said nothing.

I studied the flames in the fireplace as they licked the beech logs.

"In giving me life, she lost her own."

He looked at me impatiently. "You are not to blame for your mother's death."

"How will I fare in January, when my time comes? Will our baby survive this time? How many births must I go through before a healthy, thriving child makes its way into the world and stays with us, instead of being taken?"

Shelley left his chair, knelt in front of me and clasped my hands in his. Then he raised them to his lips. "I worry also, Mary. But don't allow yourself to be swamped by fears. Be of good courage and good cheer and then the battle will be almost-won."

It was easy for him to say…

As my lying-in period drew near, Shelley – without my knowledge – decided to ask Claire to rejoin us.

When I learnt she was on her way back to us, I confronted him. "Why?"

"Because you need her companionship at the moment, my sweet. You are estranged from your family and what you need now more than anything is not to be isolated. Claire will help in that respect. She will cheer you."

"Is that so?"

"Well, she is on her way now and the decision cannot be reversed. I suspect she will be delighted to return to civilisation. Devon was a touch too far away for her liking."

"Far enough, though, to conceal her secret."

Percy did not answer at once. "You are too near and outspoken sometimes, Mary."

"Am I supposed to lie?"

There was a short silence. "I did not have you down for a hypocrite, like the rest of them," I added.

"Claire will cheer us *both*, and she will be of help to you at this difficult time," he murmured, ignoring my jibes.

"Annie will help me. And the midwife."

"And now Claire, too. She can help lift your mood."

"And yours too, no doubt."

"You are too cold, Mary," he burst out.

"That is strange. Claire often accuses me of being cold. And yet I do not think I am."

By the time our son William was torn from my womb – joined to me by a twisted coil of flesh – in the depths of midwinter when a sprinkling of snow lay on the lawn, Claire was with us again. And it was true that part of me was pleased to see her. She watched me with my child, her nephew, and smiled at the choice of name.

"Godwin ought to be delighted," she offered. "His namesake."

I was too exhausted to speak, but Percy promised to write to my father with the news of our son's arrival.

"I hope he will appreciate the gesture and will want to see you both," Percy said.

I lay in the shadows of my birthing chamber, our little son cradled in my arms, stupefied by the agonies of birth. It is such an animal act – so visceral and passionate – and yet we keep the moaning and the blood and the fleshy slime of it secret, lest it offend anyone. How strange, that we should hide the reality! This is farmyard stuff and yet it is taking place in the bedrooms of rich and poor alike, in thousands of households throughout the land.

"We all share this in common," Annie told me, as she urged me to bear down. "In the birthing chamber, all are equals. I have helped my mother deliver my younger brothers and sisters."

"Did they survive?" I asked her.

"Most of them."

The bedchamber was quiet now. Claire was in the other room, talking to Shelley, and Annie had gone to the kitchen to make some chicken broth. I could hear their voices, drifting in and out of the half-open door, a ripple of laughter from my stepsister. William and I were left alone: I studied my son's new-born face in an attempt to get to know him.

"Here we are then. You and I," I whispered.

He opened his eyes and stared back at me. Dark, fathomless pools, fixed on me earnestly, as if his survival depended on it. Such wisdom lay there. Such innocence. There was no one else in the whole world but he and I. No one else existed for him yet. I was the sun to his planet. *Everything he has, I give to him. Everything I am, he needs.*

I felt utterly consumed by love, so that any other love paled in comparison. Nothing could compare with this overwhelming surge of emotion. It was like falling in love.

And it hurt.

Would he stay with us?

Beyond the open door and along the corridor came another loud peal of laughter. The other two were feeling the need to celebrate.

"Your Aunt Claire must like it here, in Bishopsgate," I whispered. William did not blink. His gaze was all-consuming.

"Will he stay with us, do you think?" I asked Percy when he could at last tear himself away from my stepsister's company.

Percy smiled. "You have only to look at him. He is a strong boy. He is here to stay."

"Annie says he is doing very well."

"Ah, well, if Annie says so…" Percy teased me. "You are too fond of that servant."

"Annie is more than a servant."

"I am glad that you insisted she came with us to Bishopsgate. She has been a godsend."

"Do you hear that?" I whispered to our son. "Your father concedes defeat. He admits that I am right."

"My father has asked for another loan."

I was sitting in the drawing-room, staring at the letter in my hand.

There was a tense silence.

"What else does he say?"

"He is delighted that I have chosen to call the baby William, but fears that he cannot change what I have done. I am not welcome at Skinner Street, and he would advise me to avoid our old family friends – for my own good – as I am likely to be hurt by their rejection…" I let the letter fall. "Words to that effect."

Percy held his tongue at first, but I could see the rage coursing through him. He felt humiliated and hurt on my behalf, but more than that, Godwin's rejection also wounded his own ego.

He stood up and began pacing the room. Finally, he turned on his heel and shouted, "His own grandson!"

"Don't let it trouble you, Percy. There is no point."

"Everyone rejects us, but why?" He made an effort to compose himself. "Well, I shall send your father his precious loan, to keep him afloat."

"I'm sorry," I murmured. It was not the first time my father had requested a loan, and neither was it the first time that Percy had obliged. At Skinner Street, they still feared financial ruin and the workhouse, but it was humiliating and painful to have to deal with. I used to regard my father as a giant among giants, a man of virtue and integrity, of impeccable values, but now I was forced to doubt him, and it hurt to see him reduced.

Claire walked into the room, drawing off her gloves and throwing them down on a nearby chair.

"Well?" I asked her. "How were they?"

She flounced herself down on a cushioned stool by the fire. "Oh, you know them. Just the same."

"Did they ask after me?"

She averted her gaze. "They asked after William. If he was thriving."

"And Fanny? Did you see Fanny?"

Claire paused, and looked out of the window. "Fanny does not speak much. She just obeys. She is like a shadow."

"You sound a little scornful."

"It is hard not to be. How can she bear it?"

"That's what I'm afraid of – that we abandoned her, left her to deal with the atmosphere in that house alone."

Claire shrugged. "She chooses her own path in life."

"Well, the same is true of you and I. And look what we have become."

My stepsister looked across at me, her gaze sharp. "What do you mean by that?"

I folded my lips together and said nothing.

"Mary, sometimes you are a dog in a manger. Look at you. You still have William!"

"If you are not happy with our present arrangement, you can always return to Skinner Street. You are welcome there."

"I am not welcome here?" she asked quickly.

"I did not say that!"

"But you thought it."

I bit my lip. "There is no sense in arguing. It achieves nothing."

"I feel used."

"*You* feel used?"

"When you were pregnant with William, and Percy grew tired of your moodiness, I was his amusement. I kept him entertained, until you were ready to receive him again..."

"Ah. So, we come to the truth at last?"

Claire fell silent. I studied her, waiting for more, but she had said enough for now.

"He hid you away in Devon because you were with child. *His* child?"

"I am tired," she said.

She rose clumsily, as if assailed by a sudden lethargy, and left the room.

How many lies and secrets did they keep from me? If there was a child down in Devon, Claire did not speak of it and nor did Shelley. I could get neither of them to admit the truth.

The night was dark. Percy was away in London, negotiating with his father's lawyers to settle the problem of his inheritance. We had one thousand pounds a year to live on, which paid for this house, two servants and a cook. Two hundred pounds of that amount went to Harriet, to help her raise little Ianthe and

Charles. She lived with her parents; they covered her expenses and offered her the support and comfort I so sorely lacked. They did not reject her, as Godwin rejected me.

Percy had built up a mountain of debt, which he had yet to honour. Born into money, he was not good at managing it. He bought everything on account, and because he was the son of a baronet, merchants and tradesmen would give him credit. He acquired a piano for Claire with the promise of payment in a year or two, and no one minded. Tradesmen trusted he would honour the amount because he had the look and the bearing of an aristocrat, and the title to go with it.

But Percy was not always a happy man. He had his demons, and sometimes when he was away, I was tempted to search through his private papers to discover anything I might have missed. I did not know what I was looking for – I only knew that it was an unhealthy obsession, a suspicion planted in my mind by the bitterness of my extraordinary circumstances. He left no trace of his misdemeanours.

It was quiet by the fireside with my little William.

Annie opened the door and asked if I would like some supper prepared. "I can ask cook if there are any eggs left," she offered.

"No, thank you, Annie."

"It is dark in here."

She turned up the wick of the oil lamp and the room glowed. A golden globe of light hovered, while shadows coalesced in the corners.

"Is Miss Clairmont not at home, Mrs Shelley?" Annie asked then.

I shook my head.

"She has gone with Percy, to London."

"Oh."

There was a heavy silence.

"He has much on his mind at the moment, Annie."

She waited. I was tempted to talk, to confide. I could tell her about his visit to see Godwin in Skinner Street, my father's refusal to see him or speak with him, the door slammed in his face. I could tell her about the poems he kept writing, which were continually rejected by every journal and literary press in the country. He had published *Queen Mab* and *Alastor*, but the critics either ignored him or tore his efforts to shreds, as if they were no more than amateurish ramblings. It was I who encouraged him to write in the first place. He thought he might be inclined to become a philosopher, but I told him instead that he was a poet. A poet understands more, gets to the root of life. All he wanted was to write, and the world would not listen. "Even my own father despises me," he complained. It was hard work bolstering up that fragile ego. I was worn down by it. But none of this did I confide in Annie. Besides, I had the sense that I did not need to. She was a keen observer.

"I shall leave you in peace then, miss."

Annie withdrew from the room. It would not be right for me to burden her with my worries, especially those about Claire and the reason for her prolonged visit to Devon. That would not do at all. Besides, Annie must have worries enough of her own.

On her return, Claire seemed agitated, over-excited. In London she was used to going about town on her own.

"There is an acquaintance of mine I would like you to meet."

"Oh yes?"

"You will have heard of him, of course."

I waited for her to say more.

"Lord Byron!" She dropped the name like a stone casually flung into a silence that rippled like the Serpentine.

"Lord Byron?" I repeated.

"He is a friend of mine."

A beat or two of silence followed.

"Is that so odd? Is it so hard for you to believe I might make some connections of my own without your help?"

I raised my eyebrows. "And where did you chance upon *him*?"

"In his private box. At the theatre."

"I see."

"*What* do you see?" she snapped. "You do not see at all. You jump to all sorts of conclusions."

"I have said nothing."

"Well, he is eager to meet Mary Godwin!"

"Me?"

"The daughter of Mary Wollstonecraft."

I rolled my eyes. "Ah – that again."

I had long been an admirer of Byron's, and in sympathy with his radical opinions. When I was a child he entered the House of Lords and was famous for speaking out against the Frame Work Bill. I remembered these things, because of my stay up in Dundee with the Baxters and my visit to the textile mills there. Even now, men who are hungry will take arms against the mechanised looms – like those Mr Baxter had in his factory. The penalty for destroying these stocking frames is death. Byron, like many of our acquaintance, opposed the Bill when it was first passed, and decried the harsh penalty. In spite of – or perhaps even because of – his aristocratic blood, Byron was a fierce champion of the poorer working classes. Needless to say, the Tories and the establishment mocked him for his views

I memorised his speech when I was a child, and tried to use it in my arguments against the Baxters, although no one agreed with me at the time.

"Lord Byron says…"

"Lord Byron is a man considered *mad, bad and dangerous to know*," William Baxter had interrupted me fondly. "According to his lover, Caroline Lamb, that is. You cannot quote Byron."

I had enjoyed these debates at the Baxters' table. Even though Mr Baxter had disagreed with me, at least he had allowed me to voice my views. When I sat at the Baxters' table in Dundee, defending Lord Byron against attack, I had never set eyes on the famous poet, although I admired him greatly.

I thought of that exchange now, as Claire informed me that she was apparently a close acquaintance of Byron's.

The press had vilified Byron over the years, depicting him in cartoons as a clubfooted beast, with cloven hooves. A Satanic figure! A whiff of scandal had always attached itself to his name, and they made much of that, but they forgot he was a man of the people, who sided with the underdog. He was a man with views I approved of. However, I was not so sure I approved of my stepsister's tenuous connection with him, and I wondered what would happen as a result. It could not be good…

When I met him at last, I was struck by his sensitivity and intelligence. He appeared to contradict everything I had ever heard about him, and everything they said.

"Who is '*they*'"? Byron laughed, when I admitted as much on meeting him. "I take no account of what people say."

He was dark and bold and well-built, with dark hair and chiselled features, what they call a Roman nose. Percy looked quite delicate and fair beside him. Byron struck me as pretty much well-grounded – in spite of Lady Caroline Lamb's criticisms of him. He did not flirt with me; he did not tease or dissemble. He showed nothing but respect, and listened with more attention than even Percy – Percy, who was forever flying off on a tangent, irrational and bizarre at times, excitable and full of high spirits. In contrast, Byron was quite staid. He had a sense of humour and an appetite for life, in search always of new sensations and experiences; I suspected he was calmer than Percy by temperament.

"Are you writing?" he asked me, glancing at my notebooks.

"It is Percy who is the poet in our household. I merely indulge in a few vain scribblings that will not amount to much."

"You are your mother's daughter, though."

"Yes, but that won't make me a great writer. Perhaps I have nothing to say."

"False modesty," he murmured.

"Not at all," I told him.

Claire watched us closely, her nerves on edge. I did not know what to make of the visit or my stepsister's connection with him.

"Claire is behaving very strangely of late," I told Percy. "She sparkles with nervous energy, but more than that – she is agitated."

"Is he as dangerous as they say, do you think?" Percy murmured.

"I don't think he is dangerous at all," I replied. "To me, he comes across as very respectful."

"The rumours are interesting, anyway. Accused of sleeping with his half-sister…"

Claire, who had just entered the room, lifted her head.

"What is her name? Augusta? Who knows whether the rumours are true." Percy had not noticed Claire's presence. "Well," he continued, "we are all of us used to the taint of scandal. It matters very little what people say."

"Although it does – in the long run," I added, glancing at Claire as she moved to sit by the fire. "Does it not?"

Percy looked at Claire now, wondering if she had overheard him.

It was about this time that Percy suggested we travel to the Continent again. Claire in particular was keen for us to begin the journey, and this time we were not pursued by our parents. There was no one to give chase. We were all of us glad to leave the shores of England where 'polite society' had begun to whisper openly about our *ménage à trois*.

"It is none of their business," I hissed, when I overheard a woman talking about us in public.

"*I hear they all live together, and none of them are married. And yet they have a child between them…*" Her voice fell silent when she caught me staring at her.

Instead of continuing the rest of my errands, I hurried home to the safety of my own drawing-room, and refused to leave the house again for days.

"Why let it bother you, Mary?" Claire declared. "I do not."

"Well said, Claire! Your sister is a free spirit, Mary. You should learn from her example. She cares not, but is blithe and happy and…"

Percy was silenced by a quick look, cleared his throat and said no more on the subject.

But it was incidents like this which encouraged us to consider a life abroad, where perhaps the gossip would not follow us.

PART FOUR: A MONSTER IS BORN

Switzerland, May 1816

Snow was falling in the Alps when we arrived, and we heard that the locals were disturbed by the unusual weather patterns and spoke of strange omens, predictions of what this might mean. We met a peasant woman on the road who seemed unable to tell us what season it was.

"It is strange," Percy observed, looking out at the mist obscuring the nearest mountain from view.

"It cannot be normal for it to snow this late in the year, surely, even in a place as remote as this?" he asked the proprietor of our inn.

The man shrugged and muttered something unintelligible. While Claire began to talk to the innkeeper in his own language, Percy turned away impatiently, and drummed the oak reception desk with his fingers.

Claire had come into her own on this journey so far, and took great pleasure in translating for us. Having conducted an animated conversation in French, she turned triumphantly to enlighten us all.

"He says the seasons are confused. According to Monsieur Gachet, the birds fall silent at midday, and begin to roost in the trees but no one knows why. They think it foretells the end of the world, a time of disaster and doom."

She assumed an air of importance and glowed with pride, which irritated me slightly, although I knew it was not worthy of me. Those French lessons Mary-Jane organised had stood her in good stead, after all.

As we headed upstairs the proprietor called Claire back, and muttered something else in French.

"… il y a une tempête à venir…"

"There is a storm coming," she told us. "He says we should not go into the mountains."

Percy's face fell. He had planned that we should travel to Lake Geneva, and in order to do this we had to take a route over the next mountain range.

"But how else are we to get there?" Percy insisted.

Claire shrugged.

"This is what he says," she repeated. "He knows the region. He also says there have been sightings of a strange star in the sky above the mountains."

Percy laughed. "Superstition!"

"The locals are fearful of what it might mean."

Up in our room, I looked out at the bleak landscape which had an eerie apocalyptic glow about it, despite the mist. Although it was midday, the sky was dark-yellow and ominous-looking. To the naked eye, it looked as if the sun had become obscured by a strange black dust of floating particles. It seemed possible that the sun would never shine again, nor the birds sing. It was the end of May. It had been a lean year. The crops had failed throughout much of Europe and hunger stalked the land, bringing devastation to whole towns and communities who could not afford to feed themselves. We were more fortunate than most. A baronet's son will never go hungry, or have too much difficulty in finding a loaf and some meat to feed himself and his family, even if funds become low.

I drew my son, Will, closer and watched the snow fall onto a silent world. I gave thought to the innkeeper's words, that birds fall silent at midday, and darkness covers the face of the land when the crops should be flourishing. It looked like winter outside and there was an unseasonal chill on the air. When a servant came in to light the fires, I was grateful for the warmth. I feared for my child, especially when Percy proposed that we should continue our journey and travel across the mountains to Lake Geneva, despite Monsieur Gachet's advice. I gazed at him in disbelief. He and Claire were both keen for an adventure and were united in their criticism of me. They forgot that Wilmouse was only a baby.

"But did you not hear what Monsieur Gachet told us downstairs? Were you not listening?"

"Where is your spirit, Mary, your sense of adventure?" Percy demanded.

"And where is your *sense*?" I replied.

"Your sister agrees with me, do you not, Claire?"

"My sister always agrees with you," I muttered, unheard by the other two. My lips were muffled by Will's woollen blanket which wrapped him close.

Despite my misgivings, Percy was full of excitement at the prospect of our journey the next day.

"We have enough money for a private coach all the way," he enthused, "So we need have no fear."

Monsieur Gachet, our proprietor, disagreed with him.

"If your coach leaves the track, what then? What will you do? You need men to dig you out if need be, otherwise..." he gestured towards the bench where I sat beside Claire, cradling our baby.

"Have you any men to spare?" Percy asked.

Claire translated for him.

Monsieur Gachet shrugged. "If you pay them enough, then perhaps there are some men from the village who will help you. It depends. They may need some persuasion, you know?"

"I can pay them."

"Then I am sure they will risk their lives for your stupid adventure!"

Percy and I both glanced at the man, and waited for Claire to translate. She did so with mischievous relish.

The rough track up the mountainside was barely visible. We journeyed on and when the blizzard hit, the summit became instantly obscured from view. We were lost in a thick mist, a devilish whiteout with no landmarks to guide us. The horses could so easily lead us off the track and plunge us to our deaths.

The man up front driving the horses was muffled so that only his eyes were visible, and he squinted into the swirling air. We could not hear anything he said because the wind tore his words away as it screamed past our coach.

I endured the journey in nervous silence.

Percy kept looking tensely out the window.

"We should have listened to Monsieur Gachet," I shouted above the wind.

Claire said nothing.

I held Will close, all swaddled in woollen blankets to keep him warm.

"You see those poles along the track," Percy indicated. "They will keep the driver from getting lost, even in the dark."

"I would not like to spend the night up here," Claire admitted.

Percy glanced at us both.

"That is why I took the sensible precaution of bringing men along, to assist us in the event…"

"In the event of what?" Claire said, her tone sharper than usual.

"It was not your idea though, strictly speaking, was it, love? It was Monsieur Gachet's – bless him!"

Percy chose to ignore us both, and the wind continued to scream past the curtained windows, silencing any further attempt at conversation.

All morning and all afternoon the snow fell and lay thick on the ground; the horses and carriage wheels creaked with the strain as they struggled to fight a way through. We had not made the summit yet, and it would soon be dark. When the diligence juddered to a halt, I lifted the curtain to peer outside. There was no visible landmark and the snow was falling faster than ever, enclosing us in a white shroud.

I had no desire to be stranded here, high on the mountainside in freezing conditions without any shelter in sight, with my baby son in my arms.

The driver dropped down from his seat, and the men began to shout and gesticulate as the air swirled white all about them. I heard the scrape of shovels, and Percy leapt down to help. Claire and I tried not to look at each other.

"How long will it take us to reach the other side?" Claire asked tentatively, leaning forward to look out.

"We have to reach the summit first, and then descend to Geneva. We have yet to reach the highest point."

The door opened on a blast of wind, and Percy jumped back in, accompanied by a whirl of snow. He looked red-faced with exertion and curiously pleased with himself.

"There. Nothing to worry about, my dears." As he spoke, I felt the carriage wheels lumber forward beneath me. "Onwards and upwards!" he barked, slapping his knee.

Part of me wished he did not extract so much pleasure out of putting us all in danger.

It took us all night to reach the summit, and all the while the wind screamed in a frenzy, and the snow whirled all about, and the way ahead was lost so that I was bewildered as to how the men managed at all, without plunging us over a precipice. It was still dark when we began our steep descent. I caught a brief glimpse of the lake through the snow, a tell-tale gleam in the new dawn. The sheer side of the mountain appeared to sit almost perpendicular to the water, and cast monstrous black shadows on its surface. I could hardly believe we'd been foolhardy enough to make the journey. In spite of this, I still kept my sense of wonder enough to admire the mountains and to acknowledge the startling effect they had on me. Majestic and strange, they reared into the sky, as if some unseen presence or spirit moved there. I do not believe in God, or what the Church teaches us about God, but if I were to believe in a divine being, this place would make me feel close to it.

The lake far below was agitated by the tempest: small waves dashed the base of the rocks. That was where we were heading.

"What did I tell you?" Percy said, triumphant. "I knew we would reach the summit and descend the other side."

Again, Claire and I remained silent, concentrating hard on the steep track which the coach driver and the horses had still to negotiate.

"Here we are at last, the *Hôtel d'Angleterre*," Percy announced. It was a very ordinary and unprepossessing establishment. We immediately encountered a group of English tourists in the vestibule. I had hoped we would be more among foreigners, especially after such an adventurous journey, but that was not to be the case. The whole world appeared to come here, to the fashionable *Hôtel d'Angleterre*, judging by the dowdy matrons in the foyer. I stared at them in astonishment, wondering how they all got here. Did they brave the same journey as us, in the snow? It did not seem possible.

Once we had been shown to our room amid the stares of the other guests, I placed Will in the centre of the feather bed, and sat down beside him.

"He needs changing and feeding."

"We will find a nurse for you here, Mary, in the town. You must be exhausted, and you will need help."

I had wanted Annie to accompany us to the continent, but she remained behind in England. She did not want to leave her ailing mother.

"Claire will help me."

"You need more help than that."

He was right. If I was to travel at the swift pace dictated by Percy, then I would require a little assistance. But I was happy to be here, happy to be away from Bishopsgate and London and all the accompanying gossip. What I did not bargain for was that gossip should follow us even here, to a small hotel beneath the shadow of the towering peak of Jura.

After a short rest, we walked into the dining-room, keen to enjoy our first meal. We were late coming down and most of the guests were already at table. All heads turned to stare. I strode to our table, trying not to meet anyone's eye. Perhaps I was imagining their interest? One or two diners leaned towards each other and mumbled. I ignored it.

Percy drew out my chair, and I sat.

"It appears that we are the subject of much curiosity," I murmured to him. "Even here."

Claire took her place at his other side, and gazed around the room defiantly. I couldn't help but feel a flood of affection for my stepsister. She was young, younger than me, and on occasion I was conscious of feeling protective towards her. I always remembered us standing in the hallway in our nightgowns, spying on Coleridge and my father, slipping through an open doorway and hiding behind a couch, whispering together. Now we were here, in a dining-room in the Swiss mountains, surrounded by the glint of crystal, the scrape of knives, the chink of china, and the stares of the godly and the righteous.

I noticed a woman in a feathered head-dress lean towards her neighbour. Her black feathers nodded provocatively, bringing to mind a raven.

And so, it began.

It started with a whisper, an averted gaze, a nudge of the elbow. A gloved hand hiding a smile on the lips, a look of shocked deprecation, judgement, scorn. They had heard. Our story had gone before us. We had been recognised. *How*, I do not know.

As I held Will in my arms and nursed him at table, the maid who served us bent low and exchanged a few words with Percy. She nodded in my direction. Claire joined in the discussion and translated.

"She says there is a woman in the village who can help us with Will."

Elise Dullivard had a small child of her own, but no husband and was in sore need of employment. She would become Will's nurse, and our companion.

"That will be a relief for you, my dear," Percy said, before I had a chance to offer my own opinion.

"I do not want to be parted from him," I muttered.

"Mary, it is normal," Claire insisted, leaning forward. "He needs to be weaned soon, and you need to rest. You won't be parted from Will. You will simply have some help."

Percy showed his gratitude to Claire with a slight pressure on her hand which lay on the white table-cloth.

"Thank you, Claire," he murmured.

I heard a ripple of gossip behind us. His gesture had not gone unobserved: they hissed like snakes.

Ménage à trois. Do they all sleep in the same bed? I knew

what they are saying. Is it my imagination, or did they gossip and whisper as much here as they had in the drawing-rooms of London?

Claire seemed not in the least bit perturbed by their scrutiny. She rather thrived on it. She liked the attention whereas I much preferred my privacy.

My room in the *Hôtel d'Angleterre* was a haven, away from the stares, the shocked silences as we walked into the dining-room, all three of us. Percy wanted to sail on the lake, despite the weather conditions. A light powdering of snow still fell, sprinkling the rocky mountainsides, and when the wind blew, it stirred up the surface of the open water until it became rough with waves. Percy was not deterred. He wanted to get out there, brave the weather. He hired a boat and was full of excitement at the prospect of sailing her.

Claire was keen to go with him, but I declined.

"You are missing out, Mary," he told me.

"I shall bear it, I think."

Claire was very quick to take my place in the stern. As eager as Percy to set sail and welcome danger.

I shook my head and remained indoors with Will and Elise. We attracted too many stares in the public rooms, so I took tea in my own room. I watched Elise getting to know Will better, and tried not to mind when he took to her so easily.

A stiff wind blew across the lake. I stood at the darkening window, observing the sky.

"It seems like a foolhardy thing to do," I said out loud. Elise was in the room behind me, kneeling on the floor with Will. "Why should they want to set sail today, with this wind?"

"Your husband sails well?"

I turned to Elise and smiled. "He is not my husband, and yes, he sails well. He taught himself. However, he cannot swim."

"How old is your own child, Elise?" I asked her tentatively.

She stiffened slightly, and an expression of pain and regret flickered across her face.

"She is only two months of age."

"A daughter! What is her name?"

"I called her Lisa, but I think the people she stays with may have changed her name."

I fell silent.

"It was better for her, in the long run," Elise offered.

"I cannot believe that," I said quietly.

She shrugged as she gazed at Will. "It is no matter. I have Will now. You and your husband are very kind to me, and Lisa will grow up in a household which can feed and maybe even educate her."

All of this seemed unfair to me, but I struggled to keep my rebel thoughts to myself. It would not help Elise to voice them and only cause her further pain.

"Your sister is a very spirited lady," Elise said now.

"She is not my sister," I replied.

Elise looked up in surprise. "She is not your sister – and he is not your husband. Who is what, then?"

I was struck dumb by her candidness.

"Claire and I are stepsisters," I explained. "Percy and I take care of her, for now."

"It is none of my business."

"I suppose I feel responsible for her."

Elise studied me carefully.

"Responsible?"

The conversation had taken a sudden turn of intimacy I hadn't anticipated.

"It's my fault she has ended up here, away from home, on the continent."

There was a short silence.

"I do not know you well, Mrs Shelley, but I think you blame yourself too readily," Elise murmured.

"She lost a lot when she decided to join us on our travels."

"Perhaps…" she murmured, as she bent to lift my son onto her hip. She dangled a teething ring for him and he reached out stubby fingers for it. "Or perhaps it was you who lost."

I glanced at her sharply. "What do you mean?"

"Nothing," she whispered. "I pity you, Mrs Shelley."

"Your place is not to pity me."

My rebuke put an end to our dialogue, just when it appeared to be leading somewhere, and I was immediately remorseful. Elise did not deserve such harsh words. She had had to give up her own baby and I could not help but notice that perhaps nursing my child acted as a comforter. I wondered how she bore it. The world treats illegitimate children and their mothers with cruelty. Even Sir William, Percy's father, threatened to remove my child from me on occasion, and I lived with this ever present dread, even while Percy stood by me.

A little while later, I apologised to Elise. "You are right, of course. Miss Clairmont requires some careful handling. I never really know what to expect from her, or what she will do next."

"She is very enthusiastic."

"Perhaps you could help me to manage her?" I added, tentatively.

Elise regarded me in silence and I felt sure we understood each other.

"She is eager to experience life and fears that she is missing out on the most important experiences," I added, and then wondered quietly to myself why I was still discussing my stepsister.

"She likes your husband very much. Your husband who is not your husband, that is," Elise corrected herself.

"Does she?"

"Oh yes," Elise said. "I think she does."

Elise was turning out to be quite an ally.

"And what does *he* think of *her*?" I asked.

Elise smiled and shook her head. "I could not say. I cannot pretend to be privy to the workings of Mr Shelley's inner mind. He is a man of extremes. And extreme emotions."

"You are very observant, Elise."

Will clapped his hands together and released what sounded very much like a chuckle.

"Your son is adorable, Mrs Shelley. I shall enjoy looking after him."

"And I will enjoy having you as a companion," I replied.

"Did you enjoy your trip on the lake?" I asked Shelley, on their return.

"We did," he replied. "The fresh air has done Claire some good. Have you noticed she has been looking very pale recently?"

I glanced at my stepsister as she walked across the dining-room towards us.

"Well, she does not look so pale now. She is positively glowing."

Claire joined us at our table – observed by all the other diners – and sat down with a happy sigh, her dark hair tousled by the wind.

The rest of the diners watched us, their glances sliding towards our table in overt curiosity. *Well might they stare!* I thought. It must be hard for them to work out which of us is carnally connected with my husband at present.

Byron arrived among us, as predicted, at the end of May. He did so with a fanfare and a great commotion. It did not occur to him to slip quietly into Geneva without drawing attention to himself. He turned up in an elaborately expensive coach which he claimed to be an exact replica of Bonaparte's, and brought a great quantity of belongings with him. He moved himself into a beautiful villa across the lake from our hotel, where he could enjoy the view of Jura in all her icy splendour.

The entire clientele of our hotel was made aware of his arrival, and of course Claire was red-faced with nervous excitement. She could not wait to dash across the lake and make our presence here known to him.

"Did you tell him that we would be here, Claire?" I asked her.

"I wrote to tell him that you and Percy were intending to venture as far as Geneva. He has the Villa Diodati, you know," she gushed. "I believe he has brought a doctor friend along with him, a medical man. He is a philosopher and a scientist."

"How do you know that?"

"He may have mentioned it to me before."

"Before what?"

"Before we left London."

"You are extremely keen to meet up with Lord Byron again – and on such a limited acquaintance."

She flushed with anger. "Why must you always be so keen to destroy what I have?"

"I do not know what you mean by that. In fact, the reverse is true."

Elise listened to our bickering but kept her head down, attending to my son's needs.

When we fetched stares in the dining-room, Claire was impervious to them and accused me of being over-sensitive.

"Why do you find it so embarrassing, Mary?"

"And why do you not?"

"It was you who chose this life."

"I believe you chose this too. You followed us, after all."

"Yes, and I have loved every minute of it – mostly – but you? You are never done complaining. You regret running away with Percy and you are not even brave enough to admit it. You pretend that you are following in your mother's footsteps, but you are not as brave as she! Sometimes I feel suffocated being in your constant presence, Mary."

"Then go elsewhere. Go and find someone else to amuse you. No one is stopping you."

Elise lifted William in her arms, and took him into another room. His baby face watched me over Elise's shoulder as she disappeared through the door frame.

When we met up with Byron, I winced to see my stepsister nervously perform in front of him. Part of me pitied her. She was so keen, so eager to impress. I knew my stepsister and I could see that for Claire this affair of theirs consumed her utterly. She was eaten up by it. She thought to mirror the grand romance she believed Percy and I to have embarked on.

As I watched her struggling to keep Byron's attention, I thought of a small parlour in Scotland, on the banks of the Tay, where two sisters vied for the attention of one man. I ought to be grateful and relieved that Claire's heart was diverted elsewhere, away from Percy. But I was not. I knew that trouble was brewing.

The weather continued to bring unusual darkness for the time of year. It rained constantly. Claire overheard the servants talking on the stairs. She said they murmured of strange portents.

"Their thoughts are fuelled by superstition," Percy said. "I would not pay any heed to what they say."

I felt oppressed by the perpetual darkness.

Percy longed to go sailing on the lake again, but the dismal weather kept us all indoors, cooped up like hens. When Byron pressed an invitation on us all to visit him at his villa on the opposite bank, it was a relief to escape the confines of the hotel.

Byron struck me as a man who was easily bored, and for now, we were his entertainment. And Polidori, of course. Percy was wary at first, beset by his old insecurities. I think he was wondering if the older man would take him seriously as a poet. Rain lashed down as our carriage drew up outside the villa, and I gazed up at the windows where the shutters were closed against the night. A chink of light moved behind one of them.

Claire and I hastily pulled our cloaks over our heads to avoid spoiling our carefully arranged hair, and dashed across the lawn and up the wide steps to the front door, which was immediately opened by a small servant girl, who curtsied and smiled as if we were grand ladies.

I smiled at her.

She took our cloaks, but I shook the rain out first so they were not too damp for her to carry.

"Thank you… what is your name?"

She looked a little confused, and Claire murmured to her in French.

She smiled at me again and replied "Céline."

"That's a beautiful name," I told her.

As I watched her disappear along the corridor, burdened with our cloaks, I wondered at her innocence and youth. She looked so small and young to be serving in this dark house, and she seemed almost swallowed up by the shadows.

I was not naïve. We live in a world of hypocrisy and male dominion. There are many servant girls who have no lock on their doors to protect them at night. They work in the basements and sleep in the attics of grand houses, and must hope their master is kind, and a man of principles and integrity. If he is not, they may suffer… they may find themselves staring at the door at night instead of sleeping, afraid to see the handle turn, a soft foot intrude, a flickering candle appear in the darkness, with the form of a monster looming behind it… a monster in human form.

"You are a pessimist, Mary!" Byron shouted at me later, as we gathered in the stuffy drawing-room, a fire roaring in the grate, the rain still lashing at the windows.

"Why does the sun never shine nowadays?" Shelley interrupted, before I could reply.

"It will be known as the year without a summer," Polidori said – Byron's doctor friend, a 'medical man, scientist and philosopher', as Claire described him.

"But Byron has a point, Mary," Percy added, as if Polidori had not even spoken. "You *are* a pessimist, my dear."

"I am not. I am a realist," I protested.

"The rest of us can see there will be some improvement in the lot of mankind, if science is allowed to progress."

"I don't think I am a pessimist at all. Human beings are what they are, and they will always make mistakes."

I noticed that Polidori winced slightly when Percy talked over him. He was used to being relegated, dismissed by the other two as an inferior being. I wondered why they treated him so. He was a medical man, after all, with training, knowledge and experience. Whereas they had none.

Byron was observing me closely. Here was a complex concoction of personalities with secret rivalries and desires. Claire stood very close to our host, and called him by the affectionate name of 'Albe' when he teased her – which was often. She hung on his every word. There was a sheen of sweat on her forehead which glimmered in the firelight. It was very close in the room with the fire roaring against the night.

I knew my stepsister well, and if I was not mistaken, I guessed that beneath her smiling exterior she was irritable, angry. Her flushed cheeks gave the lie to that smile. She had tried to keep Byron's attention fixed on her all evening, but it was impossible; there were too many competing interests. He was not interested in Claire as a person, and she knew it. He had used her. I knew this with absolute certainty, in exactly the same way that I knew about Isabella and David Booth when I stayed with the Baxters on the banks of the Tay.

Claire twittered on with Percy's encouragement. I remained quiet and withdrawn, watching the others as is my wont. Percy loved my stepsister. I knew this too. He loved her nonsense, her insecurity, her lack of discretion.

"I am fond," he often said, when I accused him.

So fond that he had to bury her away in Devon. What became of that thickening waistline? Claire never spoke of it. She never did tell me what happened in that remote cottage, if the child lived or died, if she gave it away? How could she *bear* not to keep it?

"How can you *bear* to stay at the *Hôtel d'Angleterre*," Polidori said, echoing the words in my head.

I looked up.

"With all those foreigners?" he stated. "The English!"

"We are foreigners too!" I laughed.

"Yes, but… not that kind."

"They stare at us in the dining-room. I have heard them whisper about a *ménage à trois*," I added.

There was a ripple of awkwardness in the room. Did the others notice it? Byron most certainly did. He was sharp and intelligent. Not much could pass him by.

"Sometimes I cannot bear it," Claire chipped in, and I glanced at her, surprised. She had never minded it before. Why did she contradict herself?

"Do not tolerate it," Byron said.

"Move here," Polidori added, at which Byron flinched a little. This was perhaps a step too far.

"There is a small house for rent, I believe, just below us."

Percy's attention was caught.

"How much?"

"Affordable, I'm sure. You can see it from here. The *Maison Chapuis*. We can be neighbours."

Claire's face lit up.

"That is wonderful. Percy, we must," she cried, grabbing his hand. I noticed the contact, and I noticed the way he nervously withdrew his hand in front of the others. Byron noticed it too.

"We can make enquiries."

"It would certainly be a welcome break from the clientele at the *d'Angleterre*. We did not come all this way in order to be followed by the dowdy London crowd, gawked at, prodded and poked."

"You ought to be flattered they recognise you," Polidori added.

"Why?" Percy rounded on him. "I would rather they read my poetry first, before telling tales about adultery and atheism and incest!"

"Is *that* what they are talking about?" Byron said, raising a satirical eyebrow.

Percy shrugged. "So Mary says!"

"Mary says nothing," I smiled.

The days and the evenings lengthened. We moved away from the dreaded hotel, and set up home temporarily in the little *Maison Chapuis*, fifty yards below the elegant façade of the *Villa Diodati*. I wondered how Byron felt about this close proximity to Claire? A little too close for comfort?

Time would tell, and time was slipping like sand through the hour-glass for all of us. Our stories would not end well. How did I know this? I felt it in my bones, unless it was the darkening sky that made me assume the worst, but at the same time I felt a bubbling of joy in my stomach. Something was happening here. I did not fully understand it, but it excited me. Always the sun was obscured by a veil of drifting black like the speckled silk a widow might wear across her eyes. The birds were still confused, falling silent at midday as if some kind of apocalypse or eclipse of the sun was upon us.

"It is as if the end of the world is coming," Claire said, trying for a note of melodrama.

"Scientists have claimed that dark spots have been observed drifting across the face of the sun," Polidori informed us.

"And what does that mean?" Byron asked.

But Polidori and the scientists apparently could not answer that.

"And then there is the strange star that has been seen up in the sky at night, when the clouds will allow," Polidori went on. "The locals have been talking about it, how it heralds a time of darkness and doom."

"The darkness is already here," Byron said, trying to lighten the mood. "Candles at midday?" he laughed, gesturing at the myriad flickering of flames on the mantelpiece and table. "It is summer, for God's sake," he cried, on a yawn, throwing himself down on the nearby couch.

I gazed out at the glassy black lake, at the snowy summits surrounding it, and felt an unexplained fear deep in the pit of my belly.

Later that night, when Byron encouraged us to try opium and laudanum, I felt uneasy. Both were exceptionally easy to obtain and offered a delight to the senses, easing the pain of life, fostering a light delirium which – Byron said – was a poet's prerogative.

"It expands the mind," he laughed, pushing the opium pipe in Percy's direction. "A closed mind is the enemy of every poet. Go on, man!"

Percy inhaled deeply, and I was the only one too timid to accept. They teased me for it. I watched the others grow pale and more languid, a sheen of sweat dampening their foreheads in the firelight. A dense fug lay on the air in the drawing-room, creating a strange claustrophobic atmosphere.

Percy lay on the chaise-lounge, the pipe affixed to his lips, greedy for more, while Claire leaned against Albe, whispering to him. Polidori sat apart, staring at the flames. A sudden headache began to build, and the others barely noticed when I rose, and quickly left the room. Out in the cold hallway I took deep breaths of cool clear air. Hearing a soft, almost inaudible sound, I looked up to see the little maidservant, Céline, emerge from the shadows. Somewhere beyond her was the entrance to the servants' staircase.

She murmured something to me, her face full of concern.

I nodded, and smiled.

"I am well, thank you Céline. I needed some air. That is all."

She nodded, a little unconvinced, and turned away. No doubt she wanted to retire to her bed, instead of having to wait on the guests who refused to sleep.

That glance between us. How much did she see and observe in a house like this? We assume that servants see nothing, know nothing, but walls have ears and the walls of the *Villa Diodati* were no exception.

Back in the drawing-room, the thick miasma of smoke was heavier than ever in contrast with the freshness of the hallway. It made me feel slightly sick and I wondered how often we would be expected to indulge in order to *open our minds*. The others thought me prudish but I excused myself on the grounds of having Will to think about.

Percy and Byron had this in common. They both loved to sail. They were like boys fighting over a precious toy yacht, competing over who had the best sails, the best chance of winning a race. They sailed together, and apart, and Claire watched anxiously from the bank, longing to go with them and desperate for Byron's attention every time he set foot on dry land. And Polidori entertained we two women, rather glad, I suspected, of the chance to shine alone without competition from the other two men. I felt a little bored by him, but I pitied him too.

When he leapt from the veranda and twisted his ankle, Byron wasted no time in mocking him. "I think you were trying to impress Miss Godwin here," he laughed, causing much embarrassment to both of us.

Percy darted a quick look in my direction. He had always maintained that he believed in free love. This is what he had taught me. He did not believe that human beings should spend the rest of their lives with one partner only, for where was the satisfaction in that? I wondered, however, how he would react if I were to follow his advice and do the same?

Polidori yelped with pain and was forced to spend the rest of the week bandaged and hobbling, barely able to leave the sofa.

Night after night we gathered in Byron's drawing-room, the fug in the air, the fire in the grate, and outside the rain would sweep down in torrents.

"Look at how it grows worse," Byron said. "These mountains can certainly conjure a storm."

The lake disappeared from view.

"It is getting late," I murmured. "We have left little Will with Elise and I worry for him."

"You will get soaked through if you try to leave now," Byron said. He urged us to stay the night in the villa. "There are plenty of rooms and the little chalet down there is probably the safest place to be on a night like this."

When I objected, Shelley glanced at me. "You would not want to risk a chill, Mary. Our son needs you to be healthy."

White light suddenly flashed through the gaps in the shutters and the sky overhead rumbled.

"The gods are cooking up a storm tonight," Byron said, his eyes gleaming with excitement.

As the night progressed the storm grew worse, echoing in the sky above the mountains. I spared a thought for Elise on her own, down in the little chalet, nursing Will. I was half-inclined to demand my cloak of the servant-girl Céline and leave, hurrying the fifty yards down the slope to our own front door, but something prevented me. The others persuaded me to stay, and I could not argue. In truth, although I felt partly uneasy, I was also loathe to miss whatever might happen next. I was greedy for it, the same as the rest.

"I think a ghost story is what we are needing," Byron cried. "Fit the mood to the purpose."

"Very well then, Albe. Amuse us," Claire said.

Byron ignored her and fixed his gaze instead on my husband, Percy. He wanted to challenge Percy, to threaten him maybe, or perhaps to awaken something in him. I was a little unnerved by this realisation. It was odd how the two men were so drawn together. The rest of us did not figure at all in the dynamic between these two giants. I once heard a rumour that during his adolescence Byron felt the love that dare not speak its name. Percy told me this, I think.

"*He has experimented in the past.*" Those were his exact words. I realised suddenly that it was neither Claire nor myself he was attracted to, but my husband. My own Percy Shelley. The revelation arrived in my head, on a bolt of lightning.

Was Percy aware of Byron's feelings? The fire spat and crackled in the hearth, and the rain beat against the window panes.

Byron had picked up a book from the shelf, but when his reading fell flat, without the profound effect he was after, he slapped the book shut. He looked hunted, bored; the experiment had not worked. "Coleridge tells a better story, one that can send a shudder down the spine," he said.

My father's friend, Coleridge. I glanced at Claire and wondered if she too remembered hiding behind the couch, listening. Claire and I, shivering in our nightgowns, trying to keep still. *And all along they knew we were there…*

"What is *your* favourite?" Byron asked.

He was addressing me.

"*Christabel*, I think."

"I know it by heart," he boasted. "Do you know what it is about?" he asked us.

No one replied because all of us realised that Byron must take centre-stage. We were under his power, his influence; the older man of the world who had life experience, whose reputation went before him.

"It is the story of an innocent young girl called Christabel who encounters a strange and mysterious woman in the forest. On taking the woman home, Christabel finds herself inexplicably drawn to her. Once inside the cabin the lady begins to slowly undress."

Byron paused, and there was a strained silence. I could hear Percy swallowing, a dry gulp which he struggled to conceal.

"Christabel is breathless with anticipation," he went on, "wondering what will happen next. It is as if she is frightened of her own feelings, perhaps."

Again, we waited.

"The lady strips…"

I heard Claire draw in a breath, a little shocked in spite of herself, as Byron leaned over her shoulder, reciting the words in her ear.

"…her clothes drop to the floor and she reveals herself to be nothing but a hideous, deformed witch."

"Beneath the lamp the lady bowed,
And slowly rolled her eyes around,
Then drawing in her breath aloud

Like one that shuddered, she unbound
The cincture from beneath her breast;
Her silken robe, and inner vest
Dropped to her feet, and in full view,
Behold! Her bosom and half her side –
Hideous, deformed, and pale of hue."

"Stop!"

Claire had broken away from him.

"What is it?" he asked, irritated that she had broken his carefully-woven spell.

The vision conjured by his words – the forest and the fair maiden and the deformed witch – faded before our eyes, and we were left with only the firelight and the dark room, and the stormy night outside.

"It is too much," Claire said, breathless. "I do not want to hear any more of it."

I glanced at Byron, who had fallen silent, but there was a wicked, cruel glint in his eye that made me uneasy. He was enjoying Claire's discomfort, revelling in it.

Another roll of thunder rumbled in the distance.

"Coleridge," Byron murmured. He did not even need the book in his hand, this time. He could recite it by memory. "Which one of us could emulate him and create a ghost story to terrify the mind, to still the blood, to send sleep to the devil?"

Percy looked up.

"Is this a challenge?"

"Of course!"

Claire was pale and ill-looking, but she clapped her hands together as if the idea appealed to her. It pained me to see her make such an effort to please him.

Byron grimaced. She was like a flea in his ear and she did not even realise it.

"A ghost story?" Percy repeated.

"Yes, man! A ghost story! Between poets. Who can write the best! The others will judge."

Will they now? I thought.

I already had my monster lurking in in the darkest depths of my thoughts, borne of pain and misery. Grief and sorrow.

"I am the fallen angel. Misery made me a fiend."

The words arrived in my head, unbidden and I suddenly longed to write them down. The fallen angel, rejected by my parents, unloved, unwanted, forced into exile, no longer welcome at anyone's hearth or home – except this one, where demons lurk and drugs are imbibed.

I had chosen my path in life, as Claire so often reminded me, but it was a lonely one and I suspected would become more so. And perhaps Claire was right, I did not have my mother's strength of character to endure it. The monster in my head gave voice to my own thoughts, my own feelings.

At two in the morning, I left the others to their discussion by the fire. We had stayed up late, terrifying one another with idle visions.

"I'll call the servant to show you to your room," Byron said.

"There's no need."

I thought of little Céline, bleary-eyed, dragged out of a much-needed sleep. That would not do at all.

Claire remained behind to pester the men. Before I could stop him, Byron rang the bell, and little Céline appeared, red-eyed and gaunt, to light my way up the staircase. The hem of her dress, as she went before me, was threadbare and worn, her ankles bare beneath it. She looked chilled to the bone. I wondered if she had the luxury of a fire in her room.

She stopped on the first-floor landing before a tall door, then stood aside to allow me to enter.

I turned to thank her, but she had already left, desperate for her own narrow cot. The room before me was huge, a dark chasm, and the bed curtains felt oppressive, like a mausoleum. Céline had left me with a light. I carried it to the bedside and set it down. Then leaned down and touched the counterpane. The bed was cold as silk, icy, and I wished Percy would come up to warm me. I took off my chemise gown and slipped under the covers in my linen undergarments.

When I placed my head on the pillow, my brain was churning with visions.

I am the fallen angel. Misery made me a fiend.

Those words again, echoing across a frozen waste of ice. A cry of despair from the darkness.

I thought of an ambitious man of science working in the cave of his laboratory, pale and earnest, a man flawed in so many ways, who believes in his own powers, that he can solve the mystery of what is the vital spark which creates life. He is ambitious, greedy for success. He will make himself immortal, famous, astound the world with his discovery. He will give birth to human life, but outside the laws of God and Nature. He will create a beautiful creature, bizarre but real. A chimera who will inhabit the ordinary spaces of the world, born not of woman but of man. Cobbled together from corpses. A creature to astound the scientific community. My anatomist will usurp God, the Creator of life. He will be the originator of mankind. He will sacrifice his family and friends, those who love him, in the interests of his infernal art.

And of the creature? What will he feel? What will he see? How will he learn to speak? How will the rest of the world greet him? I envisaged his nightmarish loneliness, his sense of abandonment and rejection, this poor cobbled-together beast, manufactured from hacked-off bits of skin and bone, stitched together monstrously with dark bloody thread. I saw the monster clearly beneath a halo of light, his features, his ugly contorted limbs, his wounds where bits of corpses had been knitted together. An ugly cross-stitch threading his naked scalp. The scars, the ugly eye sockets, the unnatural leering mouth, contorted in despair. The mumbling inability to speak properly, unable to control his lips or tongue. What is language? And what are we without it?

All of this came to me in the night. And I knew for certain I had a story to tell.

I told them it was a dream. It was easier that way. But it was not just a dream.

Anyway, what is a nightmare?

A wild horse: a mare who runs wild through our dreams at night, out of control.

But this did not feel out of control. It felt like a story I had to write. It felt like a story I had been writing ever since I was fourteen years of age and first saw a young criminal hanging from the gallows, being toyed with by a man of science in the interests of progress, as he sought to entertain the crowds. What shocked me was not simply the act itself, but the mania for gore which the crowd exhibited. Back then, I had a dream this corpse lifted his head and opened his livid eyes.

No one cared because he was a criminal, but I remember seeing those men and women being led from Newgate Prison and reflecting painfully on how they were human beings the same as us, but less fortunate, fallen on hard times. Fallen angels.

Who is the real monster? Who commits the worst crime?

Men think they can give birth to life, but is it human life? What constitutes being human? Women are torn apart and risk their lives every day to bring new life into the world, and no one tells us how monstrously difficult birth is, how ugly, how bloody, how the scalp of the babe is streaked with its mother's blood and excrement. No one speaks of these things. Byron and Percy – for all their worldliness – did not have a clue.

Polidori neither, although he was trained as a doctor. I had given birth, I had suckled a new-born infant, and I had seen that child grow still and pale in my arms. If anyone could reflect on the meaning of life – where it springs from, and why it must decay – then it was I.

I remembered hurrying through Smithfield market on my way to St Pancras and kicking that bucket of yellow entrails so that it wobbled. These are the places a true anatomist would explore if he wanted to recreate life. He would dig out the corpses, plunge his pale hands into buckets of slime, looking for spare organs, spare tissue. He would unearth wormy graves, or visit prisons and cut down corpses while they were still fresh. He would need bodies, and plenty of them.

Lightning flashed in the sky above my anatomist's laboratory – as it flashed above the mountains of Lake Geneva - while he waited for his corpse to be injected with life.

The door opened, and startled me from my thoughts.

"Mary?" a voice whispered.

He parted the bed curtains, slid in beside me. I pretended to be asleep.

He kissed the back of my neck, through my hair.

I did not want his attentions. I wanted to keep the visions in my head and write them down in the morning. I wanted my notebooks.

He nuzzled closer, while the storm raged outside.

I waited for him to fall asleep, then lifted the bedcovers stealthily. The cold air did not trouble me. I barely felt it.

There were words inside my head which I needed to write down before they faded.

I moved like a ghost, fearing to wake Percy. I wanted no one else's voice inside my head but my lonely, flawed anatomist, who had unleashed a terrible curse upon the world, and must bear the consequences.

What will he do? How will he bear it? How must he make amends?

"It was on a dreary night in November that I beheld my man completed..."

In writing the first words, I knew this to be a thread which would unspool into something magnificent, something which explored the very tissue of existence with probing fingers and hands, seeking out answers to questions which had barely been formulated. My man demanded the impossible. And the impossible would kill him. It would kill us all.

I wrote of visions that came to me in the darkest hour of the night, and I saw them all clearly before me. It was a beginning...

And it would have an end...

People would be shocked, I knew this. What kind of woman would write such a heathen story? But I did not care. I had my narrative, and I was compelled to write it.

It was like incubating a baby, a monstrous creation, in the womb of my notebooks. I knew it was there, waiting, and I grabbed the moments to write, when I could, in the pauses between meal-times, in the early evenings, the late evenings, in the dawn while Percy lay still abed. Moment by moment, I threaded my narrative together.

It was a clumsy beginning, like hacking away at a sculpture. It seemed unshapely at first, but I would impose order. First must come the rough sketch, the laying down of foundations. The rest would rise up later...

When the weather broke, Percy and Byron took their sailing boat, which was moored beneath our chalet and spent a week touring the lake together. I am ashamed to say that I barely noticed their absence. I was free to write, my mind in another place. I returned to the wilderness spaces of Scotland, on the banks of the Tay, where my adolescent mind first wove fantasies and fairy-tales.

Their departure gave me the space to write. Blessed silence filled the rooms. No more smoking sessions, the air full of opiate fug. Elise took care of Will, Claire kept mainly to her room, and I had the precious days and nights to spin out my elaborate tale. When another storm built and swept down from the summit of Jura, disturbing the surface of the lake, I paused from my notebooks and looked up at the casement. I saw my own face reflected there, back-lit by the globe of the oil lamp at my elbow. Percy and Byron were out there somewhere, in that storm. They might be moored anywhere along the length and breadth of Lake Geneva, tossed by the waves. But I was sure they were safe and would never be so foolish as to set sail in this. *They will be tied up at some safe anchorage*, I assured myself, *watching the sky from their berth.*

"They have been gone for eight days now," Claire reminded me. "Does that not worry you?"

"To tell you the truth, Claire, I haven't had time. There is so much to do, nowadays."

She looked at me in astonishment.

"Yes, you have your Wilmouse, and your writing."

"What's wrong, Claire?"

She shook her head. "You have everything, Mary. You have always had everything."

"That's not true. I do not have the good opinion of my father."

"And what does that count for?"

Claire stalked off, slamming the door behind her – the old Clairmont habit.

I wrote to Isabella in Scotland again, to tell her about little Will and my travels abroad. She did not reply.

But in the silent and majestic Alps, as long as I was away from the ferocious scrutiny of the other tourists at the hotel, I felt liberated. My mind was set free…

It was only when Percy returned and told me how close they were to drowning that I felt a tiny stab of remorse. Was he exaggerating? While a violent storm was threatening to capsize their boat, I was glad of the space and peace in which to write. My mind was in another realm. It was Claire who fretted for them: not I.

"Claire is in love with Byron," I told him suddenly.

Percy frowned. "I doubt it."

"She was concerned for you both, of course," I added, to qualify it, for I could sense my husband's jealousy.

"And you were not, my dear?"

"I was extremely busy. I had Will to think about. Besides, you were in such capable hands, I didn't think it necessary to worry."

The road beneath us was rugged and uncertain. I leant forward tensely in the saddle, listening to the silence punctuated only by the sound of our horses carefully placing their hooves. One false move could trigger a rockfall or landslide with the amount of rain we had been having. Up ahead I could see Claire and then Percy. We had left Will behind in the care of Elise at the *Maison Chapuis*, and had embarked on a new adventure at Percy's insistence, although I confess I was keen to experience it too.

Our mission was to reach Mont Blanc and the Mer de Glace – the three of us – although we had been advised against it. I wanted to cast my eyes upon the glacier, to observe for myself the creak of ice, the glassy swell. My notebook was tucked away in my saddlebag, waiting. It brought a thrill to think of it. I would not leave it behind. I had my monster and my tormented man of science to think about; I could not abandon them.

When the ascent became more rugged, and cut into more challenging terrain, we exchanged the horses for mules to aid our descent on the other side. A steep ravine cut through the landscape ahead of us, surrounded by mountains, rocky fissures and precipices. We would need to negotiate this on foot or by mule. The tumble and cascade of water was everywhere, a torrent raging below our mules, and I felt a corresponding soaring of my spirits.

I was swept along, exhilarated at the sight of the first tumbling waterfall. This is what I had been seeking. This was my landscape, one I could identify with, a kind of exaggerated version or distillation of Scotland, only more dramatic still. Broken pines littered the steep hillsides, destroyed by avalanches in winter, or storms in spring, their spines shattered. At times it looked almost like a war zone, a battlefield where the forces of Nature were pitted against each other like Greek gods. Ruined castles topped the crags at first, and occasionally an isolated cottage appeared through the trees. What must it be like to live in one of those cabins, surrounded by the spires of the Alps, pines darkening their lower slopes, while the summits remained snow-covered and cold even in the summer? How isolated it must be in winter, when the snowfall was at its thickest!

We crossed the bridge of Pelissier and another ravine opened up before us, the river raging along its basin in torrents. Percy pointed up at the steep mountain face overhanging us, but his words were snatched away by the sound of the water.

His meaning was clear. We were to ascend that steep rocky mountain in order to reach Chamonix on the other side where we would catch our first glimpse of the glacier beyond.

Claire demanded a break, so we took our rest for a few moments, while the mules bent their heads to drink at a nearby tributary which trickled off the rocks.

Claire was looking miserable these days, gaunt and languid. It was not like her to be so quiet. Even these sublime surroundings did little to lift her mood.

I worried for William and guilt tugged at my heart, but I was enjoying my freedom too much.

Elise promised me before we left that Will's care and safety would always be her first priority above all else, and I had no reason to doubt her. She loved Will as if he were her own. He was a comforting substitute for what she'd lost.

"We have a doctor up at the villa if I have need of one," she reassured me.

I thought of the spectacle Polidori presented, twisting his ankle as he leapt from the veranda, and could not help doubting his professionalism.

We dipped down into the valley of Chamonix and were met with a sight I will never forget. The environment challenged us, exacting a price, demanding worship. Icefields crept steadily towards the edge of the track where our mules walked. I heard the ice creaking as it inched forward. Halfway along we were surprised by a deep rumbling sound in the distance. It was not a storm brewing. We saw a white cloud of smoke rising in the air. An avalanche! At the end of the long valley, far ahead of those moving ice barriers, rose Mont Blanc, a pure white dome dominating one end of the glacier-filled valley.

Our mules continued, sure-footed along the track until we reached the village which would give us shelter for the night. When we finally secured a room at the only inn, I was tired but elated, still exhilarated by our journey. Mont Blanc cast its shadow directly over the building, blocking out the daylight. It felt oppressive. Our room was small and simple, a table, a bed, a chair. If I stepped outside onto the wrought-iron balcony, the mountain nudged me with its elbow. The cold breath of its shoulder touched me – a living presence.

The next day we planned to explore the glacier at our leisure and so I found myself standing beside the wall of moving ice. I heard it creak, the strain of its progress. The glacier is always moving, at a steady slow pace, advancing down the mountainsides, until it forms an insurmountable barricade, cutting off the valley in winter. A fragment broke off with a sound like thunder in the silence. Pine trees lay shattered in the wake of its advance. A thick mist cloaked the summits and high above us I saw a solitary eagle coasting the air. What must we look like to him? We must appear as tiny fragile creatures in this immensity. Here the earth was rent and torn apart, fractured by ice so that a debris of boulders was dragged along in its wake. Both rock and pine yielded to its power.

The glacier itself was perilous, full of sharp-edged fissures and deep blue hollows. The wind coursed through it, setting up a haunting cadence while sculpting the ice into sweepingly surreal shapes.

I felt my mind stirring.

As I gazed across those blinding wastelands, I suddenly glimpsed a dark hunched-up figure, garbed in black rags, crossing the white crevasses, hiding from his own creator. He loped along with a shambling gait, powerful yet broken, both hunted and hunter. This – I realised – was the perfect backdrop for the tragedy of the scientist and his creature. My man of science and anatomy, Victor Frankenstein, was father to his own objectionable creation, and he then rejected what he had made. My monster was doomed to wander the earth in perpetual isolation. Hated and despised, he must seek out places where no human contact might be possible. *This* then was my creature's domain. The monster would retreat *here* to survive in utter loneliness, living in caves of ice. The icy wastes would be his last home.

As I stood there, a wind whispered from the heights. There was no darkened figure stumbling along on the horizon.

"Mary, what are you staring at?"

Claire and Percy saw nothing.

Every day we went hiking and on our return to the hotel in the evening I sat writing in my notebooks, possessed by a fever of words, of language. My narrative and my characters took hold of me.

Ideas poured out of me in a cataract of prose and I consigned them all to the page as soon as I regained the privacy of my room. Claire kept Percy entertained, which was a blessing. They sat before a roaring fire downstairs, making desultory conversation with the innkeeper, while I lost myself in my narrative.

When I was done, I pulled the shutter aside and gazed out at the mountain hovering there in the darkness. Always I felt its presence and its power. It did not occur to me to wonder why Percy was so late to join me in our room. Besides, Claire was surely preoccupied by her thwarted feelings for Byron. It never occurred to me that Percy would comfort her.

"I love it here," I told the others. "It is beautiful. It reminds me of Scotland."

Even here, though, we were not entirely free from the prurience of other tourists. Percy deliberately tried to shock them all by signing the hotel register with the words *'Percy Shelley, poet, atheist and philanderer.'*

He knew what they would make of it.

"You do it on purpose, to shock them," I scolded him.

"If they want to imagine the worst, let them."

"And what *would* be the worst?" Claire asked, leaning forward mockingly.

"I would prefer not to be stared at when we go down to breakfast," I reminded Percy, ignoring her.

"Mary, you mind too much what people think."

"And you do not? You would not sign your name so if you did not care what people think. It is almost as if you *want* them to talk about us."

"They are talking about us anyway, my dear, so what is the harm?"

Chamonix, July 1816

Later, Claire confessed what ailed her.

"I am with child," she said quietly.

Suddenly all my pleasure in the landscape evaporated. Although I knew it was an unworthy thought, I found myself resenting Claire for being the agent in spoiling everything yet again.

I thought of her pale complexion, her strange mood of late.

"Who…?" I asked her.

"Albe… of course…"

She was angry with me for implying otherwise.

"We must tell Percy."

The room felt suddenly small and claustrophobic, and Percy had become excessively agitated.

"Then he must own the child as his," he said.

I said nothing. It was already evident that Byron had tired of Claire's attention. He was irritated by her mere presence in the same room as him.

"No doubt he was relieved when he heard about our plans to see Mont Blanc. I had my suspicions before we came away," Percy added.

"Did you?" I asked him. "You did not say."

"Yes, well… what was there to say?"

It struck me all of a sudden that my Percy might be jealous. We wove such a tangled web between us and I longed to retreat to my notebooks where my poor creature and my deeply flawed man of so-called 'progress' waited for me.

The rain kept us indoors. Claire slept in her room. I preferred not to dwell on the consequences of my stepsister's pregnancy. We would be forced to confront the problem soon enough. I allowed nothing to divert me from the task at hand.

I thought about my poor created monster and how he would fare. Would he seek out his master, the man who created him, even after suffering such rejection and hate at his hands? At first, I decided, he would punish his maker. He would seek out everyone Victor loved and destroy them, as a means of revenge. He would do this because of the treatment he received at the hands of other human beings, who came after him with pitchforks even when he tried to improve his mind. He would not understand that he was hideous to look upon until he saw the reactions of others. He would demand that Victor create a mate for him, to rescue him from his terrible loneliness, so that he was not doomed to walk the earth alone. In order to oblige him, the doctor of anatomy would find a remote hut on an island in the Outer Hebrides to set about his labours. *'Sometimes I could not prevail on myself to enter my laboratory for several days, and at other times I toiled day and night in order to complete my work. It was, indeed, a filthy process in which I was engaged.'*

My man must inevitably reflect on what he is about and

question the wisdom of creating another such as he. *'She might become ten thousand times more malignant than her mate.'*

I lifted my gaze and stared out of the window at the mountain close by, then bent my head to my notebook again.

'I trembled and my heart failed within me, when, on looking up, I saw by the light of the moon the daemon at the casement. A ghastly grin wrinkled his lips as he gazed on me, where I sat fulfilling the task which he had allotted to me. Yes, he had followed me in my travels; he had loitered in forests, hid himself in caves, or taken refuge in wide and desert heaths; and he now came to mark my progress and claim the fulfilment of my promise.'

I thought Percy would understand this passionate urge to write which grasped me, for he knew what it meant to live under the tyranny of inspiration, but apparently another rule applied to me. He accused me of being callous, continuing to write at a time like this.

"What are we to do?" he declared.

"About?"

"Your sister!"

"She is not my sister," I mumbled beneath my breath.

"She is our responsibility."

"The child is Byron's, is it not?"

"Well, yes," he flustered.

"Then Byron must deal with it."

"But you know as well as I do, he will refuse."

"We shall have to make him."

My eyes were glassy because I was thinking about my tormented anatomist in his isolated hut in the Hebrides, where the lonely wind blew fierce and keen.

Percy shook his head in despair. "You are cold, Mary."

"I do not mean to be."

"I cannot talk to you," he complained.

Then I beg you leave me in peace.

He glanced at my notebooks.

"I am surprised that you can allow *that* to take precedence over your concern for filial responsibilities."

"Why does it surprise you? Am I not a writer too?"

"But Claire…?"

"Will be protected as usual. She will give birth to a child and Byron will be persuaded to look after it. If it is Byron's," I added.

He glanced at me, frowning. "Who else do you imagine to be the father?"

"I have no idea," I murmured innocently.

"You obviously have some notion about it, so why not share it?"

"I have no opinions on the subject either way," I averred. "I merely put forward the possibility that Byron might not be the father, after all."

"So there is an element of doubt?"

I shrugged, but said nothing.

"Is that not an insult to Claire?"

"She has been very close to other men before now. I can think of one in particular."

He shot me a dangerous glance. "What are you implying, Mary?"

Then, when I still did not reply, he shouted "You are wrong!"

He swung out of the room, leaving the door ajar. I bent my head to my notebook and resumed writing. But the flow had been interrupted. I struggled guiltily to try and regain the momentum but it was lost. Why must I continually apologise for this obsession of mine, this need to write? Did Percy have to beg forgiveness when he spent an hour on his boat, scribbling lines and phrases? No, because it was expected of him.

What was expected of me? To bring forth children, merely to

watch them die? To organise food and laundry so that we might eat and survive, and so that Percy might continue to work at his poetry?

I had no notion yet, of how my story would end. In suicide, a complete annihilation of self and spirit? My poor monster would realise how objectionable he was to the world, and he would quit it accordingly, while grieving for the father who made him.

'I shall quit your vessel on the ice raft which brought me thither and shall seek the most northern extremity of the globe; I shall collect my funeral pile and consume to ashes this miserable frame, that its remains may afford no light to any curious and unhallowed wretch who would create such another as I have been. I shall die… lost in darkness and distance.'

Hastily I write it all down, the bare bones of the story. I will flesh it out, edit, hone and polish, make changes when we return to Geneva.

On our return journey through the deep ravine in the mountains, I felt obscurely as if I was carrying a precious burden inside me. Claire was pregnant with a child and I was weighted with something else. A part of me would never leave those icy wastes. The desolate plains, the snowy summits, the thunder of moving ice, would accompany me always, in my dreams, and in the deepest recesses of my soul.

When we turned at the last bend and looked back at the way we had come, I felt a surge of regret. I was leaving part of myself behind and would need to revisit this place often in my imagination – or my nightmares – to retrieve what I left there.

Back at the *Villa Diodati*, we were faced with the difficult task of breaking the news to Byron – for, as Percy said, "someone must."

Claire and I were on the terrace, playing with Will. Elise was close by and Polidori hovered, attentive as usual. I watched Percy strolling with Byron on the grassy slope below. He appeared to be telling him first about our adventures in the Alps, how it rained mostly, and we had to stay indoors.

"Which didn't seem to bother Mary in the least as she was busily writing. Claire and I were at a loose end now and then. But we did have a chance to hike across the Mer de Glace. Incredible."

Byron murmured something inaudible in return.

We watched their backs as they descended the slope away from us.

"But it was another matter I wanted to speak with you about."

Byron was suddenly alert. His posture changed. Claire was watching too. Her eyes slid towards them, a hand over her mouth. They wandered out of hearing: we could no longer eavesdrop.

Suddenly, from this distance, I could tell that Byron was angry. He threw his arm aside and shook his head.

Then we heard him: loud and clear.

"How do we know the child is not yours?" he burst out.

At first, I was not sure if I heard him correctly.

There was a terrible moment when Claire, Elise and I were all frozen in unspoken embarrassment. Polidori seemed at a loss. I dared not raise my eyes. I could not look at my sister (who was not my sister), or Elise or Polidori.

"Why do you say that?" Percy snapped back in return.

Now they were quarrelling in earnest: the atmosphere had become charged.

Byron muttered something else which I could not hear, try as I might to strain my ears.

Then I heard my husband's voice soften.

He rejoined us on the terrace, leaving Byron to walk down to the lake in silence. He glanced at each of us, and wiped a hand across his forehead. Percy – for all his faults – strove to be a peacemaker. He did not like to quarrel.

"It has given him something to think about, anyway," he muttered. "Even if he refuses to accept it."

When Byron finally walked up the steps to join us, Claire half-stood, anticipating a word from him perhaps. He shot her a look of disgust and stalked past her into the dining-room through the open French windows.

I watched her crumble before my eyes. She looked utterly dejected and forlorn.

I felt a surge of compassion for my stepsister that disarmed me, took me by surprise. I did not touch her or make any false gesture. I simply sat quietly and acknowledged inside myself the resolve I felt to stand by my stepsister and her child.

Byron would never help her and if Percy and I did not support her, she would ultimately be left alone with an illegitimate child on the way, forever shunned by society. Her child would never be accepted. That is not an enviable position for any woman to be in. I thought of my sister, Fanny, and of Elise.

Elise and I exchanged glances in silence.

The arguments continued for days. No longer did we sit by the fireside after dinner, telling stories and reciting poems. Instead, the talk was all about the practical business of who should support my stepsister.

"If you will not acknowledge the child as yours, what is Claire to do? Who will support her?"

"I don't believe the child is mine," Byron retaliated.

"My friend, I have tried to be reasonable with you. You cannot deny the child is yours. Claire is distraught."

"She threw herself at me. Do you think I would have looked at her twice otherwise? What was I to do if she was continually putting herself in my way, insisting I take her into my room?"

"Keep your voice down, man: she will hear you."

"Perhaps she should. I told her plainly I didn't love her, and didn't want her in my bed, but she wouldn't listen. What would you have done?"

"Even so, she is just a girl."

"So is her sister, but I don't see her acting with so little discretion! How can I not be irritated by her miserable wretchedness and her presumption that I should feel anything for her?"

"Well, I have promised her."

"Promised her what?"

"I will give Claire and her unborn child an allowance."

"Ah, you see, the baby is yours, after all. As I suspected…"

"… in the event of you failing her! Think of the child," Percy persisted. "What if it is yours and you fail to put your name to it? What will become of the poor wretch?"

Byron shook his head.

"It is not mine. Or at least, I can't be certain it is."

Percy stood. "Then I shall make a settlement on your behalf."

Byron was seething, his pride finally nettled.

The atmosphere was tense, all our camaraderie spoiled and marred. If the guests down at the *Hôtel d'Angleterre* could see us now, squabbling and in disarray, it would give them plenty of fuel for gossip.

"Why would *you* pay for the child?" Byron retorted. "Do you want it to be raised as yours, then? No, I can't allow that."

"So you admit the child *is* yours?"

"I admit that it *may* be so, but if the child is mine, then my sister, Augusta, can raise it."

Claire, overhearing, paled like a ghost.

The poor child was not even born yet, and already Claire must fear losing it. I felt myself grow still and quiet. Darkness settled on the room. It seeped from the vicinity of my stepsister, a cloak of despair that stretched from her to me.

Suddenly a terrible wail escaped Claire.

"You cannot take my child away from me," she cried. "I will not let you."

I guided her from the room, my arm across her shoulder, but she shrieked in Byron's face on passing.

"The child is mine. It is not yours to take."

"Get her out of my sight," he muttered.

Back at the little chalet, Claire, Elise and I sat by a glowing fire, waiting for Percy's return. He had gone up alone to have a final discussion with Byron, in a last desperate attempt to arrive at some arrangement agreeable to all.

Elise put Will to bed and made some supper. The room was quiet, but for the coals shifting in the hearth.

"Percy is a persuasive man," I murmured, my eyes on Claire. "He will help Byron to see reason."

No one answered me.

"I am sure there is no need to worry. He will be able to negotiate some kind of arrangement, I am certain of it."

I could feel Claire's fear, her anxiety for her unborn child. Her passion for Byron was slowly ossifying into hate, as she dreaded what might become of her little one before it had taken its first gulp of air.

Knowing how deeply it would wound me to be parted from Will, I shared her pain.

Elise sat in a corner, quietly attending to some mending in her lap, the supper tray discarded on a side-table. We three women all knew what it was to bear a child, and to suffer. We all knew what it meant to be alone in the world, to face ostracism and disapproval. Like the monster who limped through life in limbo, rejected and despised: we were women who had broken the rules, chosen to live life our own way, but perhaps it was not a choice…

"It is easy for men," Elise murmured out of the darkness. "They do not suffer the same consequences. Even men like your Shelley and Byron."

Claire could not speak, at first. She was too worried, too full of hurt pride and wounded love.

"I thought Byron and I would… once he knew I was carrying his child."

She did not need to say the rest.

Elise put down her sewing.

"Listen! I thought I heard a footstep outside."

The door opened and Claire half-rose from her seat.

Percy reached out an arm towards my sister.

"You are home, already? What did he say?"

He touched her gently on the shoulder.

"It is not all bad news."

"Sit down and tell us."

"I came up with a solution of sorts," he told us. "I suggested that rather than take the child away, Claire might pose as the child's aunt. That way, you can remain with the child. At least at first…" he finished uncertainly.

I glanced at him. "I do not like the sound of that *at first*."

"It was either that," he added, "or he would insist on the child being raised by his sister, Augusta."

"Yes, we have heard about his sister, Augusta…"

"Well, whether the rumours are true, he is adamant that any offspring of his must be raised in an aristocratic household rather than… rather than…" Claire looked at him, as he fumbled for the right words before finally giving up.

"Anyway, Byron finally agreed with my proposition. Except–"

Claire was feeling some measure of relief, although the term 'aunt' was not as reassuring as it might be, holding as it did no legal rights over her own offspring.

"Except?" I asked him.

Percy looked momentarily awkward. It was clear he would rather not finish his sentence.

"I could only get him to agree to the plan on the proviso that he be allowed to send for the child when he feels the time is right."

Claire's face assumed the saddest expression, as if she could see into the future. She saw the inevitable ahead of her, like a stay of execution.

She knew she had to be grateful for small mercies, but it was a harsh lesson to learn. I pitied her, as I pity her now, when there is room in my heart for pity.

We all felt for her, as we went to our beds that night. I felt a surge of affection for Percy, for the way in which he had tried to fight Claire's battle and rescue her from the pain of loss.

I kissed him on the lips when we were alone.

"You are a good man," I told him. "You try to be good. You care about those closest to you."

For all his faults, he was a conciliatory man. He showed generosity towards others, as well as myself. For that, I loved him, even while it stirred a little jealousy in my heart.

I stood in the middle of the nursery and looked out at the familiar view. I liked it here and did not want to leave. A mist was caught like tatters of silk in the snow-capped mountains across the darkness of the lake, a full moon and a sky full of stars lighting the way. It reminded me of another place where I was happy, long ago, as a teenage girl. I missed my friend, Isabella. Isabella Baxter used to confide in me. Isabella *Booth* would not even acknowledge my letters. Still, that was to be expected. There are always sacrifices to be made. And I had lived moments I would never have missed for all the world. Life in Skinner Street could never have afforded me this freedom, this giant air in which to breathe. In this landscape I had found my creation, my poor wretched monster with his hubris form, stitched together from bloody corpses. Birth is always a bloody business, a filthy process in which I am engaged.

There was a soft sound in the room behind me. Elise had come to help me pack Will's linens.

"We are nomads, Elise. Are you happy to come with us to England?"

She smiled.

"I am glad to," she murmured, folding baby clothes, linens and sheets.

"There are things Percy needs to attend to in London."

"You do not need to explain to me, Mrs Shelley."

"Have you ever been to Bath before?" I asked her, knowing she had not. "It is very respectable and stuffy. I can imagine it will be dreary in the autumn compared with here. You will not like it much, I fear. You will miss the mountains."

"The mountains will be here, waiting."

"Percy has promised us a cook and two servants. You'll have more time to play with Will."

I felt a stab of remorse. I was sure Elise would rather play with her own child, Lisa, who now lived among strangers.

It was sad to be packing up. I did not relish what awaited us in England. I would rather stay here.

I begged Percy that we might be able to return to London or Bishopsgate rather than Bath, but he was adamant. He owed considerable sums of money and did not want our creditors to find out where we lived.

We would be in hiding.

"Would it not be better to remain on foreign soil then?" I asked him.

"We can't afford to remain here, my sweet. We are in need of funds."

I thought of my stepmother, Mary-Jane, earning her keep

at the desk in our basement bookshop, translating books from French into English. Perhaps one day I would earn my own living by my pen, as my mother once did, and – I was loathe to admit it – my stepmother also. I did not like being dependent on Percy, but what choice did I have?

5 Abbey Churchyard, Bath, September 1816

Autumn. The air was dark outside, casting deep shadows within. A fire burned, crimson-bright in the gloom. The clean air of Lake Geneva and the mountains beyond Chamonix with their rending ice seemed a long way from here, merely a parting dream. I sometimes wondered whether I had imagined it all. I wanted to recapture that time, revisit those wilderness places and icy wastelands in my notebooks.

Bath was not for me.

Its streets were stuffy and forlorn with abandoned hope. People did not dream here. They did not aspire to anything other than comfortable respectability. They had no sense of adventure or daring. They wanted nothing to change. They wanted nothing more than to visit the tap rooms and baths, take tea and gossip. I avoided those places like the plague. No doubt they had heard of us there. Our reputation went before us. The League of Incest and Atheism who got up to all sorts of diabolical activities in the Swiss Alps, in our hired villa. Three unmarried women, three men of loose morals, one baby and another on the way. Who knew what was going on, they murmured to each other.

Percy insisted that Bath was a safe place where Claire could await the birth of her child.

"You must not answer the door while I am gone," he instructed us.

"That could be a little difficult."

"You must promise me."

"Elise and I will be careful."

And so we were. I knew the child was not Percy's but if Claire were to show her face at Skinner Street and they were to see her in her condition, they would assume otherwise and then the repercussions would begin.

"You and Claire would be the ones to suffer," Percy told me, and so – he argued – it was better for us to hide away here.

"But why Bath?" I complained.

"Bath will be practically empty."

He was right; the fashionable season for inhabiting this godforsaken spa town was past, and only the dribs and drabs remained. People like us, fugitives with nowhere else to go.

Percy went to London, leaving we three women alone. As the nights drew in, I allowed the dangerous thought to enter my head: Perhaps Percy would not come back? Perhaps he was even now in conference with Harriet; she was, after all, his legal wife. There was no certainty that he would return. I had his child, but that meant little. Men have abandoned their mistresses for less. And Harriet had two of his children, whom he perhaps missed more.

"What am I?" I asked him before he left. "Your mistress or your wife?"

He laughed at me. "We agreed, you and I, that we don't need to observe the rules that govern others… We are making a stand."

"For what?"

"For the freedom and independence of women."

"Is this independence then, to sit here alone and wait for you, afraid of the opinion of the world?"

"You must be brave, Mary," he insisted, a touch of scorn in his voice. I remembered then how he used to speak of Harriet. He did not like her so much when she began to complain. I remembered how he told me that Harriet demanded to be married so that she might have some financial and emotional security, but in doing so she lost her sense of self, her spirit, her individuality. She became nothing more than a carping woman he was no longer in love with.

Had I become that?

How could I be sure of him, if she could not?

The dark days stretched ahead and I received no word from Percy. No letter. He did not visit. We waited, in limbo. Our fate in his hands. He left before my nineteenth birthday. The anniversary of the day which put my mother in her grave…

Having Elise with me meant I was still free to write. There was no compulsion to go out into the streets of Bath. I could sit by the fire, watch the leaves fall and the air darken, and disappear inside my story. I could rescue my poor monster from whatever fate befell him, journey with him into the wilderness and feel his pain. His abandonment and rejection. When I first began working on the tale, my gifted and ambitious doctor of anatomy, Victor Frankenstein, was the hero, but now their roles had switched: he had begun to seem more like the villain of the piece. He was not thinking of the advancement of mankind, the improvement of life conditions for the rest of us. Like all men, he was attracted by power and ambition. I was thinking now of my own father, desperate always for more money to prop up his failing career as a writer, desperate for recognition and fame at the expense of all else. Family and loved ones mattered little compared with this. And so my Dr Frankenstein was driven by the same obsession.

It was the monster I empathised with. He was the victim in all of this… created, for what purpose? How lonely he must feel, how isolated, with no one to call a friend. He could not make himself lovable, except to a blind man unable to see his deformities. Even when he aspired to become moral and cultivated, even when he learned to read and to discover emotions through language, by observing the dealings of a small, loving family, even then he was shut out in the cold. The one man who fathered him, who made him from the rough clay of butchered corpses, hated the sight of him.

Who would not seek revenge if they found themselves so reviled?

I thought about the poor criminal I had seen dangling from the gallows in Glasgow like a plaything, while the doctor of science experimented with him and the crowds watched. It was the watching crowds who had frightened me most, their lack of compassion for the man hanging there, whatever his crime in life might have been.

So it was with my monster.

I could take my story to its dark conclusion, its logical end. The monster would be a poor doomed creature, who did not deserve to be created, if creation led only to this revulsion.

It was a sombre tale with a dark message… too dark, I was sure, for the likes of Bath.

It felt like a dirty secret I must not own.

It would be better if I were not to put my name to it, when it was done. For a woman to have created such a tale would not be acceptable in polite literary circles. They would never countenance it. It was one thing for Byron to write poetry to shock; quite another for a young woman (of dubious repute and origin… "*her mother was Mary Wollstonecraft, you know*,") to indulge in the same.

Claire wanted to visit Skinner Street. She would be welcome there, for sure, but it would only cause further unwanted strife. Mary-Jane, my stepmother, would probably forgive her own daughter anything. Not so with me. They held me responsible for leading her astray.

"If they see you in that condition, they will assume the worst," I told her.

"I shall tell them otherwise."

"They won't believe you!"

My father sent not one word of comfort or kindness. He did not even ask after William.

I was dead to him.

Again I was plagued by the vision of two little girls, walking through a flowering meadow, on their way to visit their mother's grave. A father walked beside them, as tall as a giant.

Where was that giant now?

"Who are you writing to?"

Claire was hunched in a corner of the room, furtively applying herself to a letter. It was too wet to take a walk. I had my own notebooks at my elbow, creased with much use.

She lifted her head reluctantly and her quill paused in its scratching.

"I am writing to Albe," she replied.

"You know it will not help, Claire."

She ignored me.

Some minutes passed, and I'd almost forgotten we occupied the same room. I was meeting my monster and my anatomist again, living in the pages of my notebook.

"I must persuade him to see reason. He *has* to be reasonable," she muttered out loud.

I glanced up, pulled out of my own reverie. I couldn't help wincing at the desperate tone in her voice. Much as my stepsister often infuriated me, it pained me to see her like this. I wished she could muster the self-respect to push him aside rather than debasing herself. Her youth made her vulnerable, I suppose.

"Why do you bother to write to him? It will only infuriate him."

She bit her lip, staring at the page.

"How can you ask that? *You – of all people.*"

She spoke again without looking at me.

"I am begging him to return to England. I have told him I will always love him, to the end of my life, and no one else."

"Is that true?"

She did not answer and I had the sense I wasn't helping.

"I thought you hated him. When we left Geneva it seemed as if…"

She cut me off. "Love is very close to hate. Perhaps you have not experienced that yet."

I gazed into the fireplace for a while.

"No, perhaps not. I don't hate Percy," I murmured quietly.

She looked up. "Why would you need to? He has not abandoned you or hurt you in anyway."

Beyond the window I saw figures walking, ladies in pairs, calling on our neighbours. No one knocked at our door, for which I was glad. They knew we were in here. I was sure the gossips had alerted them. Gossips the world over are quick to pass on their information as if by telepathy.

They wore bonnets that all but obscured their faces, but I saw one of them glance in at our window and whisper to her companion.

Perhaps we were objects of interest to them, dark and mysterious, living the kind of celebrated life they could not afford to risk. We represented something forbidden and dangerous, which they would never want inflicted upon their own daughters, exciting though it might seem. They were safe in their suffocating worlds; we were drowning in ours.

I think it was that afternoon by the fireside that I had a flash of inspiration. I decided to add another character to my narrative: Robert Walton writing to his sister, Margaret. An Arctic explorer risking his men's lives in search of the North Pole, his ship becomes near locked in ice and that is when he encounters my villainous hero. A master-stroke of structure, my explorer, Robert Walton, will be the one to introduce the topic of Dr Frankenstein and his unlikely tale. It would ground the story in reality, lend it some credibility. A narrative which had been received at one remove. Robert Walton will have encountered Frankenstein and listened to his terrible tale long before anyone has any inkling of it.

Letters. We all write letters. Some we never send. They could be of use in my narrative.

I sometimes dared to think I was writing something of worth or value. I had to believe it, in order for the story to progress at all… but I was worried that no publisher would agree with me.

When Claire rose and left the room, I barely noticed. I was far away from Bath now, lost in the frozen wastelands.

Claire wrote to Byron and I wrote to Percy. Letters upon letters, some of which we sent. I felt dejected. The only person who could improve my mood was little Wilmouse. Elise cared for him so well that sometimes it made me uneasy. I was glad she was still with us. What would Claire and I be without her?

"Don't worry, Mrs Shelley. He will come back to you."

I glanced at her quickly, wondering how she could read my thoughts so easily.

Of course, she knew. She had her own fatherless infant to worry about, even if Lisa was living far away with strangers.

She knew what they were saying, what they were accusing us of. They were wrong to think it, but the world is very slow in changing.

"To think differently to everyone else," Elise told me. "That was your mother's gift."

I looked at her in surprise.

"I have been reading your mother's book."

My mother's books came with us on our travels and I put them on the shelf in my temporary library.

"You do not mind?" she asked hurriedly.

"Of course not."

"I have learnt a great deal from them," she added. "Your mother had great courage."

Is it possible that three women hiding away in the centre of Bath, with nothing to do but write letters and care for little ones, could be radicals of the future?

"We are doing the important things, Mrs Shelley. The things that matter."

I glanced at my notebook and stroked the cover; then I saw Will turning to Elise first, instead of to me and it gave me pause for thought.

I found it difficult to keep my tone cheerful and light when writing to Percy. I wrote a long blast of complaint to him, about how I resented being left here, with only my stepsister and Elise for company, and sent it off before I could change my mind. I told him that I hadn't run away with him all those years ago, breaking the law and my father's heart, just so that I should end up living buried away with my stepsister, Claire, and without the father of my child by my side. Full of resentment, it was. He would not like the tone and I was aware that it could alienate him further. I would no longer seem like the dreamy, romantic girl he fell in love with, with the famous red hair and pale cheeks and broad brow. I would come across as tired and carping, not much better than Harriet. If he was capable of abandoning Harriet, then why not also me?

"Percy met up with Fanny in London," I told Claire, at supper that evening.

She seemed disinterested. Fanny was never a favourite of Claire's. The chat at table was always stilted whenever Percy was away.

"She is very unhappy at Skinner Street," I continued.

"Wasn't she always?"

I held my tongue.

"She has asked to come and live with us."

Claire's attention was caught, at last. She stopped in the act of cutting up her meat.

"And what did he say?"

"He refused. For obvious reasons. If Fanny found out you were pregnant, she would most likely tell Mr and Mrs G. We cannot risk that."

"Mr and Mrs G? Why do you call them that?"

"Why not? It's what Percy calls them."

Claire lifted a morsel of meat to her lips. "Fanny is a traitor."

"That's too harsh. They expect too much of her. She is caught in the middle."

We continued eating in silence. Elise ate at table with us. Three women, closeted together.

"Have you thought about what you will do?" I asked her tentatively.

"What do you mean?"

"Once the baby is born!"

She stared at her plate.

"Well, you cannot stay here forever," I explained. "With us, I mean."

"Has Percy said something?"

"Of course not."

She met my gaze.

"I'd always assumed he was happy for me to remain with you, for the time being."

"Well, yes, but we can't carry on like this forever," I laughed, but even I could hear the false note in my voice.

"Why not? Percy seems perfectly happy with the arrangement."

Arrangement? What arrangement? I did not like that word and swallowed back my fury.

"Yes, but we have to be *realistic*. You'll need to find work as a governess. Something that will give you a measure of independence. You can't expect Percy to meet your living expenses forever."

"Like you, you mean?"

"That's different. He is my…"

She looked up, arching her eyebrows. "Husband?"

"In everything but name!"

Elise avoided looking at either of us during this exchange – dear, sweet Elise who insisted on calling me Mrs Shelley.

I suddenly lost my appetite. I rose from the table and excused myself.

"What about your food?" Elise murmured, glancing at my unfinished meal.

"I'm not hungry anymore."

I picked up my plate, and carried it through to the scullery, where I scraped the remains into the food bin. Elise would feed it to the birds and the resident cats later.

When a letter arrived the next morning, I expected it to be from Percy. It was not.

I read it in silence and a cloak of depression dropped onto my shoulders, where it lay for the rest of the day.

Elise and I took breakfast alone. Claire remained upstairs, resting.

"My sister Fanny writes to me," I told Elise. "She is desperate to leave Skinner Street. If she can't join us here in Bath, then... I don't know what to do."

"What *can* you do?"

I tried to see it from Fanny's point of view.

"God forgive me for saying this, but it is hard to take pleasure in her company, and it has been like that for years. Not since we were little girls... She will lie for hours on her bed without moving, avoiding mealtimes, barely speaking."

Claire walked in, and sat down with a sigh, massaging her back.

I wondered for a moment if she thought I was talking about her, but to disabuse her of this notion would have been too awkward.

"Sore?" I asked her, affecting concern.

She shrugged, and glanced at the letter.

"Percy is coming home soon?" she asked hopefully.

"It's from Fanny."

She lost interest immediately. "Bad news?"

"It is always bad news," I sighed. "Apparently, she wrote to our aunts in Ireland, my mother's two sisters. She asked them if she could stay with them for a while, and they point-blank refused."

Claire shrugged again, as if she cared little either way. She had no interest in what happened to Fanny, I could see that.

"They won't let her stay with them because of her association with us – Percy and I," I continued. "According to Fanny, anyway. The aunts are worried about their precious reputation being damaged. As if Fanny is tainted by association."

Will sat on Elise's lap, eating egg yolk from a spoon. I leaned forward and wiped his yellow chin.

"You could show a little interest."

"Why?"

"She's your stepsister!" I explained.

"Yes. She's not my *real* sister."

And neither are you, mine. And yet you expect so much of me. I wisely kept these thoughts to myself.

The weather continued wet and windy, keeping us indoors, but Percy returned to us at last. He knew that I wanted Claire to be independent once the baby was born, but did not share that view.

There was complete silence from Byron. He had not responded to any of Claire's letters of entreaty. She began to lose hope.

Once the baby arrives, he will change his mind, was her belief.

When I told her that I doubted that, she took a temper fit, storming out of the room and accusing me of wanting her gone from our lives.

"Did any letters arrive for me today, Elise?" Percy asked.

"Not for you, no," she said. Something about her tentative tone made me glance up.

"There is one for *Mrs* Shelley but I wasn't sure if…"

Out in the narrow hallway, I saw it resting on the table, on the silver plate, waiting. Elise had begun to understand my dread of receiving any letters at all.

"Another one from Fanny," I sighed. I was reluctant to open it.

"I wonder what messages from Mr and Mrs G she will convey this time?" Percy called out.

As I broke the seal and began to read, I was vaguely aware of others speaking in the dining-room. I could not absorb the contents of the letter; I could not make sense of what was written there. Percy appeared in the doorway and I could hear the others asking questions, but I no longer registered what they were saying. The blood was pounding in my head.

"What is it, Mary?" Percy asked me.

I could not speak. Dread moved thickly in my veins. My legs turned to stone as if a great weight was pinning me to the earth.

"Mary, what is it?" he repeated.

When I would not answer, he snatched the letter from me and began to read. I was aware of this, but of nothing else. I did not hear the others. I did not hear Percy speak in urgent tones to Elise or the servant. I did not hear him pack and demand that someone see to the Mistress as she was in shock. I did not hear him say goodbye, for there was no time to linger on farewells.

What I did hear him say, however, was, "I will look for her." His face was close to mine, but I could barely hear him through the storm of silence in my ears. The world slowly rotated and spun around me, but I was still. I could not move. I was fixed forever in one place. With this burden of knowledge. That would never leave me. Ever.

I had let my sister down.

My true sister.

Who asked nothing of me.

Until the end.

And I denied her.

"Sit, Mrs Shelley. You must sit." Elise, speaking to me firmly.

"Where is Percy?" I asked her, in a faint voice.

"He has left already."

"Where?"

"He will look for her. He is heading for Bristol. Did you not hear him say so?"

"Why Bristol?"

"That is where her letter was addressed from."

"It will be too late." It came out as a faint whisper – a thought I dare not give utterance to.

"No," Elise commanded. "Do not think that."

She spoke quietly and firmly.

Where was Claire in all of this?

She was nowhere. Upstairs, nursing her own grief and pain, incubating her fatherless baby.

The next few days were a blur. I waited for a word from Percy. Claire lounged by the fire, nonchalant.

"Are you not a little worried?" I asked her, fighting my anger.

"Not especially," she said. "It is Fanny's choice. If she chooses to end her life, then it is an honourable course of action. And we must respect her for it."

"And let her die?" I almost howled.

Claire frowned at me. "There is nothing to be done."

"She is my sister," I said, but the words came out as a strangled cry.

Claire merely arched her eyebrows in that way she has.

"Perhaps you should have asked *her* to run away with you all that time ago – instead of me."

"Mrs Shelley," Elise murmured. "I think Will needs you."

She separated us with a few discreet words, in order to spare us the degradation and pain of another fight.

Percy, of course, was too late.

I waited four days with no letters and no communication.

The first to arrive was a quick note from Godwin. His note was so brief it floored me, because in it, he assumed I already knew. He did not realise that Percy had not had time to communicate with me yet.

His words were brief and to the point. "*Go not to Swansea, disturb not the silent dead; do nothing to destroy the obscurity she so much desired.*"

"Swansea? I do not understand."

I handed the note to Claire.

"She was in Bristol," I said. "That is where she sent the letter from."

As if that really mattered now. But somehow I needed to get the facts straight in my head before I could understand.

"Why Swansea?" I repeated. "What was there?"

Claire looked at me. "It does not matter," she said softly.

"What does not matter?"

"Whether it was Swansea or Bristol. Or Bath. Or London. She'd have done it anyway. It was her choice," Claire added gently.

"Her choice? Death is not a choice."

"It was her right. God knows I don't blame her."

"I will wait for Percy to come home. He will explain."

Claire shook her head. "What difference will that make?"

"This does not affect you," I said, more sharply than I intended. "As you said yourself, she was not your sister."

I stood at the window and stared out into the October darkness.

"She was mine," I added softly. So softly that no one heard.

"When I got to Bristol she had already fled. She had covered her tracks, but I found the inn where she was staying and spoke to the landlord. He told me that a young woman answering to Fanny's description had left on the eighth, the day she sent the letters. She caught the stagecoach to Swansea. So I went there. But then I saw an article in the *Cambrian News*, saying that a body had been found in the Mackworth Arms. *A young woman...*"

He struggled to speak, and I struggled to listen.

"I went there straight away, before... before they had removed the body. There were ongoing investigations. I spoke to a maidservant there, who said that Fanny had asked not to be disturbed. She was in need of rest."

"How?" I asked him.

"She took laudanum. There was a note. But I scored out the signature. She did not want to be found, Mary." He whispered those last words so that I barely heard him.

She did not want to be found. My sister, Fanny Imlay, had wanted to disappear.

"Because no one loved her, no one wanted her. Even me."

"Hush, Mary. Fanny suffered from melancholy."

"A family trait, apparently. My father used to warn us both against it. *Don't give in to it,* he urged us. *I saw what it did to your mother.*"

"And so, listen to his advice!"

"Am I not allowed to grieve?"

"Of course. Grieve you must. But do not blame yourself."

Rain drops pattered against the gravestones and the clods of earth. Percy stood beside me.

I thought again of two little girls walking through a flowering meadow, during high summer. *This* flowering meadow. It never rained back then.

As we stood at the graveside, Mr and Mrs G barely spoke to me.

"She died of a cold, on the way to visit her aunts in Ireland," my father said afterwards. "That's what we are telling everyone."

I looked at him – my father – and struggled to find the words.

"It matters so much? What people think?"

"It always matters, Mary. If they knew how her life ended, we should have had to leave her in Swansea where we found her."

I listened to the rain fall. An endless refrain of raindrops. I wished their sound could blot out his voice, the voice of my father. *Mr G.* It was easier to call him that, these days.

"Still, she is with her mother at last."

The only one who really cared for her... he did not need to add.

"I don't understand why my sister would do this!" Perhaps I wanted to accuse them, make them feel bad.

Mrs G looked at me.

"Need you ask that?" she said. "You knew she met up with Shelley? Did you?"

"Of course. She asked to meet him."

"She was in love with him," Mary-Jane said in a clipped voice.

"That's absurd. You are a fantasist. She asked Percy if she could come and live with us, because she was so unhappy at Skinner Street. She found it unbearable living under your roof. None of you cared for her."

"We loved her."

"You tolerated her. Barely that."

"And why have you kept Jane from us? Why is *she* not here?" my stepmother accused me.

"Ask her yourself."

Percy, who stood some distance away, watched this exchange. Our voices were so low that he did not quite catch the import of what we were saying.

"Mr and Mrs G did not ask us back to the house, then?" Percy noted, when he saw me off on the stagecoach. I was travelling back to Bath alone, leaving Percy here in London to meet with his solicitors. He had promised to join us soon, but I did not know whether to believe him.

"I will never return to Skinner Street," I told him. "Never."

"What did he say to you?"

"Nothing much. They are telling everyone she died of a cold on her way to visit the aunts."

"If it protects Fanny…" he conceded, in a tone of compromise.

"But it's not the truth," I pointed out.

"The truth does not matter in this case. If it spares Fanny from the shame of being buried in an unmarked grave at a crossroads, where no one could visit her, then what is the harm in withholding the truth?"

"No one will visit her anyway," I muttered, thinking of those quiet headstones and the tall waving grasses.

"Well, at least we can protect her reputation in death."

"I did not think you cared so much for propriety," I added, a little disappointed after all.

"I care for what happened to Fanny, and our part in it."

"My father does not. He and Mary-Jane blame us. Do you know what she told me? They claim Fanny was in love with you and that's why she killed herself."

"Oh my! How flattering! All the women are in love with me, according to Mrs G... I leave a chain of broken hearts behind me."

There was an uneasy silence.

"Did your father ask after Will?" Percy asked me.

"Not especially."

"Loving father, as ever."

But I wondered why he changed the subject so quickly.

On my return to the narrow house in Abbey Churchyard, Elise had the fire roaring. I was reunited with little Will who was eating his tea at our small table in the corner of the room. Slops of bread and milk, spooned into his baby mouth.

Claire was nowhere to be seen. I had expected her to be eager to ask questions.

"She is lying down," Elise informed me.

"Well, I am too tired to face her questioning yet."

I helped Elise to bathe Will and played with him, then I took a nap with my little son cradled in the crook of my arm. He was sleepy and content to be snuggled up with his Mamma again.

"Let me take him," Elise offered. "You look exhausted."

"No, Elise. He comforts me."

His breathing matched my own, each single breath a tiny miracle. No one must take this child from me. It was as if I was waiting for the next blow to fall.

A letter arrived for Claire. There was a strange look on her face, of deep content and delight, and at first I assumed it must be from Byron.

"Byron has replied at last?" I asked her.

"It's from Percy," she announced with delight. *My* Percy. She seemed to take a cruel pleasure in telling me so.

She left it lying on the table, and I wondered if her careless action was deliberate.

I tried to ignore it at first, but at last, driven by curiosity, I crossed to the table, and glanced at it lying there, so casually.

"My dearest Claire... Thank you too, my kind girl, for not expressing much of what you must feel – the loneliness and the low spirits which arise from being entirely left alone."

The door creaked behind me. Claire strode back in, and caught me prying.

"You wrote to him first then?" I said, deciding there was no use prevaricating.

"Of course. He is my friend and confidante too, Mary."

Elise continued sewing in the corner, watching us both. The tension in the room was palpable.

I did not rise to it.

I said nothing.

Percy wrote to Claire because she was like a sister to him. That is what he often told me. He regarded her most fondly, as one of the family.

I heard the snakes of accusation hissing in my ear, the voices of the diners in the Hôtel d'Angleterre… *"The League of Incest and Atheism, we call them." "In league with the devil more like."*

I still recall that disappearing act she made to Devon, to spend those few months in a remote cottage. We never spoke of it.

Except the once, when she cried in my face, "Why are you able to keep *your* child, when I had to sacrifice mine?"

So many things left unsaid, areas we must never trespass into.

"*Entirely left alone?*" I quoted. "You are not alone."

I longed to take him to task for that letter, but I knew that I must be circumspect. My position was a tenuous one – this was the price I had to pay for having the courage to stand outside the conventional restraints of marriage. Besides, even within them I would have had little control over the matter.

Autumn turned to winter, and Percy returned to us when I had almost given up hope of ever seeing him again. But I did not take him to task over his fond letter to Claire. A little snow fell, even in Bath, and I spent my afternoons writing, pouring all my grief and anguish into the monstrous creation in my notebooks.

"*I am the fallen angel. Misery makes me a fiend.*"

My villain's despair was absolute. As was my sister's. We are all wretches in the end.

That night as Percy and I read by the fire a melancholy mood sat between us.

"I should have told her to come and live with us," I murmured at last. "Why did I not do that?"

Percy looked tired. Recent events had taken their toll on him too.

"You had no way of knowing what she was contemplating," he replied.

"I should have encouraged her to join us. She had nowhere else to go."

But the worst crime of all is that I called her 'stupid' – a sisterly quarrel, silly and pointless.

In Bath, the plane trees were stark and bare against the whiteness of the newly-fallen snow, stripped of their autumn coverage. It was dark outside, the streets were quiet, and the night watchman called the hour. The River Avon moved smooth and dark between the golden buildings and under the arches of the new bridge.

In London, squalor and poverty bred crime in the darkened alleyways. Women fell on hard times, and had to find other ways to feed themselves and their children. Prostitution was rife. Babies were left in orphanages, and mothers were forbidden to see their children.

Darkness stalked the land. Winter and hunger took their toll.

I once saw a prostitute when I was a child, as I walked through Smithfield Market on my way to St Pancras. Her clothes were soiled and she wore rouge on her cheeks, two bright crimson spots, messily applied. She looked sick. A man draped his arm around her bare shoulders while forcing her to swallow from a bottle. When she opened her mouth I saw she had teeth missing. She wasn't old. I was about ten years old at the time. Mary-Jane had warned me against the dangers of wandering alone through the streets near our neighbourhood. The sight stayed with me afterwards. A haunting glimpse of a life I would never lead.

And yet… and yet…

Harriet was a Westbrook. She lived in a beautiful house in Grosvenor Square. She fell in love with a man, a poet, who did not believe in marriage. Then practicalities set in. When she became pregnant with his child, she wanted to be sure of him, so she persuaded him to marry her. And he did. But then he fell *out* of love with her and ran away with another woman. She was not *completely* ruined. She had her family, the Westbrooks, who stood by her while she gave birth to a little baby girl.

Then she made the mistake of falling in love again, this time with a soldier. Harriet's father, Mr Westbrook, could not forgive her foolishness a second time and sent her packing. Unfortunately, so did the soldier.

So those darkened alleyways of London became the only place

she knew, as her belly grew round with another child. This time the child was illegitimate. Just as little Will was illegitimate.

It is a sobering tale. Harriet was lost to her family. And lost to the world. Until her body turned up in the Serpentine, beneath the shadow of the bridge from which she flung herself. She floated in the light of a gibbous moon, bloated and deformed. When they drag her to the bank, they think they have found a prostitute in the water. It happens all the time. And they are right. She was…

But she was also Harriet Westbrook. Fallen on hard times. My husband's first wife.

London, 1817

History repeats itself. We stood across the street from the house of the Westbrooks in Grosvenor Square. I had been here once before, but this time it was with a different purpose in mind.

I doubt they will want to see us.

The journey to London was grim, neither of us speaking. I insisted I came along too, whether he liked it or not. We left Claire behind with Elise in Bath. I did not want to leave little Will behind, but the journey would not have been good for him. It was better he should stay at home in the warmth. The grand and austere-looking house opposite where Harriet lately lived looked back at us like a fortress, its fine Georgian windows reflecting the sun. Percy's children, his little Ianthe and Charles, were somewhere inside that building, behind that aloof and impregnable facade but it seemed unlikely he would be allowed to see them.

Life always comes full circle in the end. I experienced a sudden flashback to that other time we stood outside this well-appointed house, humiliated and dejected, while Percy spoke with Harriet inside. The boatman sat outside with us on the step and I was pregnant, with a baby that did not survive. The boatman thought we were bizarre. No doubt it furnished him with a story to tell his wife when he went home – if he had a wife.

Now we are here again. Percy was determined to ask for the custody of his daughter, Ianthe, and his little son, Charles. Harriet had left them motherless, and he would have them in his care if he could.

Mr Westbrook refused to see him, as I thought he would. The same footman as before denied us entry. I remembered his face, sour as if sucking on a lemon.

Percy was not deterred.

He wrote letters, hired lawyers and solicitors to argue his case, tirelessly campaigned. It was his new obsession. I agreed with him because I must. I would never turn away his children, no matter how crowded our household became.

We sat side by side in Mr. Pratchett's office. A weak winter sun found its way through the shutters from the streets of Chancery Lane outside. Mr. Pratchett was Percy's solicitor and I listened in self-contained silence as he explained to Percy that he would stand a much better chance of keeping his children if he were married.

"Living with an unmarried woman and an illegitimate child will do nothing to improve your prospects when the case comes to trial."

I disliked his tone and although I *had* promised to sit quietly, I could not keep quiet any longer.

I leant forward in my chair, interrupting.

"I do not like to hear myself spoken of in the third person, Mr Pratchett, especially not in those terms." I did not like Mr. Pratchett. His fingers were stained yellow with tobacco.

He looked at me pointedly for a moment or two, annoyed that I had spoken at all.

"Mary is here to assist me," Percy explained.

"Hmm…" The man pursed his lips. "The Westbrooks may not see it that way."

"Your office is very dusty, Mr. Pratchett," I observed. "Do you have a maid? Perhaps you should think about getting one."

Percy glanced at me, a little shocked at my matronly tone.

When we agreed to marry it was not quite in the manner I had hoped. It was merely part of the scheme to win custody of Percy's children. If we were wed, then he would look more respectable in the eyes of the law and stand a better chance of winning his case.

I found myself outside a church in Bread Street, a sprig of ivy and berries in my hand (there are no fresh flowers to be had at this time of year), with a shawl over my best dress.

Do you, Mary Wollstonecraft Godwin...?

The ceremony was brief and the promises short. I had never thought to be married in this fashion. I had never thought to become Mrs Shelley at all. I was happy being plain Mary Godwin, for all the scandal attached to my name.

Shelley sent a note to let the others know. Mr and Mrs G in Skinner Street. Claire and Elise in Bath. He had even dropped Byron a line. But we were marrying with one purpose in mind. To prove that Percy was a fit father to bring up his own children.

When Mr G turned up at Bread Street, I could not comprehend it. And yet there he was, in his finery, with Mrs G on his arm.

They arrived in a flurry of commotion at the back of the empty church. Percy turned, and I heard him utter the words, "Oh no!" in a low tone.

"Wouldn't have missed this for the world," Mr G said.

"Your father is so proud of you, my dear," Mrs G said.

I was speechless.

"He will be able to tell all of our friends," she added. "His daughter! Married to the eldest son of a baronet."

"We *are* talking about Percy?" I asked. "The same man you banished from the house when I was sixteen?"

Percy looked embarrassed.

"Perhaps now is not…" he began.

"Water under the bridge, my dear. Water under the bridge," Mr G said.

"Let your father have his moment, dear, after all he's been through. He is so proud. *So* proud."

It beggared belief. I used to look up to Godwin so. I used to think he was a man of huge stature and moral integrity. A force to be reckoned with. A man of learning, who stood by his principles. Although I loved him, his hypocrisy left a foul taste in my mouth.

January. Bath is caught in a mid-winter sleep. The streets are empty and smoke oozes from the chimney pots, creating a low-lying mist.

It was freezing outside. Claire had taken to her bed, to await her time. Elise sat sewing by the light of the fire, a torn garment of Will's in her lap. She was always mending in the evenings and it soothed me to watch her, her needle glinting in the firelight.

She kept her head bent over her work, but she frowned. I knew that she saw more and understood more about our household and its strange goings-on than she would ever admit. She saw the divided loyalties, the incipient jealousies, the tension. She knew what was afoot, and how I struggled with it. She never said what she really thought, but I had an inkling her sympathies lay with me. She was never particularly fond of Claire.

It was all they were talking about in London, Percy's custody battle to win back his children. I wondered for a moment what I would do if he succeeded. Accept them as my own? Love them – those two little strangers – as I loved Will? Even though I was expecting another on the way?

The fire glowed between us and I listened for a sound upstairs. Silence.

It had occurred to me to wonder whether they might not be better off with the Westbrooks, their own grandparents, whom they had lived with until now. But to suggest as much to Percy invited anger.

My musings were interrupted by a loud crash from upstairs, as if a table had been overturned.

Elise threw down her mending and hurried up the stairs. I was not far behind and peered over her shoulder into Claire's room. A strange sight greeted us. My stepsister was crawling on all fours, clutching her belly.

Elise had her up in no time, uttering words of comfort the while, but I stopped her.

"No, let her be. Let her crawl if she wants."

Elise stared at me.

"I remember my maidservant, Annie, helping me to give birth to my first child. She told me this was the way all of her brothers and sisters were born, and she was right. It eases the passage of the baby. Gravity does its work."

Claire was bellowing like a bull and I rubbed her shoulders and back, while Elise fetched hot water and towels.

Clare Allegra Byron was born on 12th January in a stuffy overheated room in Bath, where Elise had piled coals on the hearth to counteract the draughts from the window. We cleaned the baby, washed the blood and mucus from her orifices so that she could breathe, hacked away at the cord like butchers, and rubbed the child's hands and feet and back until she released her first wail. Once we heard that cry, we all breathed a sigh of relief. The tension in the room relaxed. A miniature human soul had made it safely over that dangerous threshold into the world.

"She is healthy," I told Claire. I was flooded by a sudden and surprising rush of love for my silly stepsister and her sweet little daughter. Where did that come from, I wondered? I held the tiny weight in my arms, and looked out over the rooftops of Bath, at the mist and the smoke, the ordered streets and crescents of white houses, punctuated by bare plane trees.

The way we hacked at that cord, Elise and I, reminded me of the butchery in my novel. Victor Frankenstein dipped his hands in blood and gore, and so do we, in order to bring forth life. But what man can succeed in that province? This is a female domain. Men know nothing about the butchery and gore of childbirth.

"The child slipped out of you like an eel," I told Claire.

"Your maid, Annie, was right, Mrs Shelley," Elise observed. "'Tis best when we crawl like the beasts in the field. Men would have us lying on our backs."

"Wouldn't they just," Claire murmured. We both glanced at her in shock.

"Meet your mother," I whispered.

I handed the child to Claire, and watched in surprise as she bonded instantly with her daughter. I had somehow expected less of Claire. The tug of motherly love was there. Claire could not take her eyes off her daughter; she was completely absorbed, besotted.

"She will know me as her aunt."

"Do not think of that."

The threat of this tiny mite being whisked away by her legal father was an ever-present reality which Claire must learn to live with. It was a risk we all had to live with. But in this moment in Bath we three women were united in our greedy protection of her.

Elise and I helped Claire with little Alba (as we called her) for the first few days after the birth; women closeted together in the intimate stuffiness of the birthing-chamber. Percy remained in London. He was staying with the Hunts in their cramped little cottage on Hampstead Heath. Leigh Hunt, his wife Marianne, and lots of children.

Bath stifled me, and when he wrote to suggest that I join them in Hampstead, I wasted no time in accepting. Elise promised to stay with Claire and the baby, while I took Will with me to stay with the Hunts. I pacified my conscience with the argument that it would give Claire a much-needed break from me, and a chance to bond with her child. Many women die of child-bed fever in the first few days, but I reassured myself that Claire looked robust and strong as an ox. She would not succumb.

"Leigh Hunt is a capital fellow," Percy told me, on meeting me from the stagecoach. "You've met him before."

I recalled a tall, dark, handsome man, a trace of Indian blood running in his veins, which lent him an exotic quality.

"He is a hot-headed radical who runs a hot-headed journal. *The Examiner* first, and then *The Indicator*. Sometimes the newspapers themselves cannot stomach his radicalism, and then he must needs find a journal of his own to be the editor of. We are working on this right now, in fact."

"Along with retrieving your children from the custody of the Westbrooks?"

He glanced at me in surprise. "You have become caustic, Mary!"

"Perhaps you have left me alone for too long!"

And there it was – the beginnings of a gulf opening up between us. I wondered how we would bridge that gap. Would I stand on one side, reaching out, while he grew more remote? Or perhaps it was I who turned my back on *him* at night?

"How is the baby? Little Alba? And Claire?"

"They are well. Thriving, in fact."

"You must meet Marianne," Shelley enthused, steering me lightly by the elbow. She was a sculptor and a painter, he told me, making her sound as interesting as possible. "And she does all that whilst managing a household full of babies. Imagine that."

"*Imagine!*"

He gave me another sidelong glance, but barely responded this time.

We strode across Hampstead Heath, Percy carrying Will in his arms, enjoying the crisp winter air, and opened the door of a fairly small cottage onto a scene of chaos. One child was crying, while another was half-naked, holding a soiled napkin in the air. A woman with smooth hair was calmly ignoring all of it, while another with wild hair was running around half-screaming, brandishing a wooden spoon. She was apparently in the midst of cooking a meal when the mayhem started.

"That's her sister, Bess," Percy informed me, indicating the woman with the smooth hair. "She lives with them too."

"Sounds familiar," I couldn't help observing.

"Leigh! Leigh!" a voice screeched. "Your visitors are here."

Along the hallway a door opened, and a man in a blue silk dressing gown appeared, his hair still bed-swept, looking entirely unconcerned and oblivious to the noise and chaos surrounding him.

"Ah, Percy, you have brought your lovely wife to stay with us. Capital! You can add to the mayhem."

"So honoured to meet you, Mrs Shelley," Bess greeted me politely.

"Please, call me Mary."

"I have heard so much about you," Marianne began politely, struggling to regain her composure.

As one of the toddlers banged into my ankle, I began to think with longing of our dull rooms in Bath, with their quiet solitude that had so bored me before. Will rode high in Percy's arms and stared out at the rabble, as if looking upon a choppy ocean that he dare not enter. It entertained him too. His eyes followed the other children about and twinkled as if he could not quite believe it.

Percy turned a look full of enthusiasm on me. "Isn't it charming?"

He handed our son back to me. "I knew you'd love it."

A little white later, once the pleasantries were over, he and Leigh disappeared into the smoke-filled study at the end of the narrow hall where they were presumably discussing plans for their radical new journal. The door closed on them and I was left with the clamour of the women and children. And Will, who weighed heavy in my arms.

There was a whiff of poverty here, which I was not unfamiliar with, a sour stench of baby effluence, decay and over-cooked cabbage. Shelley had been talking for months about the rarity and brilliance of his friendship with Leigh Hunt, how much the man longed to unite his talents with my husband's and share their intellectual endeavours. There was also the little matter of funding the enterprise. Leigh must have felt confident of my husband's purse strings.

The son of a baronet must always promise cash, surely? Well, the truth is, not necessarily, particularly not when your father considers you to be a menace to society and would rather see you locked up in an asylum than darken your door again. I did not breathe a word of this to Marianne.

What the world did not know would not harm them.

"When is it due?" Marianne asked me.

I glanced down. "Is it so obvious?"

"A woman who has had four of her own can tell. I feel as if I should apologise for the size and state of my home. I wish Leigh would find somewhere else for us to live, but we are not in a position to improve matters."

It was a relief to be out on the heath. The ground beneath our feet was hard and white with frost. We had left Bess and a nursemaid in charge. Marianne and I had taken to going for long walks to clear our heads.

"How do you manage to find time for your own work?" I asked Marianne.

"It is a struggle," she admitted. "Sometimes I don't. We have a nursemaid, of course, which helps. But... the house is too small. There is not enough space for us to both have a study."

"And Percy and I are merely adding to your troubles," I added.

"Not at all. It's a relief to have some company – other than my sister, Bess, of course. It is no trouble to have you and Shelley with us. The children all sleep in one room anyway, at this stage. But I could wish we had a bigger house."

"Are you here for long?"

"It depends on how Leigh's work progresses. I would like a studio, a space of my own, but it is a luxury we can ill afford at present."

"I know that feeling. I have been very lucky so far, with Elise."

"She is the girl you brought back from Geneva?"

I nodded. "I could never be without her. She is a friend to me."

Marianne considered this in silence. "And how is your stepsister these days?"

"Oh, much the same as ever. Percy is keen to hide her away in Bath. She rarely goes out, and now that the baby is born, I don't know what we will tell everyone. My father and his wife know nothing, of course."

"And has Byron...?" She left the question hanging.

"He just about acknowledges the child as his, but with the caveat that he can reclaim her at any time he chooses. I feel sorry for Claire. She lives in fear of that threat. I am surprised, I confess. She is so bonded with the child. I didn't know she had such strong maternal impulses in her. Having little Alba has changed her. It took me by surprise."

"Has it made your relations with her any easier?"

"For the time being. Percy is keen to offer her our protection."

Marianne gave me a sharp sideways look.

"We shall see how it all pans out," I murmured. I lifted a protective hand to my own belly beneath the layers of my cloak. "There is so much uncertainty at the moment – with the court case hanging over us."

"How will you cope with the addition to your household if Percy's claim is successful?"

"I don't know. I find solace in my writing, but if I could not write, it would make me deeply unhappy. Everyone says I should fight against the demons of depression that hounded my mother and Fanny… but I can hardly do that if we have so many mouths to feed."

"Oh, it's the usual problem," she sighed. "The men seem to think that if we create new life, that should satisfy us…"

"Which it does," I added quickly.

"Of course. We love our children. What mother does not? But are the men asked to make the same sacrifice?"

"I have watched maids working for us before, and seen their reddened hands. I often ask myself how many great novels might have been written, or works of art created, if women weren't forced to spend their lives sweeping floors. I am conscious of my own good fortune."

"I hear your mother's voice in you."

"I think of her every day. She would never have turned her back on me the way my father did. I think if she'd lived, she would have saved Fanny too, made her feel she belonged to someone."

We had neared a belt of dark trees in the centre of the heath and I could hear the wind whispering through the bare branches, knocking them together, finding a way through. I was suddenly conscious of the dead who go constantly before us. Rank and file of them, paving the way… to what?

"Life is full of ghosts," I said.

Marianne slipped her arm through mine. "Come, it's chilly. Let's find somewhere to take tea."

"What about the others? Will they not be waiting for us?"

"They can manage for now."

What a civilised idea, to sit among company in a pretty room, taking tea out of china cups. And perhaps no one would guess who I was, and no one would gossip.

The next day Percy told me about his little scheme.

"I haven't yet broached the subject with Leigh and Marianne, but I'm sure they will agree."

"Agree to what?"

"Claire can join us here, with Alba, and we can pass the child off as theirs."

My mouth dropped open in dismay.

"They have so many little ones that one more would go completely unnoticed."

"But… Marianne?" I began, thinking of the workload she already managed.

He cut me off.

"Then, once everyone has begun to accept that the Hunts have five children in their brood, we will adopt little Alba back into our household, tell everyone that she is a Hunt, and Claire can be as close to her daughter as she pleases."

I made an effort to hide my exasperation. "What makes you think the Hunts will agree to it?"

"Leigh relies on me for the success of his journal. He cannot get the project off the ground without my input."

"…and your money."

"He knows this, and so Marianne will be persuaded of it also."

I turned away from him.

"And Claire will agree because she has no choice," I added in an undertone.

"So much compassion for your sister nowadays! I thought you hated one another?"

"Stepsister!" I corrected him. "My sister lies cold in her grave."

I wondered quietly how Marianne would greet this latest piece of nonsense cooked up by the men.

As for Claire, she was desperately in love with her little girl, and terrified that Byron would take her away – as was his legal right.

Elise and Claire came to join us in Hampstead, despite the cramped accommodation.

The little house on the heath was like an overheated stove, about to explode. My nerves were shredded by the continual noise and chaos. I woke to feelings of nausea which did not abate until mid-afternoon. A feeling like a black miasma sat heavily on my body, affecting my mood. The world looked black. The air felt blacker. I barely had the energy for little Will; guilt oppressed me and lowered my spirits still further when I thought of Fanny.

Percy left for London early that morning. His court case was reaching its conclusion. There would be a ruling today. I lay on our narrow bed, listening to the chaos downstairs, afraid to join the fray. The positives of having the company of Marianne and the other women were quite frequently outweighed by the burden of being cramped together with so many children. I thought of those long days of solitude in the mountains, gazing at the lake; the peace and tranquillity, the space and freedom in which to write and think… our trip to Chamonix and the Mer de Glace, the great glacier stretching before us, the clean air cracking as the ice moved, the clear grey rock, the wild summits.

I would give anything to be back there now, gazing at the peak of Jura in the mist, instead of lying up here in a cramped room, listening to the chaos below, the smell of overcooked cabbage seeping its way up the narrow staircase.

I rose uneasily on my elbows and looked out at the grey February light coming in at the window. I dragged the basin from beneath the bed, where dust balls collected, and made a note to myself to get at them later with a broom. Lifting my chemise, I balanced myself over the pot and relieved myself. The stink of hot urine filled my nostrils. I pushed the pot away, out of kicking distance. I would deal with this when I was dressed.

Percy had left some water in the jug and I poured a little into the basin and splashed my face with it. The room was freezing. I had left the fire to go out, so I quickly dashed a few more coals on it, in the hope they would take. I riddled them to coax a glowing ember.

I could hear little feet pounding up and down the stairs. The Hunt children were often wild. Elise had Will, as I did not feel well in the mornings. My clothes lay on the chair. I reached out for my clean linen undergarments, dragged the thick cotton over my head and loosely laced the front.

I could not face another day in this cramped cottage, over-run with children. I glanced at my notebooks.

I picked up the nearest from the console table, and began to read. I needed to make a fair copy. Could I borrow a few hours from the chaos of the day, to remain up here and write?

Someone fell heavily against the bedroom door with a thud, and a child burst out crying.

"*I told you!*" another screeched.

I opened the door and bent to attend to the culprit lying there.

We were gathered in the parlour round the table, drinking tea while the children ran around the small space. A set of toy wooden bricks lay scattered in a corner. Claire, Elise, Marianne, Bess and I kept one another sane. Leigh was in his study, the door closed, the scent of pipe tobacco drifting down the passage.

In London, Percy would have heard the verdict of the courts by now. I glanced down at Will and wondered how we would manage if we had an extra two mouths to feed. Never once did I voice this anxiety, afraid the others would judge me for it.

"Look, it's snowing," one of the older children cried, and they tumbled towards the window and looked out.

I felt desperate for some air. The coals burnt brightly in the gloom, while more snow fell from the sky.

It was near supper time on the third day of his absence when Percy returned to the cottage in a temper. We did not need to ask what the outcome was.

"Our campaign failed," he told me flatly. "The courts rejected our request."

Marianne rose to offer him soup.

I looked at Will in Elise's arms with some measure of relief. So Ianthe and Charles would not be joining us, after all? I was careful though, for I saw Percy glance in my direction.

"The court ruled that they must remain with the Westbrooks where they have lived until now."

The court had also ruled that Percy should never see his children again.

"The things they said about us, Mary. The courts blame us for Harriet's death. That was the implication."

Her ghost rose before me, like Banquo at the feast.

Throughout March, while winds tore across the heath, I remained in my room in the mornings, copying out my novel neatly into manuscript form, making small changes as I went. I was usually up in the night, disturbed by nightmares.

Early one morning, I had my first dream about Harriet. I dreamt I heard a noise and jerked awake in the dark to see the door handle turning. A wet hand appeared, and a whispering corpse-like Harriet moved slowly across the room towards me. It took her an age to reach the narrow bed. She reached out a dripping hand toward the covers, and eventually I could make out the words she was whispering.

"I have come for my child," she hissed.

Just as she was about to pull aside the covers, I sat bolt upright. The room was not dark anymore, and I realised I had been dreaming. I blinked at the daylight. The bed next to me was empty. Percy was already up and closeted with Leigh in their office. I looked about me, dazed. Harriet's drowned corpse, still dripping from the Serpentine, had been with me here in this room, I was sure of it. Perhaps she wanted my child in exchange for her own suffering, as recompense? I shook my head and dismissed the vision as a nightmare.

But when I placed my bare feet on the floor, they touched water. Where the dripping corpse of Harriet had stood and leaned over me in my dream, the boards were still wet.

But then I noticed the tumbler lying on its side. Percy had tipped it over in his haste to dress that morning.

Harriet began to visit me almost every night after that. I was afraid for Will and the child in my womb. What if Harriet wanted to take them from me?

I did not tell Percy, or the others.

I stayed in my room, writing, determined to finish my task. I doubted that my book would make much of an impact on the world, but I wanted to see it finished, and I wanted to see it printed and distributed. An impossible dream…Sometimes my confidence would fail me, especially when I considered that this was not the 'nicest tale' to be penned by a woman.

Albion House, Marlow, 1817

In March, Percy moved us to Albion House in Marlow. There was a stable block and extensive grounds and – glory of glories – a vast library, with shelves towering high and an oak gallery above, and tall windows onto the pebbled paths and shrubbery beyond. I was ecstatic.

The library beckoned me.

I walked into that hallowed temple as if I was entering a cathedral. I found myself a desk, sat down, and let the ideas and inspiration flow. I had almost completed the fair copy of my *Modern Prometheus* and was beginning a new project, a travelogue based on our adventures touring Europe. It was a less onerous task than the other tale, which was so tragic and dark in scope and stature. This task offered only comfort and satisfaction, and allowed me to revisit those places I so missed and longed to return to. I enjoyed the nostalgia of recreating a time when life was sweet.

I missed Marianne, but I did not miss the cramped cottage on the heath. Elise looked after Will and little Alba for several hours a day. Claire remained with us. My sickness abated a little and I was feeling almost well again. I seemed to have left Harriet behind for now, in that tiny room under the eaves. She had not visited me here at Albion House, although I feared she might.

I waited for the door handle to turn at night, for the wet hollow of her footsteps, the hissing breath of her as she demanded my child... but she did not appear to have followed us here. I tried to forget the nightmares, and to dream instead of the future. Percy and I had plans: and a little one on the way, a playmate for Will.

Having the library and the space brought to mind those early days of my childhood at the Polygon, before life took a turn for the worst. I loved that house. It was peaceful there, until the Clairmonts filled it with their drama and clutter. I thought of Fanny, a quiet child even then. How we walked together to Mother's grave, and how I did not know Fanny had a different father to me at first. I thought we were the same, but it did not take long for Father's insensitive comments to make us all realise there was a two-tiered system in our household. Fanny was the cuckoo in the nest and when Mary-Jane joined us, our stepmother merely reinforced that idea. I wondered if Father reproached himself at all for what happened to Fanny?

In our strife and dispute, none of us gave enough thought to Fanny, caught between the two. She became a go-between, carrying messages simply because she was asked. The only true word she spoke that was her own was when she asked, no, *begged*, Percy if she could come live with us: she was so unhappy where she was. I forced these thoughts down, buried them deep where they belonged – my abandonment of my sister. She must have felt that I chose Claire above herself. No matter what I do in life, or where I go, or who I am with, I will never be able to make amends. I will always think of those two little girls walking through a flowering meadow, talking quietly, while a father they trusted walks tall beside them. I ought to leave them there, in that memory, but I cannot. I keep returning.

Percy came to terms with the harshness of the court ruling. Ianthe and Charles were consigned to the past and he moved on. He did not allow ghosts to haunt him the way I did.

He was happy because we were near an old school friend of his, Thomas Peacock. And happier still that we were close to the Thames. It snaked lazily right beneath the grounds of Albion House, where he had access to a rowing-boat tied against a small private jetty. He spent his days out on the riverbank, gently dipping the oars, watching the sunlight glitter against the water.

"One day, Mary," he told me "I will own a bigger boat, a yacht with sails that will cut through the water like a knife through butter."

"Is speed so necessary?" I asked him.

"Of course it is. The river is all very well, but it is the sea I would like to navigate. That's where the real thrill lies. There's a boldness and skill in that."

"My husband, the brave explorer," I laughed. "You are a sensationalist, Percy."

Being married to Percy meant that we never stood still for long; he moved us on to the next house, the next destination, always in search of the next thrill in his relentless pursuit of sensation. Boxes and crates lay unpacked in the hallway, and although I loved it here, I wondered if it was worth the bother of unpacking them.

We had a gardener called Harry and a young woman from the village called Brigid came up to cook and clean. I began to value their presence, especially when Percy was not at home.

He installed a beautiful new piano in the drawing-room for Claire. When I heard he spent seventy-five guineas on the purchase I was appalled, but he simply laughed and said he had signed another credit note for it. Man cannot live on bread alone, but the son of a baronet can certainly live on credit. Where we would find the money, I did not know.

"It won't be due for another three years!" he exclaimed.

"And then what, Percy, my love? What happens in three years?"

"Neither you nor I can answer that."

It was a neat and ingenious way of avoiding the issue.

Albion House was a beautiful location, but I wondered how long it would last. Will and I were never quite enough for him. When he suggested that the Hunts come and live with us ("We have so much space, my love!") I did not contradict him. After all, I was as delighted to have Marianne's company as he was to have Leigh's, but I could wish there were a few less children in the house. I was rather enjoying the peace of the empty rooms, the silence of long corridors where no feet trod.

Albion House, April 1817

Yellow daffodils appeared like bright flags. Every time I passed a corner I saw them waving there in the grass, a reminder of the long summer months to come. I circumvented the crates in the hallway as if they were small islands in a sea of marble. I felt like a perpetual traveller. The Hunts joined us on the sixth of April and Albion House became a little noisier. Elise and Marianne chased the children out into the garden, but she feared the riverbank and warned them against it, although they were too little to pay much heed. Leigh seemed oblivious, but delighted with his new surroundings. He and my husband met up with Thomas Peacock and the three went out rowing all day, or walking, ensconced in their plans. Leigh had a small room in our house that he could use as a study, and they were still intent on their plans for a journal. Percy was disappointed with the lack of reviews for *Queen Mab* and *Alastor*. Leigh was full of encouragement, but Percy remained despondent. Meanwhile my manuscript festered in a drawer.

"The critics barely know that I exist. If they cannot be bothered to put pen to paper, then what is the point?"

"There is always a point, my love," I told him. And besides, he knew as well as I that he would continue to write his poetry until they did notice him.

But he contradicted me. "They do not notice me for anything other than the scandalous behaviour they imagine we are indulging in."

He lost himself instead in the pleasures of friendship and rowing on the river, as a welcome distraction. However, I knew that it left a foul taste in his mouth. The critics' rejection irked him.

He overlooked one fact though, which his friend Thomas reminded him of. His book, *Queen Mab*, attacked the monarchy and it also attacked the name of God as being the excuse provided in order to invade other countries, to justify war and oppression.

"Perhaps it is better they have *not* noticed your work. You could be arrested for such seditious views!" Thomas said, lounging on the terrace one afternoon.

Despite the heat, I felt a sudden chill pass through me, and gathered my shawl close, although there was no wind.

"It's ludicrous," Shelley burst out.

"Ludicrous, but true, my friend, especially in light of recent events."

"Oh that – that is nothing. The English are too weak to want a revolution," Percy retorted.

They were referring to an incident recently reported: a pedestrian on the street had the temerity to throw a stone at the Prince Regent's carriage, and the backlash was swift and immediate.

"It may be nothing," Thomas replied, "but they're taking it seriously. They've forbidden meetings or gatherings of more than fifty people, deemed to be of radical or disseminating views. And you – my friend – would be deemed a radical." He picked up a single copy of *Queen Mab* lying on the table and lifted it in the air by one of its leather wing-tips. "Particularly in light of this. You may think the critics have ignored it, but someone will have noticed it, believe you me."

I could feel the clamour and confusion of the outside world intruding into the peace and tranquillity of this little rural haven I had created. I gripped my shawl tighter, and looked through the trees at Claire emerging from the woodland path with Alba in her arms.

I walked with Marianne beneath the shade of the trees, and listened to the voices of the men on the riverbank below. We could hear splashing and laughter beyond the willows which hung their long green hair into the water.

"They are happy," Marianne observed.

We watched Claire in the distance, holding little Allegra. Alba, as we called her, had begun to crawl recently and squirmed to be released onto the grass.

"Claire is very close to the little one," Marianne noted. "Do you think she will be able to keep her?"

"I hope so, for her sake. Although…"

Marianne gave me a sharp look. "Although?"

"I don't know how she will manage in the long run, as an unmarried mother with a child to care for. We had friends over recently, before you came, and they asked after Claire's relationship with Alba, noticing how the child clung to her. They did not seem particularly convinced by the label of aunt."

My thoughts turned dark and inward. If Claire was to have any chance at all of an independent existence, she must not be suspected of being the unmarried mother of an illegitimate child. My own mother defied the world and its petty laws, but she suffered because of it. Twenty years ago the world was in a ferment, overturning the old order. Anything seemed possible.

But the status quo was quick to be re-established, and with it, the expectations of what a woman should or should not do.

"I do not want Claire living with us for the rest of her life," I confessed to Marianne, my voice a whisper. "She needs to be independent."

"And you think she cannot do that while posing as Allegra's aunt?"

"Not if the world does not believe her."

I glanced at Claire lifting Alba in her arms, while the little girl flung her chubby little arms around her mother's neck. "Would you?"

"You're a traitor," Claire accused me later, with much melodrama. "You want me gone."

"I want you to be independent."

"You want Percy to yourself."

I stared at her, aghast. "He *is* my husband."

"What does Percy want in all of this?"

"You should have an eye to the future. Think about what you might do next."

She glared at me with such resentment. "You always were a dog in the manger, Mary."

"You keep saying that and I don't know what you mean."

"You never wanted to share Godwin."

"My father?"

"He was my father too!"

"No, he wasn't, Claire. He never was. You and your family, you were the intruders. Fanny and I... we..."

"Why bring Fanny into this?"

"Why not? She was my sister..."

"And what am I?"

"You are not my sister the way she was!" I cried.

Suddenly the grief came spilling out of me.

228

A step in the hall made me turn my head. Percy was standing in the doorway, watching us both.

"How long have you been there?" I asked him.

Claire put on her hurt look.

"Long enough," he replied.

There was a long silence. For a moment I thought he would leave us to it. I felt agitated by his unaccustomed silence. It was not like Percy to be so circumspect.

When he did at last speak, it was not what I wanted to hear. "Mary, it is my wish that Claire and Alba remain with us for as long as they need to. They have nowhere else to go…"

"I realise that, but eventually…"

"Eventually Byron may ask for the child," he interrupted.

I heard a sharp intake of breath from Claire. "But for now, we cannot know that, and all we can do is care for one another."

Claire smiled her gratitude at him. I felt the warmth between them. He held out his arm and I watched as she slid into his embrace. Brother and sister. A filial love – so they claimed. I watched in silence. I wished that Marianne were there to see it, to confirm for me that I was not imagining it.

I swept past them and left the room. Percy half-turned, made as if to stop me, but I pulled my hand away.

Did it give Claire any satisfaction to see us quarrel?

I passed Marianne in the hallway. I recall she spoke to me but I was in no mood to be stopped.

In the library, I found a quiet alcove between shelves, where no one would find me if they happened to glance in. A storm of emotion travelled through me in waves, but I stilled it with an effort. I refused to subject myself to the humiliation of jealousy. This is what matters, I told myself, placing the flat of my palm against the burden beneath my gown. This child. *This* matters more than anything Claire can offer, more than Percy's love even, more than his little Ianthe or Charles.

Not more than William though…
These two beings would fill my whole world.

Covent Garden, London, 1817

I sat fidgeting in the dusty office, watching the ticking clock on the mantlepiece. I did not know what to expect, but I was nervous. Outside the window I could hear the rumble of cart wheels: hooves striking the cobbles and voices ringing out below. We were waiting for him to arrive. *He. The man.* The publisher who would decide my fate. My manuscript lay in Percy's lap. We had agreed that it might be better not to put my name to the title.

"This is such a dark tale, so radically gothic in its imagining, that the public would not receive it well if it were known to come from the pen of a woman." This was the advice of the last publisher we visited, who then promptly rejected it out of hand.

"It's too monstrous, too… I don't know, it's as if a young sixteen-year-old girl wrote it, barely out of the nursery. Far too fantastical."

"I was nineteen when I wrote it."

"Well, exactly… perhaps that's the problem," he said.

We left that office disappointed.

Now we were here, waiting for another meeting. I was less sanguine than before, after that first rejection. I could not believe that he had not seen the worth of the story. Perhaps I was deluded, after all?

Percy stood by me. For all our differences with regard to Claire, he believed in the worth of my story and would not allow me to give up.

We glanced at each other.

"What keeps the man?" Percy hissed under his breath.

Eventually the door opened and Mr Smith stepped inside and closed the door behind him, apologising the while.

"I am so sorry, Mr and Mrs Shelley." He bowed to each of us. "I was held up." He coughed and wiped his chin. "Unforeseen circumstances." I could not help observing that he had a dribble of egg yolk on his jacket, and I longed to point it out. Now would not be a good time.

Percy leaned forward and placed the manuscript on the desk. "This tale," he said "is truly remarkable. I believe there has never been anything written like it before."

Mr Smith looked immediately sceptical and glanced sideways at me. I lowered my gaze. I knew when to act the fair maiden. One strident gesture on my part, and this deal would be lost forever.

However, what I did not anticipate was that it was lost before we had even started. "Yes… I've given it some thought…"

We could both hear the note of rejection in his voice.

"But you haven't read it yet."

"Yes… we published something similar not so long ago now."

"Similar? How can it be similar?" Percy cried. "If you read the story, I think you would be compelled to agree that…"

"Hear me out, Mr Shelley," Mr Smith interrupted. "I just do not think this is one for us. Another publisher might well feel differently and by all means try approaching another reputable house, but I cannot see that there is a future in this kind of tale. I am sorry to say…" he added, glancing sideways at myself again, as if I was an object of mild disgust to him.

"Well," Percy said, rising. "I thank you for your time, but I think you are making a grave mistake. My wife and I must be compelled to look elsewhere."

Mr Smith watched him in silence, looking a trifle uncertain. "I would love to be of assistance but I do not see how the general public will receive a book like this," he went on. "Particularly if they knew it came from the pen of the fairer sex."

"But we have already agreed that Mary will not put her name to the book. It could be published anonymously."

"Yes… well…"

I could see the hope draining from Percy's face. He had given up. We might as well be shown the door now.

Out on the street, I tried to hide my dejection. The manuscript was under Percy's arm.

"I am beginning to wish I had never written it," I confessed. "No one is going to publish it." I thought of the wonderful feelings that accompanied me when I wrote the tale, how certain I was of its worth, how empowered I felt, how inspired. Now it all seemed like a waste of time and energy. Discouragement sat heavily on my shoulders. I thought of my children back at Albion House and longed to return to them. From them, I felt no sense of personal rejection, no sense of failure or disappointment.

"What do they know?" Percy cried, marching off in search of a conveyance to take us to our next appointment. "They know nothing."

Albion House had been quiet in our absence, according to Elise, even with the Hunts in residence.

I sat with the others in the drawing-room and told them about the humiliating rejections from men who had the power to refuse.

"I hoped for much and have been bitterly disappointed."

"You found no publisher at all willing?" Marianne asked.

"Oh, we found a small undistinguished press called Lackington's. They were the only publisher prepared to print it, in the end," Percy said.

"They have promised to do a small print run, cheaply made," I explained. "I will keep the copyright and a third of the profit – if there is any. My name will not appear on the text. Percy has written a short preface to the book."

"Is that wise?" Marianne asked.

I shrugged. "It is done now."

The others could feel my disappointment.

"Besides, I have other tasks to contend with."

Marianne began to protest. "Yes, I know you have Will to contend with, and the baby due, but surely…"

"My travelogue, I mean," I told her. "*A History of a Six Weeks' Tour*. I can write it while I wait for the baby to be born."

Writing took my mind off the fear of child-birth.

Percy was glad to be home at last, away from the dirty city streets. He spent his time walking by the river, or perched in his boat, writing copious amounts of verse. When he showed me extracts from his long poem on freedom, *Laon and Cynthia*, I was struck by the fact that he must ever return to the theme of incest. It irked me.

"Why does it occupy you so?"

He gave me a flat glance. "I don't know what you mean."

"Denial is a wonderful thing…"

"If you have something to say, Mary, then out with it."

"Very well. I sometimes suspect that you are living out a fantasy through your words."

"What fantasy?"

"You and Claire? I am not blind, Percy."

The sunlight on the water seemed suddenly complicated, darts of white light shooting through the dark. I had said what could never be unsaid.

I watched him walk away from me. Would the next child bind us together any faster? If only Claire were not with us still, the worm in the apple, eating away at the fruit of our love.

It was still a crowded house, and I tried not to mind. My husband throve under Hunt's encouragement.

When the Hunts left at the end of June it was almost a relief. I missed Marianne's company, but even a house as large as this began to feel crowded when the Hunt children were about. They were so wild that not even Albion House and its extensive grounds could absorb them. Percy accused me of being bad-natured and fractious.

I gladly returned to the calm, cool, quiet of the library and copied out my manuscript in a fair hand. There was a physical pleasure in this, the scratch of the ink against parchment, the odours of gall, sulphur and tannin.

My quill was in my hand when I felt the first pangs of child-birth. Clutching the side of the desk, I struggled to stand upright and tipped over the jar of ink. A strange sound escaped from my lips. An animal-like groan. Something dark and primeval. I remembered how helpful Annie had been, but she was no longer with us. Drops of black ink pattered to the floor like blood. I cried out, but no one heard me.

Percy was boating on the Thames with Thomas. Elise was elsewhere, with Claire and the little ones.

The September sun glanced off the windows and I waited for the ripples of pain to subside. *There. I could stand again.* I should have a good while yet between contractions. I placed my manuscript out of harm's way and glanced about for something to mop up the ink.

Then, before I was ready for it, another assault took me by surprise. I rode the crest of the wave, but was surprised by a flow of hot wetness beneath my chemise. It was coming too fast.

Flinging the door of the library wide, I called out into the empty hallway. My voice carried up the staircase into silence and emptiness. Where were the others?

I was continually complaining that I needed space to finish my task; they had taken me at my word and were nowhere to be found.

"Claire! Elise!" My voice emerged as a piping squeak of pain. "Percy?"

No answer.

Clutching my swollen abdomen, I looked up. Along the corridor came a figure, darkening the light from the window, but it was not Claire or Elise. The figure moved slowly but inexorably towards me, by inches. Her bare feet dripped water. She left stains on the wooden floor as she approached.

Harriet.

I blinked the sweat and fear out of my eyes, but she was still there.

And I could hear her whispering, "*I have come for your child.*"

A hoarse whispering, barely louder than a breeze in the wainscot.

I wanted to move, to run, but I could not. I was fixed to the spot as the creature moved closer. So close now that I could see the yellowing waxy texture of her skin. Waterlogged, corpse-like, living yet…

When I woke, I was in my own bed. I do not know how I got there. Elise explained that they found me at the bottom of the stairs, lying unconscious.

"You fainted with the pain," she told me. "But now the hard work is coming."

"She wants to take my children," I murmured. Elise looked at me in confusion. I raised my head from the pillow in desperation. "She told me!"

Claire and Elise exchanged glances. They wiped my forehead, soothed my pain, made me comfortable, and stayed with me through the labour, as my little daughter, Clara, clawed her way into life.

The threshold opened for her, and out she came, screaming into the blue air. Eager to be born. Eager to live.

Please God, let her live.

Let Harriet leave her be. Don't let her take my children from me.

Clara was the little girl to replace my lost first-born. She was compensation. She was everything to me. She would grow up to become my confidante and friend. A companion in arms against the powers of male dominion ranged against us.

As she latched on to my breast, we bonded instantly. Flesh of my flesh. Her feminine rolls of flesh seemed so different to little Will when he was born. Where Will was wiry and lean and spare, Clara was all curves and softness. Male and female are so evident even at birth. This is what struck me. The differences.

I tried to banish the vision of Harriet from my mind. I tried to forget that taut whispering threat. I could not be left to my own imagination. Then I thought of my gothic tale, sitting in Lackington's office, waiting to be printed on paper and distributed to bookshops. Five hundred copies which five hundred potential readers would hold in their hands.

That tale came from a deep, dark place. I cannot even remember where I sat when I wrote it. It just seemed to emerge. But despite what my friends think, there was plenty of planning and plotting and editing and hard work involved. No one knew how much – apart from Percy. Flashes of inspiration alone will not make a novel.

I gazed down at my little daughter, who would be a friend for life. I would stand by her, no matter what she went through, in exactly the same way that my own mother would have stood by me if she could. And please God we would not be separated the way my mother and I were.

Life is uncertain, beautiful in its brevity. We must live in the present. And guard against the ghosts who would take our children from us. I had Clara to think about and little Will. I conjured charms to protect them against the curse of Harriet. But I was also capable of rationalising my fears. I knew that Harriet's corpse represented my own guilt. She was a figment of my imagination: not a reality. Corpses do not walk, unless in stories, and I was *not* the heroine of a story.

It had been a dank October. Storms had battered the house, and Percy had not been able to spend as much time on his boat as latterly. This house, which had seemed so pleasant during the summer months, was revealing itself to be a damp residence. Perhaps that explained the inordinately low rent. It reeked of mould and I found a strange form of fleshy fungi growing in the larder.

"Well, if all else fails we can always eat them," Percy said "if the larder is bare."

He was insufferably light-hearted and refused to talk about practicalities – like food and money.

I preferred not to think about these things either, but I was forced to.

A new nursemaid, Milly Shields, arrived to help Elise and I with the children.

"With her support you can continue to write your travelogue," Percy told me.

"Perhaps if Claire were to shoulder some of the responsibilities?" I suggested.

"Claire has worries of her own," Percy reminded me.

As ever, he was quick to leap to her defence.

I watched as he and Claire grew closer. She made him laugh; she sang to him, and avoided bringing up dull subjects related to household management.

When the Hunts arrived to pay another fleeting visit, my nerves were stretched to breaking point.

"Your mood is so low," Marianne told me.

"What can I do? I am exhausted!"

Little Clara was sleeping in the corner of the room. When one of Marianne's brood bashed into the cradle and almost knocked it over, I leapt up and scolded the child so vehemently that Marianne was embarrassed and offended. An awkward silence fell, from which we never quite recovered.

When Percy heard about it afterwards, he reprimanded me. "They are our guests. We owe them."

"What is it you expect of me? I need some time to myself. I cannot bear the noise. It upsets Clara."

Percy stared at me. "It upsets you, you mean."

"It's much the same thing."

"Very well then," he announced. "You shall have your peace and quiet."

A wind tore through the dark trees outside, battering against the house and making the eaves creak. Percy had taken me at my word. He went to stay in London and he took Claire and Alba with him.

"As you find extra company so objectionable, I shall relieve you of it."

The Hunts had left too.

I was alone with my two small children. Milly Shields was

here, but Elise left with the others, to help Claire. I was all alone in this damp, dark house, surrounded by trees and leaf mould. Will had begun to cough at night, and I lay awake, listening to him, my fears getting the better of me.

My mood was so low. I thought of Father's warnings to Fanny and I. "Guard against the Wollstonecraft melancholia."

Every night I lay listening for the wet tread of Harriet's living corpse on the landing. Had I invited her in? Did I invent her, the way I invented the creature? From what dark and dismal corner of my mind did she creep?

Again, the little rasping wheeze from Will in his corner of the room. I kept both children with me at night, against the storms and the cold.

I stood guard, vigilant all night long, but the effort exhausted me.

Milly was capable, but she was not Elise, and she was young.

I was desolate. I felt as if I had no one. And the burden of keeping these two little ones alive hung heavy on my heart. I could not bear the sense of dread. Where did it come from? Was I right to fear the future and what might come to pass? I felt that this terrible pessimism would be the death of me.

I kept my darkest imaginings to myself, and confided in no one, which compounded the problem.

The nights drew in. I walked with my small boy along the riverbank during the day, Clara strapped to my chest in a linen sling. Will ran forward excitedly, his little legs buckling beneath him. He could barely walk at all.

My two angels.

We were a unit of three.

I thought of them as my little human cargo. I was a boat, bearing them along on the current of life. My freight. *Where I drift, they drift also*. I tried to keep my mind clear of nightmares.

When the rain stopped, I walked between the trees, enjoying the fresh air. We collected leaves to make a collage.

I wanted to educate my children, teach them to worship Nature, and it was in the little things I succeeded. The night-time terrors were balanced against this daytime bonding, when I insisted on getting outside to enjoy the seasons. Leaves lay thick in our path, and Will gathered them up excitedly.

"Not so many," I told him. "Only the best."

They burned like a small fire in his arms and lit up his face.

We took them home and drew with them, arranging them into shapes and patterns, painting the backs of them and pressing the paint down so that a tracery of spiny lines appeared on the page. Will was delighted.

The wind picked up by four o' clock and those leaves which remained on the trees were tossed wildly about, while the rain lashed down in furious torrents.

We had tea by the fire, and for a while I began to feel safe. Milly's presence in the house comforted me. She helped me when Clara began to cry.

But when the crying didn't stop, Milly watched, helpless, while I became agitated and afraid.

I could tell no one of my fears. I must face the long dreary night, alone.

The shadows increased, pierced only by firelight, candles and the one or two paraffin lamps. The rooms became larger and darker still, and the staircase seemed to hold unseen dangers. Shadows shifted. The ceiling above my head creaked, although there was no one up there to make any sound. I was afraid to go upstairs alone with the children. I kept them with me in the library, beside the fire, even though I longed for some peace.

"Here," Milly tried to take Clara from me. "Let me!"

"No," I clutched my daughter to me, unable to let her go. If I surrendered her into someone else's arms, the charm might not work. She might be cursed. For who would protect her as vehemently as her own mother? Milly might not notice if she stopped breathing. I must concentrate on her little chest, the trembling in and out, the rise and fall, in case Clara should forget to breathe again. Her survival depended on me. If I tore my gaze away, I might lose her to the maw of death – like my first-born.

How could I explain any of this to Milly, a maid of no more than fifteen years of age?

I could not.

"The library is not a good place for her to be," Milly insisted. "Let me take her."

"There is no need. I will take them up to bed with me soon."

Milly watched me with some concern and bewilderment written on her face. I had no doubt she would like to confide in one of the other women – Elise or Claire – and tell them that Mrs Shelley was barricading herself into her room at night with the little ones: but there was no one for her to tell. We were alone.

Will tottered ahead of me as we left the library, but I grabbed his arm to pull him back, more roughly than I intended. He looked at me, hurt.

Who knew what was out there? On the poorly-lit staircase and landing? Every door we passed could open to Harriet's tread.

A footstep made me turn. It was Milly, watching me. She turned away.

I passed another long, lonely vigil over my sleeping children.

I knew I did not have the energy for many more nights like this.

"Mrs Shelley?" I jumped in alarm. My thoughts were entirely elsewhere. Clara was feeding, and as she did so I felt the life force move from me to her. There was an art in this. Her little lower lip trembled so that it let down more milk. How did she know to do this?

"Why do you not ask Mr Shelley to come home?" Milly asked.

"I wrote a letter a few days ago."

"What did he say?" she asked timidly, and it occurred to me then that the girl was frightened. Perhaps too much was being asked of her? It was Claire's fault, I decided, all of it.

"He cannot come home yet. He is trying to organise a meeting with his father's solicitor."

"That's a shame," Milly murmured.

The great house loomed all about us as we waited for the approach of another nightfall.

The days darkened into November and then one evening he returned to Albion House, without Claire. It was a fleeting visit, but my mind unravelled to see him. I needed to tell him... I needed to tell him what had been happening in his absence. The fears, the darkness...

"I am so glad you have come home," I began. "I have been so lonely here. The rooms are so vast and cold at night."

He laughed, as I flung my arms around his neck. "You used to complain that the rooms in Bath were too small and cramped."

"It's not the size of the rooms I am complaining about, but the loneliness."

He did not reply.

"You think my complaints unjustified!"

"In the summer months you loved it here."

"And now it is damp and cold, and you are not here with me."

"But you have the children to occupy you. You don't seem to need my company much these days."

"That's not true. Our children need their father."

Any mention of his offspring melted his heart.

He looked about the room, at the smoking fire, the dark walls. "It is damp, I suppose... How are the mushrooms in the larder?"

"Still there."

I avoided his gaze. "The nights are lonely. The house is… it makes strange noises. Harriet has followed me here."

He looked at me in disbelief.

"Harriet?"

He thought me mad. But there was a trace of guilt there too. I could see it in his eyes. And if he did not feel it, he ought to.

We spent the next afternoon with the children, strolling by the river. He carried little Clara in his arms, while I held Will's hand, the ideal family grouping. Behind us the dark facade of the house peered at us through the trees.

"I have tried to be a good mother," I told Percy. "Perhaps it's this house, I don't know…"

Percy looked at me with sudden concern. "Come back with me to London, Mary. Milly too. We will shut up the house for now, and return in the spring."

When the time came to leave, it was strange how I felt some measure of regret. Glancing along the path beside the riverbank, where Will and I had walked and gathered leaves, I realised I wanted to hold that moment in time. Preserve it. And perhaps over the years I would forget the nights of terror which followed such peaceful afternoons. I would retell the narrative of my life, creating a version which edited out the anxiety, the dread, the hurt look when I grabbed Will's arm so fiercely that it left a bruise.

Hampstead, February 1818

S now fell and buried the heath.

Leigh Hunt and my husband were closeted together in the cramped office/study when Marianne and I returned from our walk with the children. It was several weeks since the publication of my dark tale, *Frankenstein, A Modern Prometheus*. We had waited patiently for the reviews, to see what they would make of it.

Percy called me. They had a copy of *The Quarterly Review* on the desk.

He read aloud from it.

"Listen to this. Just listen…. I quote, '*a tissue of horrible and disgusting absurdity.*' Idiots! Do they not realise that's the whole point?"

Mr Smith sprang to mind, sitting in his dusty office in Covent Garden and declaring the book to be infantile and bizarre, too fantastical to be borne.

"They speculate about the identity of the author," Percy went on. "Apparently they think I wrote it, as my name is on the preface, and the book is dedicated to William Godwin. Also, it is clear, according to this idiot here," he tapped the paper with his finger, "that the author is an atheist. So, of course, that leads them to suspect I wrote it. As if I am the only atheist in London!"

"That won't stop them speculating though," Leigh said. "They'll leave no stone unturned in trying to find out who could be mad or demonic enough to write such a dark tale!"

I lowered my eyes.

"No one would suspect the daughter of Godwin, would they? Even though the novel is dedicated to my own father?"

"What? A woman? Write such a tale as dark as this?"

"Especially not you, my love!" Percy said. "Quiet, deferential, polite Mary Godwin, not given to demonstrations of violent emotion?"

I glanced at him sharply.

"Well, perhaps the general shock and outrage will help sales?" Leigh suggested.

He was wrong.

The book did not sell.

Neither did *A History*.

As for Percy's long poem about liberty and freedom, *The Revolt of Islam* did not even receive one single review. It sank without a trace. Neither of us made a penny.

"Percy's disappointment is worse than mine," I confided in Marianne. "Bitterness devours him, as if he is being consumed from the inside. The only one who can comfort him, it seems, is my stepsister, Claire."

Marianne was wise enough to make no comment.

"Why must he be so fond of her?" I demanded.

"Why indeed?" she murmured. "But perhaps, Mary…" she hesitated to say it. "Perhaps you are imagining it?"

"You think I'm jealous? Possessive of my husband's attention?"

Marianne was quiet.

"I just wonder if perhaps you've not been sleeping very well in recent months and your mind has got the better of you."

I was about to cut her off with a protest but she added quickly, "I've had my own battles to contend with. I know what men are like."

I did not want to quarrel with Marianne.

At some point, I knew, I would have to return to the huge empty house in Marlow on the banks of the Thames. After all, we could not camp out with the Hunts forever.

Would Harriet be waiting for me? By the river? Waiting to walk her way slowly up the drive, and into the house, and up the staircase and along the landing, until her hand came to rest on the door handle and slowly turned it…

Even here in Hampstead in the tiny, busy cottage of the Hunts, she inserted herself into my dreams…

The next day Percy came home from one of his obscure meetings looking worried. I expected him to avoid my company as usual, and turn to Claire instead, but he sought me out.

"I need a word with you," he whispered. "In private."

"Milly, will you take Clara for me?"

Milly gently took the baby from me and silently dealt with her without a word, efficient and calm as ever. So young. Where did her wisdom come from?

Percy took my elbow and led me upstairs to our room.

"What is it?" I asked.

When he did not at first reply I said, "You are frightening me now, Percy. Tell me what is wrong?"

"They've threatened to take the children."

This was it! The thing I had been dreading had come to pass.

"What? Who is they?"

"The law-courts. They have suggested that the way we live…"

"What is wrong with the way we live?"

"The elopement. The scandal…"

"But we are married now…"

"It makes no difference."

His fingers were gripping my shoulders. I could feel the impression through my thin gown.

"Rumours are beginning to circulate that a woman wrote the book."

My face paled.

"You know how they're clamping down on people like us, with views like ours. Imprisonment, transportation. We are not immune, Mary. If those rumours gain pace and they realise you are the author, they will cry out that a woman with such monstrous imaginings cannot be trusted to bring up her own children. Do you understand me?"

I understood. I understood all too well.

"We have to leave here, Mary. We must leave England, and make our way to Europe, before any of these rumours gain the power to hurt us."

I whispered Harriet's name but he barely heard me.

"We need to tell the others. I'll not run the risk of losing Will and Clara as well."

In the midst of my panic, relief flooded through me to hear these words. Percy's love, when it was given, was full and clear like a river in full-spate, and I knew that nothing could separate us. Not the Westbrooks, not Harriet, not even Claire…

When we returned to Albion House to pack, it was as a large group. The Hunts, Milly and Elise, Claire, Alba, Shelley and all the little ones. The house loomed ahead of us, at the end of the long sweeping drive, and I thought of the lonely nights I had spent here in the autumn and winter, while Shelley was gone from my side.

Perhaps when we leave this place – I thought – *and the shores of England, Harriet will no longer have a hold over me. She will lose her power to harm us.*

I held Clara against me and watched little Will stumble with his father up the broad steps and into the vestibule. The silent house waited for us. I watched them go on ahead of me, but I could not tell them what I feared…

That she was up there still.

One more night.

One more night to be endured under this roof, then we would be gone and my children would go with me, safe and sound, out of Harriet's reach.

We packed hastily and in an abandoned part of the library I came across the pictures we made in the autumn, the brown leaves crisping to powder beneath my touch. *Now it is March and we are leaving for the continent, and we shall never look back.* I felt sick at the prospect of travel, and how my little human cargo might fare. I would not be easy in my mind until we had left this place.

"I would rather the children slept with us tonight," I told Percy.

"Milly can take Clara. It would be best if you had some rest, my love."

"No," I insisted. "Not here. Not now."

He looked at me, alarmed. "There is nothing to fear, Mary, but fear itself."

"I will have Clara with me tonight. And Will."

"Then must I sleep elsewhere?" he sighed.

"You may do as you please, but I am not sleeping another night in this house unless the children stay with me. In the same room."

"Very well."

When I prepared myself to spend the night on the large bed with the two little ones nearby, Percy made as if to leave.

"Will you not stay too?" I asked him.

"There is not room for all of us, my love."

I grabbed his wrist. "I want you to stay."

"Why?"

It was on the tip of my tongue to murmur her name. *Harriet!* But I knew he would not believe me. I could see it in his face already.

"Harriet is not here, my love," he muttered. "She is gone."

Fear gave me the power to read minds and I could read my husband's mind like an open book, whether he wanted me to or not.

It was a long, lonely night, my last under that roof.

I watched the door handle. I waited for it to turn. I listened to every footfall on the landing. I almost thought I saw her glassy eyes dripping with river water and pain and lost love.

I wondered if Percy had found somewhere comfortable to spend the night. There were plenty of empty rooms to choose from…

Claire was a few doors down along the corridor. Little Alba did not sleep with her tonight, but with Milly. The two nursemaids were preparing to flee these shores alongside us – for Milly, it would be the first time.

I imagined my stepsister lying in her lonely room, waiting for morning, wondering what the future held. And I imagined my husband, Percy, bored of marriage, tiptoeing along the corridor to meet her.

"We are close," he always told me. "Like brother and sister!"

Like brother and sister? I do not think so.

I woke to the sound of Clara snuffling for comfort like a puppy in search of paps full of milk. There is something so animal about childbearing and motherhood. It pulls us sharply back to our base instincts. The anxiety of our impending journey had dried my milk.

Regretfully, I went in search of Elise.

We finished packing in darkness, and only when we were ready to leave did the sky begin to lighten. Farewells were said, with fulsome promises to meet on the continent if events allowed us.

I stared back at the locked-up house, at the tree-lined path where I walked with Will in the autumn months, gathering leaves. The façade was dark. It was ready now for the landlord to send servants in to clean it.

Marianne glanced at me.

Harriet walks there, I wanted to tell her.

Instead I smiled and said to her, "Europe awaits. And the future waits…"

PART FIVE: SORROWS

Tuscany, March 1818

The Hunts were extremely sad to see us leave the shores of England, and once again we three were thrown together. Claire became curiously self-contained, besotted with little Allegra, and while Percy and I were glad of a cousin for our own two, William and Clara, my stepsister posed a threat to our domestic harmony.

We stayed in a half-ruined villa in Tuscany. Claire would sit in the shade of her room, listening to the trickle of the fountain in the courtyard beneath, always in the company of her precious daughter, Alba. It was a delight to see her so happy with motherhood. Alba was a strong child and thrived under her care.

She still posed as the child's aunt, but I doubt many were fooled as the little girl was frequently seen to lean upon her knee. If Claire left the room, Alba's head would swivel round in search of her. It would not take a fool to work out the real relationship between the two, but, thankfully, few visitors ventured to our ruined villa.

I knew that Claire needed to be independent one day and I did not see how she would do that with an illegitimate child to care for. I tried to reason with Shelley, to make him understand that we could not live like this always, as a group of three, that it was not *normal*, but Shelley had a convenient way of looking at the situation. To live like this was proof of our radical beliefs, and anyway, he declared, he did not much care what people thought and neither should I. Whose business was it but ours?

I couldn't make him understand that it was not the good opinion of others I cared about, but a chance to be alone with my husband and my children, as a family, without the burden of my stepsister.

He doted on little Alba and Claire.

"We are family," he always told us, at which Claire would thrill a little, while I fought down inappropriately jealous feelings which did not seem worthy of me.

Was I deluded? Was I mad? Surely there was nothing between them?

Shelley and Claire had an ingeniously clever way of making it seem so. I wondered if they could see the glimmer of ice in my eyes.

There were fruit trees growing in the orchard, although they did not bear any fruit when we first arrived, as it was too early in the year. Claire was content. She claimed that it was good to escape the cold of England, "the coldness of polite society where women like I are scrutinised, and then ostracised."

She may have no regrets, as she watched her daughter stumble towards her across the broken flags of the courtyard, but I did.

Elise would lean in the doorway, watching us. She was a silent shadow among us, her destiny linked with ours since that day we found her on the shores of Lake Geneva.

"Careful, miss," she said in her French accent. "She will be wanting to play with William. He is like a big brother to her."

I was up in my room above the courtyard with the shutters open.

"Where is Will?" I heard Claire ask.

"He is with his father. Mrs Shelley is indisposed with a headache."

"Mrs Shelley always has a headache," I heard Claire respond.

"You look pleased with yourself, Percy," Claire said then.

I sat up in bed and drew closer to the window. Percy was below, with Will in his arms.

"And so I am, sister," he murmured, leaning close to her. I couldn't quite see them, but I strained forward, like a spy in my own home. "I have written to Byron, asking him to come join us here."

Claire froze. "Albe? Do you think he will?"

"I don't see why not."

At once I had visions of repeating our Geneva summer by the lake at the Villa Diodati, when the thunder and lightning played across the forum of the sky. Here, in this beautiful palace, with the ruins and the waterfalls all around, we could repeat that dream, re-live it.

"If he comes to join us here," Claire whispered, gazing at Alba in hope "then he will see how beautiful and adorable his little daughter is becoming. He would not be able to resist her then. Would he?"

"Indeed," I heard my husband say. "Who could resist her?" But I could hear the false note in his voice.

"You do not believe that he will love her, as I love her, do you?" Claire pressed him.

"We shall see what he says," Shelley added. "It would certainly lift Mary's spirits too. A company of freethinking writers living side by side, sharing ideas as we did in Geneva."

"Do her spirits need lifting?" I heard Claire ask him.

"*Always…*" he allowed himself the indulgence of this one tiny criticism, and I stored it away, another little nugget to add to the pile that was growing.

There was resentment in my heart, and jealousy, I own it, but at least in our ruined villa in Tuscany I was not troubled by Harriet. I began to persuade myself that I had left her behind in Marlow, in that house with its fungus growing in the basement.

Claire knew that her situation was delicate. She knew it, but she hung on, knowing I wanted her gone. She told herself the lie that once Byron arrived, and cast his eyes on his own beautiful little daughter, he could not help but love her, and by extension, love her mother. So my stepsister continued to delude herself, and to some extent, I could understand why.

"Where are the others?" I asked Elise.

The great kitchen of our ruined villa was empty, the flags swept bare, the cupboards and shelves filled with jars and pots of food which Elise had managed to acquire.

"I think they went out for a walk," she replied. She stood chopping bundles of leafy herbs at the table. I watched her in sheer admiration. What would we all do without Elise? Shelley had not employed a cook yet, but Elise was always happy to take on any task required of her.

I tried to hide my disappointment from her sharp gaze.

Elise missed nothing. She frowned as she returned her gaze to the chopping board, resuming the rapid movement of her blade against the leafy bundle.

"Clara and I will go on our own little walk then," I murmured.

Elise was still busy with her hands, but I knew she was studying me carefully. Nothing slipped past Elise. She had been with us since our summer in Geneva, and she knew the way things worked in our 'family'.

"Will you be gone long?" she called.

"Only a little while."

"Would you like some company?"

I shook my head.

Some time alone with Clara would suit me well.

The gardens around the villa were overgrown, full of tumbling green verdure. There was no gardener to keep it tidy. My stepsister Claire maintained she rather liked the romantic effect, saying that it reminded her of Albe's poetry, full of wildness and untamed beauty. When Shelley worriedly suggested we should employ someone to create some kind of order, she objected.

"When is Nature ever tidy and ordered?" she argued.

"Well said, sister!" he replied smartly.

He backed her up so easily in those days, even as he and I maintained a charade of happiness and contentment.

"One of us must remain practical, at least," I reminded them both.

I walked beneath the trees, carrying the baby in my arms. She wriggled to be put down, but I held her off the ground. I wondered briefly where my stepsister and husband had gone, which path they had taken. There was no sign of them so I headed instead for a sandy track beside the river, shaded from the midday sun by the leaves of the laurel trees.

"It's beautiful here, is it not?" I sighed.

I reached up and plucked an early pink blossom from a branch above my head, and handed it to little Clara. She clutched it in her stubby fist. Life is new to her, I thought: she soaks it all up like a sponge. I felt such pride as I watched her.

I remember that afternoon for one good reason...

As I neared the villa, I glimpsed the outline of a horse and rider. We were so remote here that visitors were rare. The rider was galloping away from our secluded palace, not towards it, hooves pounding the sandy track. I hastened into the courtyard, where Elise stood holding a letter.

I snatched it from her. It was addressed to Mr and Mrs Shelley.

"It's from Lord Byron," I muttered, examining it. I tapped it against my wrist impatiently while Elise watched me.

"How long did my husband say they would be?"

"I do not know," she murmured. "They will be back before supper time."

I could not bear it; that was an age away. What business did they have, disappearing into the countryside on their own for so long, leaving Clara and I alone?

Clara, who had picked up on my anxiety, reached up her arms, as if to take the letter from me.

"We had better wait for Papa," I told her.

Hoisting her onto my hip, I walked with her to a chair in the courtyard, sat down near the fountain and waited for my stepsister's return. The letter sat waiting on the table before me.

"I will make you some tea," Elise offered, and disappeared inside.

The trickle of the fountain normally soothed my thoughts, but this time they would not be pacified. I needed to know the import of that letter. I knew that Claire's destiny and that of her little daughter Alba, was bound up with its contents, and the not-knowing was agonising to me.

We choose our own destinies. Claire told me later that she was still glad – even then – that she ran away with us. She said that she did not want to exchange the life she was leading for one spent in Skinner Street, listening to Mother's woes and Godwin's complaints about the way the world treated him.

My fingers edged towards the letter. It would be a simple matter to break the seal, and Percy would surely understand that I could not wait for him.

Elise appeared with a tray.

When Claire and Shelley returned they looked like the proverbial happy couple, strolling in a pastoral idyll, smiling and content, leading the two little cousins by the hand. They ambled along the sandy track towards the villa, in no hurry to be home. When Percy released little William's hand he ran forward to greet me.

Percy noticed the letter right away.

"It is from Byron. It came an hour ago."

He broke the seal with his pocket knife. As he read, his face grew pale and he refused to meet my eye.

Something was wrong. I could sense it in every bone of my body, and I would know what it was, even while I dreaded its import.

He strode off into the shade of the house, his back to us.

"Percy," I called after him. "What is it?"

Claire, who had also gone pale, followed him into the hallway.

"What?" she demanded. "Please tell me, Percy. I need to know."

He had his back to us, but slowly turned to face my stepsister. That look he gave her!

I could sometimes swear he loved her more than he loved me.

"Byron is not coming," he told us, and I felt my hopes plummet. But there was worse to come. I knew it, I could tell from Shelley's demeanour.

"He wants Alba," he said softly, in a voice so quiet I was afraid I had misheard him.

Claire leaned forward to catch it again, "He wants…?"

"Alba," he repeated quietly, still unable to meet either her gaze or mine.

"He writes to say that she must come and live with him. He is sending a servant in a couple of days, to give you time to… prepare."

"But…" Claire wheeled about and the dark cavity of the room whirled about with her. "He has never wanted her before. He has shown no interest, no care in her… She cannot go with a stranger, halfway across Italy, without me… She is fifteen months old…"

As we watched, Claire appeared to be choking.

Shelley watched, helpless. He did not know what to do, how to save us from this.

"My poor sister," I murmured, stepping forward to comfort Claire, but she shrugged it off and walked away.

Over the next few days little Alba developed a mild fever, and Claire nursed her constantly, smothering her with kisses. It was getting steadily hotter, and we tried to convince my stepsister that it was merely the weather which made her temperature rise.

"You are making her hot with all the attention you give her," I told her.

"She is burning up," she protested. "Her forehead feels hot and clammy."

"We are all hot and clammy."

"Why do none of you believe me?" she cried. "She will die if I let her go. And you would be happy with that – yes, you would!"

These few days were a torture to my stepsister, and I knew it. If a medieval executioner were to devise a new method of inflicting pain, this would be it. To allow Claire to enjoy the last few remaining hours with her daughter, knowing that she would soon be snatched away forever, to live among strangers.

Shelley, Elise and I looked on regretfully, knowing that there was nothing we could do.

"We could refuse him," I suggested.

Shelley appeared to consider this for a brief but hopeful moment.

"If we oblige him, then perhaps he will let Claire see her in the near future. Whereas if we refuse him now, he may do the opposite."

We all knew that he had the legal right to do that.

"But he has shown no interest in her wellbeing or happiness before now. He has not even cast eyes on her."

"When he does, he will love her," Percy reassured Claire, "You said so yourself."

"Yes, but that was when…" her words trailed off. That was when she still believed she had a chance of being reunited with Byron.

I felt for my stepsister, in spite of our differences. She was about to lose her daughter, her little Alba, who was fifteen months old and so attached to her mother that she would surely suffer from the separation.

"But… strangers?" Claire muttered. "How do I know they will care for her adequately? They will not love her as I love her."

Elise turned away and busied herself elsewhere, unable to bear the sight of my stepsister's pain, perhaps a raw reminder of her own…

Then Claire began to appeal to me.

"You are such a fighter of injustice and wrongs. Your mother fought the battle. How can it be that I have no rights over my own child, whereas an absent father…"

"There is nothing we can do," I said. "It is the law."

"And did you have to give up *your* children?" she asked me quietly, in a voice loaded with meaning.

Then she turned to Percy. "You have always stood by me, Percy. Always. Would you see them take my daughter from me?"

He did not reply.

"You promised to be our protector," she begged him.

"That is enough, Claire," I interrupted her coldly. "You will upset Alba and make her fever worse."

Claire lay in her bedchamber upstairs, the wide shutters thrown open to the breeze which found its way through the gaps in the walls. Alba was with her. It was early. The others had not yet risen, although she could hear Elise moving about below. We all knew that Byron was in Venice at the moment. How long would it take for his servant to get here? Poor Claire calculated the hours, while seeing a vision of those hooves churning up the dusty miles, making light work of them.

My stepsister studied her daughter's little face as she slept – the faint upturn of her nose, the lift of her rosy lips – as if she would imprint that face on her memory forever. She reached out a finger, traced her brow with it, fearing to wake her. She could feel the stir of her breath, the vital spark that gave her life: in, out, a regular comforting rhythm. Who would ensure that she continued to thrive, if Claire was not there to do it? Who would notice if her spirits seemed low, or her countenance pale, if Claire was not there to watch over her? Only a mother notices such subtle changes, and stands guard against the darkness which continually threatens. No one else would be as vigilant of her care.

When we heard the dull thud of horses' hooves in the courtyard below and a clipped exchange of voices, despair took hold of my stepsister. Time was running out, as through an hour-glass. It hurt to watch it fall, grain by precious grain.

Voices outside and the door of her bedchamber was flung open. Elise's face appeared, frantic with worry.

"Byron's manservant is here," she whispered.

Claire rose from the bed, leaving Alba sleeping and went towards her. The rooms were vast in this villa, great echoing spaces.

"Elise, I cannot do this."

She slipped an arm around my stepsister.

"You can. Be strong."

Claire leant on her, and shook her head.

"Alba is not well. Her temperature is soaring. I do not think a journey would be wise at this time."

Elise glanced at Claire, then at the bed where the child lay sleeping.

She placed a cool hand on the little girl's brow, then shook her head.

"Will anything be gained by delay?" she asked.

"I don't care. It is the truth."

Elise left Claire alone for a while, and my stepsister went to the wide table between the two tall windows, and splashed water on her face from the jug. She smoothed her hair and put on a fresh gown. Then, leaving Alba still sleeping in her bed, she went downstairs to greet Byron's servant. All of this she confided in me later, as we talked by the light of a single candle, sharing our grief.

The man was standing in the kitchen below, helping himself to some of the food Elise had prepared. He was a tall man, rather handsome, dressed in soft brown clothing of good quality. His boots were rather fine for those of a servant.

He stood up when Claire entered, and bowed his head politely.

"Miss Clairmont?"

"Your name, sir?" she asked him.

"Claire," I began, stepping forward at this point to smooth the way. "This is Paolo Foggi."

"Well, Paolo, I think I must send you back to His Lordship, disappointed."

He paused, and looked to the rest of us for confirmation. No one dared speak.

"My daughter is not well enough to travel," Claire said. "She has a fever. It would be dangerous to move her just yet."

His brows met. "My instructions are to bring the child back to His Lordship in Venice without delay. I cannot be riding all the way back without her."

"I understand that to be the case, Signor Foggi, but I doubt that His Lordship would wish to risk his daughter's life."

Then she appealed to me. "Mary, Alba is not well. We need to explain to Signor Paolo that she cannot possibly travel today. It would be tantamount to murder."

"Claire," I whispered, "I know it is hard…"

To my horror, she began to weep. "I cannot… She is…"

I led my stepsister to a chair and pressed her down into it.

"Where is Alba now?" I asked her.

"She is sleeping."

"Elise, can you fetch her?"

Elise was eyeing Paolo carefully. He was a handsome man, with a touch of swagger about him.

When Elise returned, she had Alba in her arms, sleepily cradled there with her arms around Elise's neck.

"I am sure that Lord Byron would not want his daughter to suffer any injury," I said firmly, glancing at Paolo. "You must understand that it is hard for a mother to part with a child, knowing that she will go to strangers."

Alba opened her sleepy eyes, and regarded us all in silence – those familiar to her, and those not.

"Mamma?" she murmured, and leant towards my stepsister. Claire took her daughter from Elise and held her close for one last heart-breaking moment.

I don't know why I suggested it, but it seemed the only sensible thing to do. The words were out before I could stop them.

"Perhaps…" I began. "What if Elise were to go too?"

Elise's eyes widened, and her head shot up quickly, as if taken utterly by surprise. I stared at Elise… Elise who had always loved Alba, and treated her well.

I leaned closer to my stepsister. "Elise would take care of Alba, and ensure that no harm comes to her," I whispered.

"Elise?"

Paolo was watching all three of us with eyes like a wolf in search of prey. The thought of allowing Alba out of our sight, to be accompanied only by this man with his soft leather clothes and his sly smile, was inconceivable. Claire could not bear it, and neither could we. But with Elise by her side, Alba would at least be cared for and protected by someone who loved her.

As for Elise, her face was blank, the expression in her eyes unreadable.

"I will go with Alba," she whispered quietly "if that is what you require."

Alba was watching the adults, her head turning from one to the other as if she was trying to work out why the atmosphere was so tense.

"I will get the child ready," Elise said quietly.

Claire spun round and followed Elise from the room.

I was left alone with Paolo in the kitchen.

I ordered him to take a seat, and told him to wait.

When Elise returned I half-rose, and began to apologise.

She shook her head, and I sensed then her palpable regret that she was being forced to leave this villa behind, where we had only just lately arrived. It was half a ruin, but a beautiful one, with rooms and walls exposed to the air in places, staircases leading to the sky, but I knew that Elise loved the kitchen here, which had quickly become her domain. She had cleared its shelves and tables, swept away the piles of dust and heaps of spilled flour and grain that remained, and made it her own.

She rallied a little, in an attempt to hide her pain.

"I have never been to Venice," she added. "It will be an experience for me."

I felt guilty, but I was trying to limit the damage, that was all.

We were all young women then, with no economic independence of our own, but I could not help but wonder what it felt like to be Elise, a servant grateful for a roof over her head, forced to go where others dictated.

It took another hour of preparation, getting the horses ready and a carriage organised which would take them all the way to Venice. I could hardly believe this moment had arrived.

By noon, Elise and Paolo were gathered in the courtyard and ready to leave, with Claire's daughter alongside them. Claire was in shock. She could not comprehend what was happening. Events seemed to unfold in slow motion. I noticed details with absolute clarity, as if I had never seen them before; the shine of Paolo's buckle contrasted with the dust on his boot, the loose thread that hung from Elise's skirts. She did not have much to take. Her belongings were contained in one small satchel.

"It will not be for long, Elise," I reassured her.

She glanced at me quickly.

"How can you promise that?" Claire snapped. "Will Elise not remain with my daughter for as long as necessary?"

Alba was looking at us all a little anxiously now, but no one had explained to her that she was not simply going away for an afternoon stroll in the countryside. She would never come back.

Claire cupped her pale cheek, kissed her soft head, breathed in the familiar scent of rose petals which came off her, released as if by magic from the top of her skull since she was a new-born baby.

"Be a good girl for Mamma, and I will see you again very soon."

The sight of her mother's tears made Alba uneasy and her face crumpled.

"Mamma?"

"… will see you again very soon."

But it was a lie, and we all knew it.

For a moment Claire considered telling her daughter the truth. She wrestled with it, wondering what to say. *As she grows up, will she imagine I have abandoned her? She is not yet a year and a half. What will she understand, or even remember of this day?*

Claire reached up, unclasped the locket from her throat and placed it in Alba's little fist.

"There," she told her daughter, while silent tears coursed down her cheeks.

There was an awkward silence and Percy was the first to break it.

"Give her a lock of your hair," he whispered.

He raised his own pocket-knife, lifted my stepsister's dark hair by a single curl, and gently severed it. They were conscious of me watching them, I could tell. Paolo and Elise too. Percy took the lock of hair, twisted it, and placed it inside the locket, then handed it back to Alba.

She took it in her chubby fist, where it dangled precariously.

"Elise will keep it for you," he whispered, and planted a kiss on the little girl's forehead.

Claire retreated upstairs at the last, unable to bear the sight of them leaving. Alba burst into tears, and held out her arms for her mother, but Claire was inside by then, lying upstairs, listening to the sound of the retreating horses' hooves, the rumble of the carriage wheels, fading away.

Afterwards, there was silence, while Claire began the long process of grieving, knowing it would last a lifetime.

It was the end of April, and the villa felt empty and abandoned without little Alba and Elise. We missed them both. There was a restless vacuum which none of us could fill. I tried to, as did Percy, but our efforts were doomed. Even little William and baby Clara failed to fill that void. Claire kept herself apart from the rest of us and we worried about her.

Milly tried to breach the gap left by Elise's absence, taking on her workload, but she was a poor substitute.

I sat alone for hours in my private room with the shutters open, listening to the trickle of the fountain in the courtyard beneath.

"I will need to make friends with my grief in order to survive," Claire told me, days later, when she finally spoke. "For where I go, it will follow, my constant companion. I know this."

But she also believed there was still reason to hope.

"What if we were to kidnap Alba, and bring her back?" she said, her mind working overtime. Her imagination ran through the possibilities of a furtive night-time rescue.

"But Byron will always find you again. And if he does, he will refuse to let you visit her ever again. Then there really would be no hope."

I knew that despite my advice, Claire continued to think about running away with her daughter, to a place far away where none of us could find her. But what would she live on? Who would support them and offer her protection? If she earned her living as a lady's companion or a governess, she would not be allowed to bring a child in tow, especially one without a father.

As the season advanced, it grew hotter and dried up the water in the fountain. Percy and I were continually fretting over the problem of what to do with Claire.

"She will need to find employment in the long run," I began, "something that will engage her, take her mind off…"

"But we promised to protect her…"

"*You* did, Percy! Not me! She cannot live with us forever."

Percy fell silent. Above the courtyard where we sat one of the open shutters moved slightly. I glanced up.

Was she eavesdropping? I wondered.

I cared for my stepsister's welfare and I cared for little Alba, but I could not see how our own little family could survive under this shadow any longer.

Percy did not reply.

He walked away from me.

I glanced up at the shutters of Claire's room again, where I fancied I saw a shadow move.

We all wondered how they treated little Alba in Venice, if they protected her from the humid airs that hung upon the over-heated canals. How could it be possible that Claire – her own mother – had no say in all of this?

The downstairs kitchen felt abandoned without Elise at the helm. A cleaning woman came in every day from the nearest village, but I found her sullen and difficult, resentful of the 'rich strangers'. She was not the same as Elise. I came upon her sweeping the corridors. I felt she had already made her own judgements about us. Claire was the only one able to communicate with her properly, as Percy and I spoke no Italian, but she grieved alone in her room, while Percy and I took to the hills. We went on picnics into the countryside, leaving my stepsister behind to sit in her room and listen to the sweep of the cleaning woman's brush. She had no desire to accompany us, so we let her be.

It was hot out in the hills.

Then one afternoon a strange thing happened.

Claire told us about it afterwards.

It was late, towards tea-time. She was waiting for Percy and I to return, and she said she could hear the cleaning woman's brush in the corridor outside, rhythmically moving against the broken marble. *Sweep, sweep.*

Surely she has done by now, my stepsister thought?

"The sound continued relentlessly, so that I had recourse to cover my ears with a pillow to block it out," Claire said later.

It was twilight before we returned, and she seemed glad to see us for once, as the half-ruined villa was beginning to seem too empty and vast in our absence, its vacant rooms filling with shadow.

"Were you able to rest at all?" I asked her.

"I would have done, but the cleaning woman has been sweeping the upstairs corridor all afternoon. The sound kept me awake. But I do not think I would have slept anyway."

"Livia leaves just before noon," I said lightly.

"Well, she stayed much later today. I heard her."

I shook my head. "You must be mistaken. She does not normally work through siesta time."

Claire described again the *swish swish* of that broom, moving slowly up and down the corridor outside her room.

Something about our exchange made me a touch uneasy. I was thinking about Harriet.

"I always believed that the ghost of Harriet visited me at night, in that huge abandoned house in Marlow. Albion House. I loved it there in the summer, but come the winter, the damp and cold crept up from the foundations, and with it, I believe I saw Harriet walking the corridors." *She wants my children*, I had thought. *She has come for Will and Clara. As punishment.*

But as it turned out, it was not Will and Clara she came for at all – but Alba.

So I thought.

"My little Alba was the price we had to pay, while you kept your children close," Claire murmured.

Had Percy's first wife, who drowned herself in the Serpentine, come to haunt us even here?

I don't think Claire believed it, but she could see the fear in my eyes.

"Percy, I don't know that we should stay here too much longer," I surprised us all by saying at supper that evening.

Candles glimmered along the length of the table in the courtyard, and my food lay untouched on my plate. Moths fluttered near the candle-flames, mesmerised by the glimmer and endeavouring to end their lives with one swoop.

Percy stopped and gazed at me. "But I thought you were happy here?"

"I am!" I said, avoiding my stepsister's glance. "I was!"

"It's beautiful – you said. The ruined villa with its peaceful setting," he persisted.

"It *is* beautiful."

"Then why leave?"

"I am just not sure if Claire needs a change of scenery."

"You have never suggested this to me before."

"Well, that is because it has only just occurred to me. I am suggesting it now."

"And what do you think of this, Claire?"

Claire shrugged. "I have no opinion, either way," she said quietly.

The next evening I disappeared into the hills, leaving Percy to mind the children, and returned late, eventually finding my way back to our beautiful, decaying, half-ruined villa, with its now-silent fountain, its broken paving and its marble staircases to nowhere, vines hanging heavy against the soft ochre walls.

As I entered the hallway I noticed someone walking away from me.

I called out, thinking it was perhaps Milly, or Livia the new cleaning woman, or even Claire.

But *this* woman did not respond to my call.

She kept on walking.

As she mounted the spiralling staircase and began her ascent, she kept her head resolutely turned away from me.

It was then I realised that this was not Milly, or Livia, or my stepsister Claire.

It was no one I knew.

Although perhaps I did recognise the turn of her head, the

particular rigid stance of her spine from the one or two chance meetings I had with her, years before.

Something inside me froze.

I stared after her..

The children were sleeping upstairs, on the floor above.

I hurried up the staircase in the wake of the disappearing figure, but when I reached the landing, she had vanished. Both corridors were empty…

I decided not to mention the encounter to the others. They would think me mad.

As the summer progressed, Percy took to bathing naked in the nearby stream under the shade of the trees. When he tried to persuade me to join him, I refused, and he looked disappointed.

Claire sat beside me and asked me what was wrong. "You've become so silent lately."

I told her that I missed Elise deeply. "She was a practical help, but more than that, she was a friend."

Percy could not hear us. We were sitting on the rocks, the baby in my lap with William playing nearby. Of course it begged the question.

"Then why did you ask her to leave?" Claire demanded.

"You know why," I said quietly.

When Percy suddenly emerged from the water, I turned my face away and handed him a linen shirt.

He laughed at us, and shook his head so that droplets of water showered us.

We shrieked, and Claire cried out, "Percy, you are like a stray dog!"

Percy sat upon the rocks, half-naked, without a care in the world, scribbling and doodling in his notebook, like a child.

Claire and I sat some distance away.

"Would you think me mad if I told you that I have seen a woman in our villa, on the stairs?"

I was cleaning little Clara's face and arms with a linen cloth to cool her body, and wipe away the dust of the meadows. I was distracted, intent on my task, but I knew Claire was listening.

"I hurried after her, but when I reached the top of the staircase, there was no one there."

Claire was silent, her brow furrowed.

"Perhaps it was Milly you saw, or Livia."

"No." I shook my head. "Do you think it was her?" I asked.

"Who?"

"Harriet."

I lifted Clara's delicate little arm, and sponged beneath her tiny armpit where the ridges of skin were puckered and seamed with adorable baby flesh.

"I confess I don't know," Claire said.

"It is her. I know it."

Neither of us spoke for some moments, and Claire shook her head, still frowning.

"You are imagining it, Mary. The heat is making you feverish."

Eventually my stepsister reached out a tentative hand to stroke little Clara's cheek.

In mid-August the heat spell intensified, so that a languid air of torpor hung over the half-ruined villa, leaving us enervated and weak. Two things happened. Clara began to develop a mild fever, and a letter arrived from Elise, urgently declaring that she was desperate to be rescued from Byron's clutches. She believed she was in danger, and little Alba also.

Panic seized Claire. No one could keep her from rushing post-haste to Venice, to retrieve her little daughter.

Percy said he would go with her: they gathered a handful of

necessities to throw into a travelling chest, and immediately left for the city.

I watched them leave from the steps of the villa, young Milly Shields by my side, trying not to feel afraid. Little Will clung to my knee while I held the baby in my arms. I was conscious, as they left, that the villa was remote, and part of me could not help recognising that both Milly and I were inadequate to the task of protecting the children in that lonely spot, if we had a need to. I glanced up at the windows behind me, and thought of my fear of Harriet – a fear I had almost come to believe in again – that she walked yet, and followed her nemesis to foreign shores, to distant places and houses she had never set foot in when living. What was her purpose?

I did not think Harriet was given to thoughts of vengeance when alive, but whatever was haunting me seemed intent on revenge. Perhaps Claire and Percy were right, and it was just my own imagination playing tricks.

I focused my mind instead on Elise's plea to be rescued, and Claire's daughter who was perhaps even now in danger. I did not know what Byron was capable of, but I knew he was no angel, and if Elise claimed to be frightened then she would have good reason to be.

It is painful for me to recall what happened next.

While I was alone in the villa, I received a letter from Percy, imploring me to hasten to Venice. He wrote to say that Byron had agreed to consider the possibility of handing Alba over, but only to me. He would not hand her over to anyone else, and would enter into no agreement with my stepsister.

Little Clara was suffering with a mild fever and I was in two minds about travelling with her, but I packed our few things and came on by carriage with the two little ones, and Milly the nursemaid.

Percy also wrote to say that he had found Elise to be with child but managed to persuade Paolo to marry her, and raise the child as his.

"Why should you go to such lengths to protect Byron?" I asked Percy later.

"I am not protecting Byron," he replied. "I am protecting Elise."

"But why?"

This is a question I would frequently ask myself over the coming months, to which Percy never gave a satisfactory answer.

We were still ten hours' journey away from Venice when Clara's temperature rose and I began to fear for her life. There was nothing I could do. There were no doctors to hand, and the other passengers seemed indifferent as I held my little daughter in my lap. Will was silent, patiently sitting beside me, as I struggled to hide my anxiety and despair from him. I whispered to Clara, and tried to keep her awake, but her head lolled to one side on her little neck, and her cheeks grew inflamed.

When we clattered into the city, it was too late. I had sent word ahead to Percy and he ran to greet me, but I collapsed on the floor with Clara already limp in my arms. I had been unable to revive her. Percy tried in vain to rub some life into our little daughter. I held her and wept, and would not let anyone else take her from my arms.

I remember Claire taking William from my side, and leading him away from the scene of suffering and disaster, his pale face looking back over his shoulder at me. He didn't want to leave our side. He wanted to stay with his little sister, whom he already loved so much. He and Clara were always close, and when I think of them now, I think of them as a pair, consoling each other, whispering and laughing together, wherever they are now.

But back then grief emptied me of any conscious thought. All I wanted was my little Clara, alive again in my arms, warm and breathing. Her pale stillness was an affront to nature, her blue lips parted in their final breath. I could not bear to look on her, and I could not bear to let her go.

"She has gone," Percy had to tell me, hours later, when I would not let the others prise her from my grasp.

We buried her on the shore, in the wet sand, with no stone or marker. I dropped a few flowers on the grave. There was no one in attendance with us. Claire was still too distraught about Alba to attend, and Percy and I wanted no one with us. She was our daughter, our little girl: her life was so short it left a barely a trace, except in my heart.

I wanted to be alone with my grief, so the others obliged. Not even Claire dared to disturb me. I was inconsolable.

Harriet had got her way, at last.

During our short time in Venice, I had time to reflect on what might have happened if Percy had not insisted I rush to join them in the city. Would our little daughter still be alive? In our secluded, shaded villa I would have had space and peace in which to nurse her; she would not have been subjected to the discomfort and heat of the over-long coach journey, and she might have survived. Percy always demanded that we should leap to Claire's aid, but now the cost had been too high, and I told him so.

"Our daughter would be alive today if you had not asked me to travel halfway across Italy with her."

"I'm sorry, Mary. I did what I thought was right. I was thinking of Alba."

"You put Alba higher on your list of priorities than our own daughter. I cannot forgive you for that. You ask too high a price of me, Percy."

I could feel my stepsister watching the cooling of our ardour and passion for one another, as my heart began to atrophy.

I did not approach Byron and ask for Alba. My heart was broken and I had no energy to fight Claire's battles. I apologised, but told the others I had no appetite for any more negotiations.

Claire made little protest. She knew that I had my own grief to bear. At least her little Alba was still alive, as I reminded both she and Percy. Percy knew better than to press me on the issue, and so Alba remained where she was.

We left Venice without her.

Little William was now my only consolation. He did not understand where his little sister had gone, and I was incapable of explaining it to him.

I did not even have a graveside to visit.

Clara lay under the wet sand, and the tide came in and covered her, and to everyone except little William and I, it was as if she had never been. The marks of our footsteps in the sand as we grieved for her were washed away.

I return to that desolate scene in my mind often. I hear the distant sigh of the sea and I feel the wet ridges of sand beneath my feet as the tidal shore extends all around me for miles, wet, flat, and glistening, and only a few flowers remain, scattered where I left them.

Naples, December 1818

We moved to Naples in December, to a tall narrow house on the Rivera di Chiaia; number 250. Vesuvius stood guard over us all. When I stepped outside on to my balcony and glanced to my left, it looked as if it lay at the top of the street almost. I hoped it would remain dormant for now.

I was trapped in the chambers of my own past. I could not move forward, for to move forward was to leave my little Clara behind.

I envied Claire. There was still some hope that she might see her daughter again, but for me, there was no hope. We left Clara on the sands, and the tide covered the spot and swept away the few flowers I left there. Nothing remained. She was gone.

I did not blame my stepsister for what had happened. It was Percy I blamed. And so an uneasy peace reigned between we stepsisters, a truce of sorts, as we were locked together in our dual grief.

Harriet has had her revenge, I thought, as I stood at my window, and gazed out across the sea towards the Isle of Circe beyond. What a price Claire and I had paid for our so-called freedom.

Newgate Prison used to be the view from our little room at the top of the house in Skinner Street. Now we had different views, always a new city to explore, new vistas to contemplate.

But what a price we had paid!

The houses in Italy were not built for the cold. A spell of winter was not what this country needed. The walls were thick, the floors of bare stone, and the windows narrow, barred and shuttered to keep out the sunlight during the stifling summer months. Which is all very well, but when the temperatures plummeted and a chill wind blew – as now – we froze indoors: the little stoves were inadequate to do battle against the cold.

We were a strange and motley household. Percy retreated upstairs to write his poetry, and mourn the lack of appreciation he received from the literary world at large. If he was fortunate enough to be noticed at all, it was only to receive a scathing review, which was almost worse in his view than nothing at all. I had word that my novel was stirring some strong opinions in London among those who had read it, veering from disgust to horror. People were talking about it, at least, and a few copies were selling, although a first print run of 500 was not much to speak of.

Claire and I were both outcasts from society, cast on the mercy of the men we fell in love with, and – according to the word on the street – we had both been punished for our wrongdoings. This is what Marianne wrote to tell us from far-away Hampstead. She kept us up to date with the rumours.

I cared not one fig for what they thought in London.

We gathered on the steps of the house in Naples, in order to bid a fond farewell to Elise. She had been with us, part of our troubled little household now, since our adventures began on the shores of Lake Geneva. She became William's nursemaid, and comforted my stepsister and I through two further pregnancies and births. She witnessed our terrible losses, and now – heavily pregnant with her own child – she was to marry the dashing and rather handsome Paolo.

Would she be happy?

I doubted it.

Percy seemed inordinately delighted and relieved to see Elise comfortably settled with Paolo, especially as she was so near her time.

"You will take care of them both," I heard him whisper fondly, patting the man on the shoulder.

I stared at Percy for a moment. What was this constant urge to protect the women in his life, as if he felt he was the ultimate Protector of us All? He fancied himself a god-like figure, as if he was the man we should all thank and look to for guidance and protection. It was part of his fantasy.

Elise looked uncertain, but I tried to be optimistic for her sake. This was a marriage of convenience, to save Elise from scandal and ostracism. Paolo had always had the dubious air of a man on the make about him, but I hoped we could trust he would be a good husband to Elise. This is what I told myself.

I had been told the child was Byron's. I had no idea what to believe.

As we embraced Elise on the steps, with many false promises to see each other again soon, I watched Percy carefully.

Why was my husband so keen to see Elise comfortably married to Paolo, so much so that he promised them a small annuity – although he could ill-afford it – to help them set up house together, where the child could be adequately cared for?

Who would go to such lengths?

I kissed my friend and servant Elise on both cheeks, and she wept as she said goodbye to little William.

I suppose none of us will ever know the truth.

*

There is a tiny, but sad little postscript to this story. Elise never did return to us. Her days with us were over, despite our friendship with her.

She went to live in rented rooms with Paolo and I suspect her life was very hard. She had to shift for herself, and tend the new baby when it arrived, without the aid she offered to Claire and I when we were in the same position. She also had a husband to tend to, to provide him with meals and clean linen. The laundry would not get done by itself, without servants.

We heard from her now and then.

I often wondered if she was happy with the handsome Paolo.

In February news arrived of a baby girl. Claire and I went along to visit her and found Paolo standing sullen in a corner of the room, while Elise lay exhausted in her bed. There was no fire lit – despite the cold – no food on the table, and dirty linen piled in the corner.

I whisked up the laundry and declared that I would have it sent back to them later. There were plenty of laundresses in Naples.

I then bent to light the fire.

There was something about Paolo's demeanour that made me uneasy. He seemed resentful of the baby – that was it – and disappointed with Elise. He showed no interest in the new-born.

"What will you call her?" I asked.

"Elena," Elise replied "Elena Adelaide. It was my mother's name," she said sadly.

"Percy must come to see Elena too," I smiled. "He will be delighted."

"Oh, Mr Shelley has already seen her," Elise said.

There was a beat, a momentary pause, during which I glanced at Paolo, who appeared to glower with resentment. The child, of course, was not his. We all knew that. He had merely agreed to step in. But at what price? Did he drive a hard bargain? Was my husband in debt to him? Did Shelley pay for Paolo's silence?

He stared at me defiantly now, and added "Mr Shelley took the child to register the birth."

I did not like the way Paolo lay such heavy emphasis on Percy's name.

On the way home, I was very quiet. I was remembering that time a few years before, when my stepsister had disappeared to a remote cottage in Devon for a few months. I had never asked her about it. And neither will I...

"Do you think...?" I asked Claire later, when some time had passed, and I had sent the laundry out, and then returned it fresh to Elise's rooms.

"Do you think that a man like that is capable of blackmail?"

She looked up from her plain sewing.

"Paolo?" she asked.

"Exactly! Paolo," I nodded.

I was reading by the light of the fire, but was unable to concentrate on the page for more than a minute at a time.

Claire shrugged. "I don't know. Perhaps."

The child – whoever her father might have been – died six months later, in the heat of summer, when so many young babies in Italy are stolen by fever.

Elise, however, remained bound to Paolo for life.

Rome, May 1819

We moved to Rome in late February, at the insistence of Percy ever in search of his elusive muse. In spite of my grief, I allowed myself to feel excited about the ruins and broken columns which lay scattered about the streets like so much precious rubble. The remains of an ancient empire lay tumbled together with the living, so that travellers stepped over the ruined temples and buildings and between the fallen statues. In Rome, the present was intimate with the ghosts of the past, who inhabited every corner of the city.

I was used to ghosts by now. I had plenty of my own.

It was hot and the sunshine baked the stones beneath our feet. We sought the shade of the trees, and the cool marble rooms which were built to withstand the heat.

Percy and I became a little reconciled. We would walk for miles, leaving Claire behind in the villa. Percy had organised singing lessons for her every Tuesday with a local master. She took refuge in the piano, and her lethargy and sorrow about Alba meant that she did not intrude between myself and Percy as an unwelcome third.

There was still a little tension between us. I remember that Percy complained I retreated into the past, but I don't know what he expected of me. I had lost a daughter. She had died in my arms, and she was not the first to do so. I could not help recalling that grey dawn in London, in Margaret Street, when I tried to revive the pale mite I'd given birth to a week before.

"I can't get her to feed," I'd told Annie, as I struggled to encourage the limp little girl to latch on.

But now we were here, in Italy, with its grand romance and its gallery of statues open to the public gaze of every passer-by. And the child who really haunted my waking dreams was Clara, the little girl I left in the sand.

Percy liked to hear my stepsister sing. She did have a beautiful voice in those days, and I wondered if she ever wished for a larger audience. When I asked her, she laughed.

"To appear on stage would be yet another scandal for Godwin and Mamma to bear… almost worse than the many others they know nothing of."

It was an uneasy truce we enjoyed, the three of us balanced precariously on a knife-edge.

While I remained angry with Percy over the death of our little girl, my stepsister did not reproach him at all. She said it was her own choice to run away with us that July night in Skinner Street.

No, it was many years later that Claire began to reproach Percy for what he did, but he would be deaf to her accusations by then. She could slander us as much as she wanted, and Percy would never feel the sting of it.

*

In Rome I made friends with an artist who moved in radical circles like ourselves. Amelia Curran, who earned her living through portraiture mostly. She promised to paint a portrait of our little William.

She spent a great deal of time in our villa then, in the drawing-room on the first floor. With her brushes and paint, Amelia attempted to capture Will's ephemeral spirit, while I kept him occupied and docile.

Claire – who was never an early riser – joined us at noon one day, just before siesta time, when the sun outside was at its hottest. While Amelia concentrated on her canvas, Claire stepped behind her to admire her work.

"You have his likeness," she said. "His pale features, his soft blonde hair with the middle parting, the eyes – like Percy's – a little close together."

I could see it myself, a languid sweetness in his expression.

"He is like an angel, Claire, is he not?"

Amelia was frowning, a little distracted, as she painted a broad sweep of rose tint to his pale cheeks.

"He feels a little hot," I added.

"Perhaps we should stop for a while," Amelia said laying down her paintbrush.

There was a look in her eye I did not much like.

"Mary, perhaps you should think about leaving Rome soon," she suggested later.

"Why ever would we do that? We are as happy here as it is possible to be, given what we have suffered."

Amelia paused as if she did not wish to alarm me. She had spent the past seven days studying William closely, observing every minute detail which she then transferred onto the canvas

"Roman fever," she began tentatively "is more virile here in the city than in other parts of the country, and is to be guarded against. I would not advise staying here for too much longer."

Fear rose inside me and swooped like a bird of prey with talons. It cast a shadow so vast it eclipsed the bright sunlight pouring into the burning streets outside.

I rearranged Will's shift, which fell from one shoulder, and smiled at him, pinching his dimpled chin.

Sometimes, when Percy and I walked in the evenings, Claire agreed to look after Will. I thought it must give her pleasure to be with her nephew, to alleviate her own pain.

What she told me afterwards of their time together sent a chill through me.

She said that she sat with him that evening, the shutters open, looking down at the street below.

"Aunt Claire," William lisped. "Who is the lady in the drawing-room?"

"What lady?" she had asked.

"The lady who is always there."

"Amelia, you mean? She is the lady who paints your portrait."

Little Will shook his head and frowned. "No, not her. The other one."

Claire maintained that she was only half paying attention at this point as she was gazing down at the couples strolling among the ruins in the gathering twilight.

"The one who stands in the corner of the room. She is always there. She never speaks. She has a very white face."

"Now he had my attention at last," my stepsister told me later. "I stared at him in silence. Although it was so hot outside, I felt a chill suddenly, and lifted my shawl to my bare shoulders. There was a strange dread in the pit of my stomach."

She did not tell me this that night, but weeks later, when it was too late. She chose to keep it to herself, for fear of alarming me – she said.

"Why did you not tell me this at the time?" I asked.

She would not look at me. "I was in two minds about whether to broach the subject when you and Percy came home. But...I chose to say nothing."

Amelia returned every day to join us in the drawing-room where my little son continued to sit for his portrait – his first and last.

It was almost completed, a perfect likeness.

Claire noticed his eyes continually sliding towards a certain corner of the room.

"I followed his gaze," she said later "but could see nothing there. Just a porcelain vase on a pedestal. But when I came near to him, he leaned close to me and hissed 'Who is she?'"

"Why did he not tell me, his mother?"

"Perhaps he did not want to frighten you," my stepsister said.

"What did he see?"

"It was the fever in him," Claire said. "His brain had become feverish by then, and he was hallucinating."

"But why did he not tell me? I'm his mother. Was his mother."

Livorno, June 1819

Another wide stone villa, another city to explore. Percy had found us a new address to rent as easily as hailing a cab. This house boasted a glassed-in balcony where my husband would retreat to write in the afternoons, bathing in the hot sunshine which flooded his empty page. Nevertheless, for all its charms, it was a sad household we occupied.

We avoided each other. We lived under the same roof, but that was all. We no longer took long leisurely walks together. I did not know how Percy could take any comfort in writing. All of my words had dried up. I had nothing left to say. I had lost everything. The two children who meant – who still mean – so much to me, had been taken from me. Someone once said to me that a life is not any the less valuable for being short. Such little lives they had, my little Clara and William, and I will never leave them behind completely. I carry them with me, as ghosts, a permanent ache in my heart.

I took some comfort from our location. I often walked alone to the shrine on the hill, whose pink dome glinted in the sunlight.

Percy accused me of superstition. "You have never been of a religious bent before."

"It gives me comfort," I told him.

I, in turn, accused him of lack of feeling, of callousness.

My stepsister watched us both, and kept apart.

William did not come with us to Livorno. Amelia was right. We were too late in leaving Rome. The fever caught him first. All I had of him was the finished portrait which I took with me, but I would rather have had my son.

When Claire told me about her last conversation with little Will, babysitting him as Percy and I walked in Rome, I replayed it inside my head, as if in punishment. Why had I not read the signs? Why had Claire not told me?

"Who is that lady?" he had asked her in a whisper.

Harriet.

Even here...

The shrine I visited was dedicated to the Virgin Mother and her Child. I would stare at the statue in the cool shadows, out of the sun, and think of my own losses, knowing that she was one woman who might understand. In a world governed by and for men, she offered a different perspective – the one which so many of those I loved had endured – my mother, my sister Fanny, even Claire (God help her). All of us had loved and lost, and were paying the ultimate price.

In the peaceful hush of that place, I came to a conclusion of sorts. I realised that little Alba was the catalyst for all this pain: the day we rushed to Venice in the hope of retrieving her, was the moment when all of my losses began.

I reproached Percy, and I found it very hard to forgive Claire too.

"If you had not encouraged me to travel such great distances to Venice then Clara would not have fallen sick... She would be alive today."

"That is not true," he pleaded.

"The child was sick, and what she needed most was rest in her own home, not a ten hour carriage journey across the Italian countryside."

Sometimes I could not even bear to look at Percy and Claire. It would be a hard journey back from that road. A place of no return.

Alba remained with Byron, and for Claire, it seemed that her only chance of rescuing her daughter was lost, but there was nothing any of us could do. That ship had sailed, as far as I was concerned and she would have to accept the loss, just as I had had to accept mine.

For Percy, the way out of his pain was to write verses and stanzas and odes to grief, in his glassed-off balcony at the top of the house, bathed in brilliant sunlight.

Meanwhile, I lived in the shadows. Words were no consolation now. My pen had run dry.

Livorno, July 1819

I felt as if I wanted to die, follow the lonely path that both Harriet and my sister Fanny had taken, but there was a reason I could not. I was four and a half months gone with another child, although I had little faith that this one would survive or fare any better in the cruel world than poor little Clara or Will.

One day my stepsister said to me, "We have been through so much since we left Skinner Street together."

I looked at her, wondering what she intended to say. We did not usually speak so candidly with each other. Often we just passed the time of day, with grumbles about household management, meals, linen, who should organise what... I would complain that she did not do enough around the house and she would retaliate with the accusation that I always liked to assume control.

We were sitting quietly in the drawing-room of the villa, resting, taking tea, while the sun beat down on the hillside.

"This experiment...?" she said then.

"What experiment?"

"You know…"

It took me a while to understand what she was saying.

"I was only ever aware of living," I said finally, "not experimenting."

"Was it worth it in the end?" she persisted.

"You have asked me that before."

I remembered it well, when we stood outside the steps of Harriet Westbrook's house in Chapel Street, Grosvenor Square, on our return from Europe. We were shabby and worn with travel. Claire was sixteen, I had just turned seventeen, newly pregnant, and not impressed by the hardships we had had to endure, nor by the fact we were forced to beg at Shelley's wife's door, in order to pay the boatman.

"And you never gave me an answer," she added.

"And I will not now."

Percy heard nothing of this. He remained upstairs, free to write, unmolested; always granted a room of his own in which to follow the calling of his Muse.

"Well, I shall answer it for you," Claire said. "You do not believe it was worth it in the end, Mary. I can tell."

"So, would you have me sitting in Skinner Street still, having seen nothing of the world, having written nothing, risked nothing… lost nothing?"

"You know as well as I do, that what we have suffered at their hands is not fair."

"Not fair? Child's talk! Nothing is fair."

"Percy – like all men – has done you and I an injustice, I think. He encouraged us to leave Skinner Street, to break all the rules of society, but who is it who pays the price in the end? Is it Shelley? Is it Byron?"

I gave my stepsister a long look.

"I wonder what Percy would say if he knew his sweet little sister-in-law betrays him like this," I said quietly.

She shrugged. She was beyond caring now, I could tell. She had burned her bridges and she knew it.

"It is true. We are women… we will always be overlooked, while the men are free to do as they please. If this adventure has taught me anything, it is that!"

After this a coldness and distance grew up between us. I did not know where it would lead, but I felt sure there would be no return to what we once had. A parting of the ways was approaching, and we all sensed it.

"You are the songbird of our trio," Percy told my stepsister.

Well, he did not realise it, but his songbird had plans of her own.

Florence, September 1819

As the time for my confinement drew near, Percy eventually moved us to the city to be near to Byron's physician, Dr Bell. We were still in touch with Byron, despite all that had happened between us concerning Claire's little daughter.

Percy thought that my stepsister would be a comfort to me at this time, but she was of little practical help. I think she begrudged our closeness to Byron, and wanted to make it clear she was still a presence to be reckoned with.

Percy lost no time in accompanying Claire on sightseeing expeditions. While the others enjoyed the city of Florence, I concerned myself with morbid imaginings. I could not help myself. I did not believe the child I had conceived would survive. I was certain it would die, this last little fledgling.

And perhaps I would die with it.

Childbirth is a risky business, a threshold between life and death.

My own mother had not survived the passage a second time,

so why should I? This was my fourth child. None of my little ones had survived, so how could I have faith that this last would thrive?

I sent the novel I had been working on to my father, who promptly informed me by the next post that it was disgusting and refused to return my copy. I was heartbroken. I had worked on Matilda for months, painstakingly, pouring all my grief and pain in to the manuscript, only to have it so violently rejected. It is a writer's lot in life to suffer rejection and disappointment. I know this now.

In November I gave birth to a little boy. Claire sat with me through the labour. He appeared to be healthy but I did not dare to hope yet. I called him Percy Florence, for obvious reasons.

As I fed the new little arrival on my breast, I thought of Will's last words to his Aunt Claire, "Who is that lady? The one who watches me?"

"I will not let Harriet have you, my little one," I whispered.

He did not look like Clara, or Will.

He looked like – himself.

As he does still.

Snow began to fall, and little Percy lived. Harriet's ephemeral spirit – malevolent or otherwise – did not pay us a visit, in spite of my fears. We occupied the spacious top floor of the Casa Frassi on the Lung' Arno. Food there was cheap, and the bills easily manageable so that even Percy Senior ceased to complain about our finances for now. But there was only discord in our household, never harmony.

My stepsister continued to be a burden upon us and refused to accept the need to move on, to become financially independent.

"Shelley promised to be my protector," she reminded me. "Mine and Alba's."

"And so he has. And so he did," I said. "But where is Alba now? That time is past. My husband cannot be your financial provider forever, Claire, you must see that."

"Then what am I to do?"

"You have five languages. You could become a governess, or set up a school of your own."

"A teacher?" she said dully.

"Yes," I said. "A teacher."

Percy was reluctant to lose her, but eventually she surprised us all by asking him to look out some friends of ours she might stay with.

Mrs Mason, a friend of ours from England, had some acquaintances in Florence, and Percy got in touch with them to ask if they might accommodate Claire for a while.

I could see that it pained my husband to let her go, but the time had come.

I thought of the catalogue of disasters and tragedies which we – as a guilty little threesome – had left in our wake.

Before she left, my stepsister gave me one last piece of advice. "A house with an unhappy wife at its heart is like winter. Outside the sun may shine, but inside all is dark. If you don't offer Percy comfort, there are others who will."

While I fearfully and anxiously nursed our little son, my husband was no stranger to society, to the parties and gatherings of the fashionable people of Florence.

When we left Florence, Claire remained behind, in the house she now occupied with friends. One obstacle was removed, only to be replaced by another.

While my world shrank, and I concentrated on my little fledgling – the only one to survive – Percy's world expanded to ever new horizons. He was always being feted, or entertaining folk.

He might have lost his little songbird, but shortly afterwards he met and was charmed by his cousin, Sophia Stacey.

Another city, another grand villa in Tuscany, another group of friends and acquaintances to keep my Shelley amused, and life continued, while I shielded my eyes from the truth. The snow fell on Pisa, the next town we lived in, and the distance between he and I grew colder, and I was too afraid to challenge it.

He was happy, at least.

But even that did not last. My husband always maintained that he loved me, that I was his soul-mate, his mentor and only friend, that we enjoyed 'a meeting of two minds'. However, he was always in pursuit of his Muse – and I was not always it.

I merely held my breath, worked alone on my manuscripts when I could find the time, and concentrated on the survival of my son. Little Percy seemed solid, strong, a sturdy little fellow with no flights of fancy. He lacked the whimsical qualities of his older brother, William, but I loved him no less for that.

He loved the water, even from that early age; he would beg to sail paper boats on the Arno when we visited Aunt Claire, because that was what Papa had taught him to do – when he was at home.

And then Shelley fell enamoured of a new girl. I do not think he ever consummated any of these passionate attachments. They were affairs of the heart, merely. He dallied with the idea of a physical relationship, and almost thrived on the frustration of never seeing it consummated. He enjoyed being in love. It made him write like a dream, and for him it was an opium of sorts, to keep him high.

It hurt me, yes, and I tried to ignore it. Half the time I did not even believe it was taking place, but Shelley was always known as 'the priest' – women loved to talk to him, tell him their problems, and he loved vulnerable women.

What can I say?

Florence, October 1820

The casement window stood open to the street below. I could see the yellow Arno snaking its way lazily through the city, boats plying their trade, the easy dip and sigh of the oars, the walls of the buildings agleam with sunlight.

I had gone to visit my stepsister, taking little Percy with me.

"Mrs Mason told me that Byron has moved to Ravenna," Claire said, gazing fondly at her nephew. It had done us good to put some distance between us, and there would always be some affection between us despite our differences. We had been through too much.

I nodded. "Percy is there all the time," I told her. "He visits him often to discuss plans for a new literary magazine. Hunt is in on it too. He wants to call it The Liberal. They are thick as thieves again, ever plotting to take the world by storm."

My world had shrunk once again to the circumference of a small child's needs and desires. I lived on that island alone now. Percy was never at home. Elise had gone. Claire was no longer with us: but I did not regret pushing my stepsister out of the nest. We had needed the space from each other.

"My daughter still remains in Byron's elusive care," she murmured. "I use the term loosely, for I do not think he ever cared for her very much at all, except as an acquisition stolen from an adversary."

"Don't be bitter, Claire," I advised her.

"It is hard not to be. I am no longer part of your charmed inner-circle," she added, smiling.

"There is no charmed inner-circle," I sighed, thinking, There never was.

"I have become surplus to requirements," she went on. "I am not a literary genius or an intellectual giant. I am a songbird, merely. If even that…"

I gave my stepsister a long steady look. "Percy has become rather fond of a governor's daughter, Teresa Viviani."

She laughed. "So he has moved on from his sweet little songbird, after all," she said, and in that moment I felt Claire finally mature into the woman she would become, fiercely independent of Percy, and of all men. In the years to come, when she needed money, it would be me – her resented stepsister – she would turn to.

"She has become his new muse," I said quietly, deciding to be candid. "He has renamed her Emilia… as if he can order the world to his liking. But she was not the first. Before her, there was Sophia."

"His cousin?"

"His cousin."

"Our Percy likes the thrill of the forbidden," she added then. I bridled at her use of the word 'our' but I did not want to quarrel with her.

"Have you said anything to him?" she asked me.

"About?"

"Teresa!"

"I pretend to be sanguine about it." I kissed the top of little Percy's head. "For his sake."

"Why?"

"Why do you think? If I challenge Percy directly, he might abandon us. You know how much he values his freedom. He has accused me of curtailing his freedom before now – which is, of course, against the Wollstonecraft ideology we have always lived by, and pledged our souls to all those years ago when we fled the home in Skinner Street."

Claire sat back and whispered, "How these men do ruin us! They will be the death of us…"

My stepsister has changed, I thought then, but it was only later – as events took a turn for the worst – that I came to appreciate just how angry my stepsister had become.

Pisa, January 1821

I returned to Pisa, with little Percy, leaving my stepsister to her own concerns.

The affair with Teresa ended, and then Percy introduced me to some new friends of his – Edward and Jane Williams – who appeared to me at that stage to be utterly delightful. I enjoyed their company immediately, and had no qualms about sharing our lives with them.

Jane was not the most intelligent of companions at first, I admit, but I grew to like her. She gave birth to a little girl, Jane Rosalind, and had a toddler to care for, having fled the man she was forced to marry at the age of sixteen, only to bear her lover two children. The preoccupations of small children were a shared interest, and it was pleasant to have someone else to turn to, especially in the absence of Elise and my stepsister.

I thought the Williamses liked me.

I had no suspicion they bore me any ill will.

I did not know that it was Shelley's approval they sought, and that he alone commanded their interest.

I was naïve, as my stepsister Claire has oft reminded me since.

We shared a villa together, at Shelley's insistence. We took the top floor, while Edward and Jane occupied the ground floor. Jane had her baby – whom we all called Dina – to care for, and the fact she had a one-year-old son the same age as Percy helped to create a bond between us.

We were two young families, turning to each other for amusement and support, and no doubt other young families, on seeing us, envied our arrangement. Here we were in Italy, enjoying the fine weather, the glorious vistas and grand architecture, with constant companions by our side. Edward was a naval man and Jane and I watched from the balcony as the two men messed about in a small skiff, up and down on the Arno. Shelley sailed for miles along that coastline, one day even getting as far as Livorno where Byron was staying, but he never learnt to swim.

"Real sailors don't need to swim," he told me defiantly. "It's bad luck. Shouldn't tempt fate."

But he tempted it anyway.

Claire was still in Florence, attempting to live her own life, and it was only much later that I learned the next part of my stepsister's story.

When Claire learned that Byron had sent little Allegra to a convent in Bagnacavallo, not far from Ravenna, to be raised by nuns, she was devastated. She wrote to him, venting her outrage and disappointment, but he ignored all of her letters. He wanted no communication with Allegra's mother and according to my stepsister, he planned to drive a wedge between mother and daughter in the years ahead.

"She will grow to see me as a disreputable woman – one she must have no further dealings with."

"She is five years old," I reminded my stepsister.

Claire shook her head and maintained that I did not understand.

"You favour Byron," she told me, and perhaps my stepsister was right. Perhaps we did all let her down in the end.

She wrote to Shelley, urging him to take action and if he would not, then she begged us to help her kidnap her little girl, for she was having dreams – she said – nightmares in which Allegra was sick and crying for her mother.

"In my dreams I see the woman who visited little Will – and I fear she has come for my child this time, not yours."

Claire became convinced that Allegra was ill and unhappy, near death's door, but to my own shame, none of us believed her.

Claire was on her own at this point, and much as I struggled with her company at times, I felt for her plight and the difficulty she faced. When I later learned that she travelled to Ravenna to visit her daughter against Byron's wishes and without his prior knowledge, I did not blame her. What else could she be expected to do? Leave her little girl to suffer alone?

She came upon the convent one dismal afternoon, and found it dark and cold, with nuns who would 'glide in silence' and had 'eyes of ice' as she described it to me. She was made to wait in a small cell-like chamber, which was chilly and unheated. She could imagine from this, she said, the discomfort her own daughter was subjected to. When she heard a child crying in a distant corridor, she demanded to see Allegra at once, but the nuns refused. There was much locking of doors and the only windows had bars across them like a prison. Claire saw all of this by the light of one dim candle, which did little work to relieve the gloom.

She returned the next day, and then again the next, but the nuns followed Byron's instructions to the letter and did not allow Claire to see her own daughter. She humiliated herself by begging them, and it was then she wrote in desperation to Shelley and I, outlining an elaborate plan to kidnap Allegra.

Shelley wrote by the first post to tell her it was an ill-advised scheme which would only alienate Byron still further, and convince him that mother and daughter should be separated forever.

So Claire took matters into her own hands.

She bribed a servant, gained access to the convent dressed in a long dark habit to blend in with the nuns. She got as far as seeing little Allegra in her room.

"She looked small and cold. Her room was chilly. She wore a white dress and a black silk apron like a child being prepared for her place in Paradise long before her time. Like a little ghost," Claire told me, her heart breaking.

"She was pale and quiet, lethargic even. She was not the same bubbling little girl I remembered. She would not look at me, at first, which was the strongest reproach to me, as if I had abandoned her. Perhaps that is how she saw it. For who can explain the truth of a complex situation to a five-year-old, and expect to be believed or understood?

"I wrapped her in a warm blanket, held her close, and told her that we were going to visit her Papa. I don't know why I lied," Claire told me. "Perhaps I was afraid she would not agree to come with me. But the convent was such a sad dark place, so cold and loveless, I did not think she would mind. And in truth, she did not.

"We managed to convey her all the way to the front entrance, hidden from view in my long robe, and no one stopped us. Until we were three feet from the door. Huge. Bolted. A wooden barrier which I have imagined opening and fleeing from a thousand times since, in my dreams. If only…

——Claire grows sad at this point.

"But that is not what happened in real life. In reality, I never reached that door, did not manage to grasp the great iron ring. I am caught forever in mid-action, my hand reaching out, the space between too insurmountable a barrier, too vast. A few feet became a million miles – my whole life hung in the balance – and in that failure to open the door my whole fate changed. But more importantly, so did Allegra's."

I knew what she meant by this stage, but did not express an opinion.

"They caught up with me before I could release her from her bondage. They tore my daughter from my arms, yet again, just as before when she was a baby, and they would not let me near her. Those nuns with their black scowls and cold eyes had me forcibly removed and told me they would inform Allegra's father directly that I had tried to kidnap his daughter. They told me I was a sinner, and that I should go away and beg God's forgiveness."

Claire paused in the telling of her story to wipe the tears from her eyes.

"Allegra felt so thin in my arms. I knew they were not feeding her properly. And there were small marks on her wrists where I think she may have been grasped too roughly. You remember when Shelley visited her and said that she was still the mischievous little girl we all knew, ringing the chapel bell without permission so that the nuns began to file out from their cells? Well, I don't think that was the full story. I think in time they managed to subdue Allegra's spirit. They did not look kindly on her little pranks and her sense of fun. Instead they punished her – but of course they will have hidden the truth from a concerned visitor like Shelley."

Claire's moonlit adventures in Ravenna, smuggling herself into the darkened convent by night and almost succeeding in running away with her daughter, is a narrative she told me much later, when we had many losses to mourn between us.

I think of Claire's story often and wonder what life would have been like for her if she had succeeded in spiriting Allegra away that night. Surely they would have caught up with her, and it would not have ended well?

In later years, Claire did move to Vienna, and then to Russia to become a governess. She sought adventure and took her grief with her. She never had a good word to say about either Byron, or my husband, Shelley, and of course she had her reasons. She grew to hate us all and I cannot blame her. So when, even now, she turns to me for money, or asks me for assistance or a loan, I give her what she needs, even though my son Percy and I are short ourselves and life is a continual struggle. There are no grand villas to live in now, no private coaches and fashionable hotels, no trips abroad. This cottage is all I have, and it is not even mine. I rent it from an overbearing landlord, so you could say that the only thing I have – other than dear Percy, of course – is the snowstorm of papers and letters and manuscripts which litter my desk, and fill the wooden chest beneath the window. These are what I have, as ephemeral and insubstantial as memories, liable to fading and damage.

So why do I give Claire, my stepsister, the loans she asks of me – even now, after all these years?

Because of that story she told me, of little Allegra and her attempt to kidnap her from the convent. Perhaps I feel in part to blame.

For when she warned us of her nightmares, and her fears about Allegra's death, none of us believed her.

Shelley even went so far as to suggest she was being hysterical. And yet he'd always loved her and fought her corner. Even he deserted her in the end.

That is all I have to say about my stepsister. We don't see each other often now. She lives abroad, and writes occasionally. She has plans to establish a school of free-thinking like-minded women. She fought for her own independence, but it still eludes her insofar as she requires a loan now and again.

The only time I ever hear from her now is when she needs money.

Shelley did try to persuade Byron at the time to take little Allegra from the convent and let her live with people who knew and loved her, but Byron was stubborn on the issue.

Claire never forgave him. Or me. Or Shelley.

When people asked, she wrote the truth about the two foremost poets of the land. While I built up Percy's reputation, word by word, brick by brick, editing his poetry and those volumes of his collected works – never mentioning the scandals or the hypocrisy or the atheistic views – while I continue to salvage, Claire tears him down, but very few listen to her.

Does that make me a hypocrite?

I don't know.

All I know is that Shelley's poetry is too good to be lost and forgotten, and the only way I can establish his reputation is by withholding the truth from the public eye, making less of the scandal and more of the art.

"You always were the pragmatic one," Claire accused me recently.

Perhaps.

But needs must.

Pisa, April 1822

When Claire arrived in April to join the rest of us, she was still smarting about her failed kidnapping attempt, but hopeful that some arrangement could still be made. Allegra was still alive at this point. We three went on a trip to the Gulf of Spezia, where Percy declared it was just like old times, and that wouldn't it be marvellous if we all spent the summer there together, away from the city?

"You would have peace and quiet to write, my love," Percy said.

"You mean – you will!"

He shrugged it off.

"Edward and Jane must come with us too, so that Percy has a little playmate, and you'll have companionship, Mary."

I glanced across at my stepsister, as he flung his arm across Claire's shoulder and continued to enthuse. "We will heal each other's wounds. Try to forget…"

"I don't want to forget!" I bit the words back sharply. I did not need to add the unspoken words "…my children."

Claire was quick to agree to the plan. She did not like being left out in the cold in Florence, far away from the rest of us. She needed company too, she said, to help bear her forced separation from Allegra.

It appeared I was over-ruled.

I was pregnant again. I had known since February, and the first three months were always the worst, as I suffered from nausea and exhaustion.

Shelley and Edward were making plans to build a boat that would rival Byron's, but I did not trust their ability and had reservations about the scheme. Edward boasted that being a naval man, he knew what he was about. Shelley – although he barely knew him – trusted him.

"He's a sailor, Mary. He has sailed the high seas."

"So he says!"

"So you think he is a liar?" Shelley accused me.

"I have no idea. But neither do you."

"We've lived with these people, Mary. We know them."

"Perhaps not as well as you think," I countered.

If only we both had known them better.

Claire had already left with Edward and Jane, in order to hunt for a house for us all on the coast, so Percy and I were able to talk freely for the first time in months.

We argued a little, and he pointed out how lucky Edward was to have a wife like Jane, who raised no objections, took everything in her stride, and seldom complained.

"Take a leaf out of Jane's book," he scolded. "She is happy to float with the tide. As Shakespeare says, There is a tide in the affairs of men…"

"She has both her children living," I muttered under my breath.

"And we," he said, laying a gentle hand on my stomach, "have another little one on the way."

I thought of Clara, my little girl, how she died in my arms, and how she might be alive still if Percy had not insisted I travel to Venice to help resolve my stepsister's problems yet again.

The words hung unspoken between us.

Accusations could multiply if we let them, but all I wanted from Percy was understanding. I did not want to be accused of being a harpy, and a bad wife. I wanted to be able to grieve after my own fashion.

Little did I know there was more bad news on its way.

I took a breath, wanting to explain to my husband, wanting to breach that gap between us, but even as I did so we were interrupted by the arrival of a carriage pulling up outside our villa.

When it became clear that the occupant of the carriage was Teresa, Byron's new mistress, and that she had missed Claire by only a few hours, we were initially relieved. An encounter between the two of them would not have been wise at this stage. Percy and I had welcomed Teresa into our circle, and I knew my stepsister would not be best pleased by this.

But the purpose of Teresa's visit was not a social call: she bore terrible news.

She told us that little Allegra had died at the convent a few days ago.

I felt the floor beneath my feet give way. If Allegra had died, if Clara and Will had died, then why not my little Percy also? I felt utterly unable to trust life. It seemed only a matter of time before I would lose him too.

Shelley and I discussed how we might manage Claire when she returned from house-hunting.

"How will we break the news?"

"We won't," Shelley said. "Not yet. We will take her with us to La Spezia first, where she won't be able to attack Byron. If we tell her now, here, she will go straight to him."

It was agreed that Claire and I would travel ahead with little Percy, and the others would follow behind, while Shelley explained to Edward and Jane in private what had happened to poor little Allegra.

We both felt uneasy about the plan, but we did not know what else to do.

Casa Magni, La Spezia, May 1822

The house loomed above us across the water, a hollow-looking façade with five dismal arches. We arrived by boat, as that was in fact the only way to arrive at Casa Magni. The sea sloshed in over the high wall and moved about inside the building itself, where the nets and boating paraphernalia were kept. Dark cypress trees crowded the hillsides above it, and a dismal air hung about the place. It was no palace and it did not live up to my romantic expectations of a house overlooking the Gulf of Spezia.

A short distance away was a tiny fishing village comprising a few modest huts. There was no road, just an inaccessible shore of huge rocks and boulders.

The boat landed us at the rocky pier. Claire and I thanked the boatman, who helped us with our things, and then we stumbled over the shore to find a way into this desolate fortress, Claire carrying Percy in her arms to spare me. There was no door at the front, only the five arches where the boats were kept. Eventually we found an outside staircase around the back of the house. It was difficult to negotiate, what with the weight of my skirts and the pregnancy, but once inside, I looked about me.

Instantly, I felt trapped.

There was no way out except via the steep staircase we had just managed, no way down to the shore, no road leading across the hillside to the nearest town.

We were isolated.

The only traffic arriving here would be by boat.

There was one main room, unfurnished, bleak, boasting only a few chairs and a table, and from here the huge archway looked out across the sea like a giant stage set.

I turned to Claire, trying not to be gloomy, but it was hard to hide my despair. I watched her, knowing what I knew. She was holding my son in her arms and when she declared that he seemed a little hot, instantly the panic and dread overwhelmed me. If anything were to happen to Percy here, before the others arrived, how would we fetch help? I felt the full terror of our sudden isolation burst over me like a wave. Once the boat left, we were alone.

I could hear the waves washing against the arches below, slapping against the outside of the building, creeping steadily into the cellar beneath, which was more a boathouse than anything else.

"It was all we could find," Claire said, shrugging. "It will do fine," she added, but I could not bring myself to agree with her.

When she, Edward and Jane had arrived back from their trip the day before, they were puzzled by the speed with which Shelley hastened us on our way.

"You and Mary go first, take Percy with you, and then the rest of us will follow."

It was almost comical to observe their bewilderment, if it had not been so tragic. Far from seeing Shelley and I quarrelling and procrastinating – as they had expected – we were in total agreement as I packed Claire's bag for her and promised that the others would follow with the rest of our things.

Now here we were.

And I carried a double burden.

I could not tell her what I knew, and yet I grieved. But worse than this was the fear that my own child might succumb at a time when anything seemed possible. Allegra had died. Why not little Percy?

I suffered an agony while we waited.

"I don't know that this is ideal," I admitted to Claire, as we sat alone by candlelight that evening, looking out across the Gulf.

She frowned at me. "But it was your idea!"

I said nothing, and watched the moon rise over the sea.

My son Percy was asleep in the room I intended to share with him. I knew that when his father arrived, Shelley would probably want to sleep in another room, one where he could write poetry and read, far from the petty concerns of small children.

Claire watched me carefully that night, but if she suspected anything, she said not a word: I hid the truth from her so successfully.

But when I went to sleep that night, trying not to mind that the beds were damp and the air smelled a little foul, I listened to the sad cadence that the waves kept up, washing in and out of those archways beneath our living rooms.

It felt mournful, bleak and sad.

I did not know how the others would feel about it, but I suspected that Shelley would enthuse about our proximity to the sea. If the only access was by boat, that was all to the better in his eyes.

"We are nautical men," he joked when he arrived. "And we will rise to the challenge."

But he did not look as if he could rise to any challenge. He looked positively haunted. He felt guilty about Allegra and our part in it, I could tell.

If we had managed to persuade Byron to return Allegra to her mother… if we had given in to Claire's plea to whisk Allegra away by cover of night…

Then most likely we would all be in prison by now. I soothed my troubled conscience by justifying our lack of action to myself.

It was late at night. The others were still talking in the main room, but I had retired to my bed, exhausted. Jane, Edward and Shelley had arrived with the crated furniture the day before, and the task of establishing a comfortable home for us all had fallen largely to me, while Jane sat out on that wide balcony, her little baby in her arms, the two men dancing attendance on her. The task of occupying the two toddlers also fell to me. Jane seemed oblivious to her little Meddy's requirements, wrapped up as she was in nursing her little girl who was only a few months old.

No one spoke of Allegra, but I gathered from Shelley that he had spoken to the others before they left for La Spezia: he had informed them of Allegra's death and urged the need to keep Claire calm. All of us knew – apart from Claire – and none of us dared break the news. We were sworn to secrecy.

We would wait…

For what, we did not know.

The right moment, I suppose.

But the right moment never came.

Jane and Edward had chosen a room next to Shelley's. They had brought their own servants with them, but there were no extra rooms for them to sleep in so they were forced to camp out in the hall with the children, which they were, of course, displeased with. Immediately I was aware that it was not a very satisfactory arrangement, but I barely had a moment alone to tell Shelley what I thought about it all.

He, of course, loved Casa Magni the minute he arrived.

He stubbornly refused to look at or acknowledge the innumerable problems we were facing. The lack of transport, the difficulty obtaining supplies, the lack of bedrooms to accommodate us all. All of these 'petty concerns' fell to me. It was I who had to speak to the servants to find out how and when we might buy enough food to feed us all. No one else seemed to care. Jane floated about in a sea of calm tranquillity, admired by all, not bothering her head about where the next meal might come from, or what her own children might eat. They could live on air as far as she was concerned.

Whenever I raised the subject, she and Edward glanced at me, and kept their opinions to themselves, but I had the sense that I was failing in their estimation in some way. I was not the good wife to Shelley that I ought to be. I ought to complain less, worry less, be more sanguine.

"You love a remote location," Shelley argued with me. "You said as much."

"But what if anything were to happen to Percy?" I pointed out. "How long would it take to fetch a doctor?"

He glanced down at my swelling waistline.

"Nature always finds a way," he murmured.

"Yes – so my mother discovered!" I snapped back.

My raised voice alerted the others to a confrontation and when I sensed them all listening, I fell quiet.

Now I lay down on my lonely bed, trying to get a little rest, while Shelley went to rejoin the others.

Their voices in the main room murmured on into the small hours, while a white moon rose up above the sea and bathed our battered villa with an eerie light. It made me think briefly of my time up in Scotland with the Baxters, and how Isabel and I used to lie awake at night in the cottage, after long evenings of discussion with her brother-in-law downstairs. Now she was married to that brother-in-law. I wrote to her once, but she never replied. That life, those days when I was so young and hopeful, and on the cusp of my future, seemed a million miles away, as if they had happened to another person who no longer existed. Grief and sorrow had come between me and that child I once was. I had lost three children, I had travelled great distances, an itinerant lifestyle, restless, in search of… what?

Always following Shelley around in pursuit of his dream.

The sea was calm tonight, but still I could hear the insidious movement of the tide stirring in the cellar beneath, a hollow sucking sound.

I slept on and off, and when I woke again, the room beyond was quiet. They must have all retired to their beds. Shelley had the room next to Edward and Jane's.

There was a faint tap on my door.

Claire stood there, in a shaft of moonlight. "Can I sleep in here with you?" she asked.

I nodded briefly and she camped out on the chaise lounge, dragging a sheet over herself. It was not ideal, but it was either that or share with the servants in the hallway.

Other than the big main room with its view over the bay, there were only three bedrooms and the hallway beyond. Certainly not enough room to accommodate us all comfortably. When Claire and I had arrived the day before I had to sweep the litter of last year's leaves aside, which had gathered in the corners and rattled across the hard floors in the stirring of a faint breeze.

Once the floor was swept, it still presented a desolate picture and I could not feel at home.

In the morning Shelley was excited to set up his telescope on the balcony and scan the waters hopefully for the arrival of his new boat, which sailed into the bay later that day, a graceful narrow vessel with a tall mast, and many sails.

He would call her Ariel, he said, and they would sail her every day around the Gulf of Spezia. He and Edward were elated by their new plans. It was the perfect location, he said. Every morning, he hurried down the outside staircase, stumbled the few yards across the rocky shore to the pier, rowed the little skiff out to the yacht, and so began his day.

The sea was his playground, while the Casa Magni became my prison.

When the sun shone and the weather was calm, he propped himself up by the main mast and sat there writing poetry and working on his play, doodling in his notebooks, sketching, working… particularly if he could not find any peace in the villa from the constant activities of the children – and, I suppose, the scolding of his wife.

Claire found me sitting listless on my bed, after another exhausting morning of trying to keep the toddlers occupied.

"How are you?" she asked, with a rare trace of sympathy.

I shrugged. "Is he still out there?" I asked, and she nodded.

There was a long companionable silence, while I thought about poor little Allegra and all that we weren't telling her.

"I suggested to Jane that I was a little worried about the boat."

"What did she say?"

"She said she wouldn't dream of doubting either Shelley or Edward. They are perfectly capable of taking care of themselves. She made me feel a fool."

Claire made no comment, but she was frowning a little.

Did she suspect that we were keeping something from her, did she notice the sudden silences when she entered a room?

I don't know, for I never asked her.

On the rare occasions when I see my stepsister again, we never talk about that time.

"Do you like Jane?" she asked me now, out of the blue.

I looked shocked. "Of course. Don't you?"

Instead of replying she asked me another question. "Do you trust her?"

"Why wouldn't I?"

Claire sighed and thought for a moment. Could this be happening? My stepsister fighting my corner, on my side for once?

"Perhaps you shouldn't!" she said.

"Why?" I sat up. "What have you noticed? She and Edward are as happy a couple as I could imagine. Still in love, despite the burden of two small children."

Claire shrugged again. "Well… you know Percy."

And with that mysterious comment, she left me to my own imaginings.

I watched my husband very carefully after that.

Of course, it was obvious he adored our new friends. He wrote a long poem about being shut out of Paradise and slipped it under their door. He envied them their blissful state of union – whatever that might mean – and he implied that his own relationship with me fell short of such delights. I knew that, and I took the criticism because I had no choice. I had other matters to preoccupy me, not the least of which was feeding us all, taking care of the toddlers, managing the servants who were beginning to complain and quarrel among themselves, and of course trying to deal with the waves of nausea brought on by another pregnancy.

Shelley and I had no time to ourselves. There was a total lack of privacy in the villa.

The weather continued fair and it became very hot. I worried constantly about little Percy developing a fever.

We were gathered one evening in the main room, the four of us, while Claire was elsewhere. As far as we knew she had taken a short walk down to the shore.

"What about Claire?" I whispered to the others.

"What about her?" Edward said.

"We need to tell her… about Allegra. She has a right to know."

"One of us will need to keep her calm," Shelley said, and I could see that he was agitated at the thought of witnessing the storm of anger and grief which would surely follow. Perhaps he still felt his own part in it, his own failure, and was afraid that Claire would lash out with accusations.

What none of us knew was that Claire had returned from her walk, and was listening in the hallway, on the other side of the door which stood slightly ajar.

"She will be devastated," Jane murmured. "If I lost my little girl…"

Suddenly she stopped speaking. The door creaked. Claire appeared in the archway like a ghost.

A terrible silence fell.

We waited for Claire to speak, to unleash a storm of tears or anger, but she said nothing.

She was preternaturally calm.

She stared at Shelley first and spoke the words none of us dared utter.

"Allegra is dead."

She said it so softly.

He looked down at the floor, unable to meet her gaze.

Claire said nothing, but she crossed the floor to my room, went inside, and closed the door behind her, shutting us all out. It was the only privacy she could find.

"Perhaps you should go to her," Jane said.

I shook my head.

"She is your sister!" she added, frowning a little, and I should have seen it then, the air of judgement, the vindictive purpose beneath the smile, but I did not.

I did not bother to explain what I knew, that Claire needed to be alone. For how could Jane know that, having lost none of her own children?

Claire grieved quietly. She did not cry, or quarrel with us, or

322

raise the issue of whether we should have saved Allegra and rescued her from the convent where – Claire maintains – she had known all along that her little girl would die. Her nightmares had proved to be accurate forecasters of the future. She did not reproach Shelley and I, because it would not bring her daughter back. I saw it in my stepsister's eyes.

It is too late for all of that, her glance seemed to say.

Not long after this I fell ill with a fever. I remember very little of that time. I know I complained of being unwell and that the others did not believe me. I overheard Jane whisper the word 'attention-seeking' but wondered if I was imagining it, her smile was so sweet and her expression always so benign.

I walked down to the shore and bathed in the water to try and bring my temperature down, soaking my skirts in the process. I did not care that the cloth clung to me afterwards and there was no way to clean the salt water from my gown. All I cared about was getting some relief.

Then I began to bleed.

And the bleeding did not stop.

And at last even Jane began to believe that my complaints might be well-founded.

I don't know what happened next, for I slipped into unconsciousness, but when the doctor finally arrived by coach from Livorno he maintained that Shelley saved my life by ordering a bath of ice to be got up, and plunging me into it. It stopped the bleeding, otherwise I would have bled right out.

I lost the baby, another casualty to the war – although I am not exactly clear who the enemy was, or who we were fighting – other than the status quo, the conventional morals which keep women captive.

Shelley treated me a little better after this. He was patient and kind. At first.

Then we received a letter from Byron telling us that the Hunts were staying with him. I thought of Marianne, our walks together across the heath in Hampstead to escape the small cottage full of children, and I longed to see our old friends again.

Shelley was adamant. "I'll sail across the Gulf to pay them a visit. It will take seven hours' sailing, at most."

My stomach sank, as if I had just swallowed a stone.

"In Ariel?" I asked.

"Of course in Ariel. How else would we cross the Gulf? Magic carpet?"

"But I don't know that's wise," I began, the dread and anxiety surging up like a black cloud, darkening my vision.

I could sense Edward rolling his eyes behind my back.

"Ariel is the fastest, most beautiful…"

"But are you sure she's seaworthy? She has not been tested to such an extent…"

They cut me off.

"Edward is an experienced sailor, Mary. We know what we are doing."

Jane sighed, sanguine as ever, and turned away as if she found my continual worrying a bore, and a drain on her energies.

After a while, I recognized a look in Shelley's eye. That look said, "don't cling, don't suffocate me. I cannot stand it."

I had seen that look before.

He valued his freedom above all else, and he admitted to me that he found it claustrophobic being stuck at the Casa Magni with me, that he found my low mood and dark imaginings unendurable.

"You find it unendurable?" I cried. "You find it claustrophobic? At least you can escape, while I am stuck here, a captive and a slave."

"A slave?"

"Where will I go? What will I do?"

The others listened to the shouts ricocheting against the walls with their peeling plaster and pretended not to hear – although there was nowhere else to go to avoid hearing us.

"You always said you loved to be remote!" he shouted, exasperated.

"Not this remote!" I shouted back.

"You are impossible."

"And you are selfish. And delusional!"

He stared at me. I had taken a pin to his inflated ego and burst it – an unforgivable crime in his eyes, and – as it turns out – in the eyes of Jane and Edward Williams, our so-called friends.

"If you love this house and its location as much as you claim," I finished, "then why are you so keen to flit it?"

"To spend time with my friends!" he bellowed.

"Our friends!" I hurled back at him.

When we emerged from our room, the others avoided eye contact with me, but I felt the air of judgement emanating from Jane and Edward in particular. No one spoke.

Shelley went out onto the balcony to brood. I went back to my room, the only place where there was any privacy to be had, and it was not much at that. Within seconds Claire had joined me, leading little Percy by the hand.

I was woken by screaming in the middle of the night. Shelley dragged me violently from the bed and pulled me to my feet, his eyes starting from his head.

Claire leapt up from the chaise longue where she was sleeping, to aid me, and pulled him off.

He'd had a nightmare, he said, so vivid that even now he thought it was real. He'd seen the sea pouring over the edge of the balcony and rushing into the rooms of the villa.

"Then why go?" I asked him. "Why make the journey?"

"To see Byron. And Hunt. I need to see my friends again."

"You will see them soon enough. Stay here, with us, where you will be safe."

It was the wrong thing to say, and I knew it as soon as the words were out.

A day later they set sail in the Ariel, and Jane, Claire and I watched from the balcony as the wind caught in her sails and she began to fly across the waters before a stiff breeze, making good headway.

Before he left he promised to write the minute he arrived at Livorno.

He was in good spirits, full of his ideas to involve Hunt and Byron in a joint venture to launch a new literary journal. He was hopeful, optimistic, no doubt glad to escape the prison which the Casa Magni had become.

We women stayed behind, and waited.

Jane pretended to be patient with me, and the only criticism she let slip was that I worried too much. Claire watched her, but said nothing.

My stepsister had changed in recent weeks. She had grown into a formidable force. She knew more than she was telling. And she now saw more than the others realised, myself included. I should have trusted her, instead of giving Jane the benefit of the doubt.

"You know why he called the boat Ariel don't you?" Claire said. "In honour of her." She nodded her head slightly towards the closed door, on the other side of which sat Jane with a cross-stitch lying idle in her lap. "Jane. He's in love with her – and she knows it! She laps it up like the cat with the proverbial cream."

Casa Magni, La Spezia, 8th July 1822

A letter did arrive from Shelley. He had arrived safely, wrote that he missed me, us, and that he would return on 8th July as promised – no later.

That morning the weather began fine. I knew to expect Shelley by the evening. Perhaps once he had enjoyed his week of partying with our friends, indulging his need for company and stimulation, he would come home in a better mood, more satisfied with his lot, less plagued by self-doubt and the disappointments of a writer's life.

That is what I hoped.

Then, around mid-afternoon, I saw an eerie blackness attach itself to the horizon, and spread outwards, like a heavy cloak.

I stood on the balcony and fixed my eye to Shelley's telescope, and scanned the waters. Nothing there at first. Perfectly calm.

Then the swell began. A high rolling of the waves, a heavy movement of the entire surface of the sea, back and forth, longer and wider.

By the time the storm hit, we ran indoors while the rain

unleashed itself across the bay, hammering down onto the stone balcony beyond until it flooded.

We had to move the furniture away from the archways, as the rainwater swam inside.

Claire and I exchanged glances, and I paced the room.

Jane was dismissive.

"Edward is an experienced sailor. He would know what to do in a storm. Besides, they probably decided not to set sail in this. Don't you think?"

I latched onto this idea. "Of course. They would never set sail in such a storm."

It was a wild night and I hardly slept. I nursed little Percy in my arms, more for my own comfort than his, while I listened to the sea hurl itself onto the rocks below.

Dawn came and with it a certain calm.

The storm had passed over.

Shelley and Edward would come home today.

We kept watch on the balcony. There were one or two boats out there, but none of them headed towards the Casa Magni.

The next day then, they will return the next day…

But the next day came and went.

I wrote to Shelley at Livorno, convinced he must still be there, partying with his friends, but it was Byron who replied. He told me by the next post that Shelley and his friend had set sail on the 8th as planned.

So began a terrible vigil.

We waited for news.

We scanned the horizon for any sign of the Ariel. We even hired a carriage to take us via land to Byron at Livorno, but all to no purpose.

Finally, they found him, washed ashore, wearing his nankeen breeches, his copy of Keats' poetry, water-stained and damaged, in his pocket.

His face was half-eaten by fish.

The nightmare he had suffered had come true, after all.

The sea had poured in, over the top of the balcony and flooded our house.

It took a while to piece together the truth and all these years later I now know that Percy had headed home on 8th July as promised. The others claimed he was in a hurry to get back to me. They didn't see the dark clouds piling up behind them and when the storm hit, they tried to outrun it. There were no other boats out by that time. They had all headed to the nearest landfall, while Percy and Edward unfurled their heavy sails to full speed, and raced on. The Ariel was too narrow and light a vessel to manage such a weight of cloth. They had misjudged the weather badly and they had misjudged the building of their boat.

"He is gone," Claire wept in my arms. "Percy is gone!"

And as I held my stepsister in my arms, I thought I glimpsed a figure out the corner of my eye. A woman in waterlogged clothes. I recognised her at once.

Harriet came in the end – but not for me, nor for my last surviving child.

She came for Shelley.

That was her revenge.

London, September 1825

Claire and I became close in the immediate aftermath of Shelley's death. I tried to be strong for Jane who, at last, no longer seemed sanguine and indifferent to the possibility of loss and tragedy. She was distraught.

Although, I fancy, not for long.

Claire went to Vienna to live with her brother for a time, and so ended the long years of our meandering adventures together.

We never lived under the same roof again.

All that was past and done with.

It had been a long journey and we had come to the end of it. For better or worse.

I stayed with the Hunts in a great gloomy fortress of a palace in Genoa for a time, but there was a frosty atmosphere between us, although at the time I did not know why. I did not attend Percy's funeral, but let others take over with that. They burned his corpse on the beach where he was found, but the formalities and litigious complications of dealing with foreign officialdom alienated me completely from the process. I was not interested in what they did, or how they marked the occasion, his poet friends.

I would grieve in my own way, with my child in my arms.

I was not aware that they judged me for this, and thought it displayed a lack of feeling – nor that Jane fed them these poisonous lies when my back was turned. Out of my hearing she implied I had been a bad wife to Shelley, that I had continually criticised him and driven him to despair, that I was bad-natured and carping, that I alienated everyone around me.

I said nothing in my defence, for I had no idea that my old friends, Marianne and Leigh Hunt, had believed the rumours or that they judged me in this way.

I did not understand their silences, or their coldness.

That autumn the large villa and its palatial rooms were so cold that little Percy and I ended up huddled next to the fireplace with the Hunts and their children, despite the frostiness in our relations.

The children would gallop through the house, while I sat, stunned, showing little or no emotion – so they thought.

It is my way to bottle things up, to bear the pain.

I am not a creature of hysterics and never will be.

My friends apologised to me eventually for believing Jane's lies and gossip. Years later Leigh and Marianne asked to meet with me and tried to make amends. It was not that I refused to forgive them, but more that I was disappointed in them for turning against me in the first place, and while I understand they made a mistake, an error of judgement, I cannot forget it.

Only one of our group remained loyal to me.

Byron was living in Genoa too, at the time. He kept in touch and helped me make ends meet on occasion, offering me a sum of money to copy and edit his poems. Despite all he did to Claire, and despite the rumours Jane encouraged about me, he never thought ill of me. He remained a loyal friend. I don't know why, but I have always appreciated the kindness.

But he is gone too.

Like all the rest.

In the autumn of 1823 he went on to Greece, to become a soldier and fight for independence, ever the idealist, but he died of a fever in April the following year.

It was August 1825 when I tired of the Hunts and knew it was time to head home.

It was a rough journey by stage coach, trying to keep my young son comfortable – and failing.

It took several days, and we had to stay in cheap inns because there was no money to be had. Sleepless nights spent checking for bedbugs, and waking up to painful sores and scratching.

Shelley's father, Sir Timothy, was not inclined to help his son's widow and grandson, since he deemed I was the woman who had ruined his son's life and reputation in the first place.

I did not tell him what I knew (for it would not have helped matters much) – that Shelley had perhaps succeeded in doing that, all by himself.

London was a different city on my return. Gaslights had appeared on all the streets, and where once the neighbourhoods had been dark and empty as soon as dusk fell, now they were aglow with an eerie sulphurous light. Factories sprang up: tall chimneys burned against the sky and noisy mills rumbled like thunder in the distance.

I was not sure that I liked the change.

Some said it was exciting, that Progress was on the march, but I couldn't help remembering that flowering meadow where my mother lay and the lanes I had walked to get there.

There seemed less birdsong, and the air tasted different.

Soot began to plume in the sky, black clouds of it over London and other industrial centres where people swarmed to find work and employment.

Was it a good thing?

"It's progress, Mary. Science," Godwin told me.

"Do you really think it's progress, Father?"

I met up with Godwin and my half-brother, William, on my arrival in London. Mary-Jane did not come to meet me, but that was to be expected. She lived in a depleted household now, and no doubt she still blamed me for Claire's defection and Fanny's suicide.

Claire would never come back to Skinner Street and her mother knew it.

I felt sorry for Mary-Jane to some extent, when I had time to consider it.

I found cheap lodgings in London, not far from my father's house.

Godwin and I went by landau one night, to the opening performance of a play. Nothing so remarkable about that, you might think, other than the fact my father and I had not spoken to one another for so many years.

The play being performed was based on a book.

My book.

Frankenstein. The Modern Prometheus.

No one had asked my permission to perform it, and no one needed to. I would not earn a penny from the production – more's to the pity, as I could sorely have done with it.

We went out of curiosity.

A small crowd of protestors were gathered outside the theatre, with placards, declaring the content of the play to be obscene and ungodly, blasphemous and shocking, particularly considering it had flowed from the pen of a woman. A nineteen-year-old girl, no less.

We walked past them and no one knew me.

We took our places in the auditorium.

As I sat there in the glow of the gaslights, gazing around at the tiered seating, at the row upon row of eager faces, I confess

I felt proud. The curtain was raised and the auditorium fell silent.

I saw rapture on those faces, an intensity of pleasure and pain which made me feel like Frankenstein himself, a person with too much power – and oh, the thrill of that feeling, to be so powerful, to wield so much influence… in a life where I had always felt powerless.

I had a voice. And if it made them angry, did I care?

But no one knew me.

I sat in that audience, beside my father, knowing he was proud of me at last, and no one guessed that the monster and the scientist who played out their drama on that stage were my invention. They had crept out of the darkness of my own imagination.

"Well, Mary, what did you think?" Godwin asked me in the landau on our way back to Skinner Street.

I waited a beat or two.

"I think they should have asked my permission and paid me before performing it." There was a short silence. "Percy and I could do with the money."

Godwin smiled. "You are your father's daughter, I have to say."

That comment I did not like so much. I remembered how Father spent most of my childhood complaining of his debts, and begging Shelley and I to save him from debtors' prison.

Still, I tried to smile, because we were enjoying a period of harmony, and it seemed wise to let it pass.

Putney, February 1839

I woke late this morning, for I was up most of the night sorting through Shelley's papers. It's painful to know the truth. He was unfaithful to me often, even if only in his heart rather than in the flesh. But I am not here to argue with the dead. I am here to resurrect Shelley's poetry, to ensure that it is not forgotten, and to be paid for my efforts.

Percy and I both need the money.

I no longer inhabit palatial rooms in grand marble villas on the continent. I am no longer the bride of a baronet.

I am Mary Shelley, daughter of Mary Wollstonecraft who once tried to change the way the world thinks about women. It made no difference. They forgot her.

They will forget me too, I have no doubt, once the first shock of my 'monstrous tale' fades, but I will not let them forget my husband or his poetry.

I am still dozing when Lizzie appears, all wrapped up in shawls against the bitter cold.

"At least it has stopped snowing," she tells me. "How is your headache?"

"Much better, thank you," I lie.

A night spent sorting through the past has done nothing to help it.

The fire has gone out, and she lights it for me. We are both glad of the warmth.

"I shall look forward to Percy's visit from Cambridge soon," I tell her. "In a week or so, when the thaw arrives."

"We shall all look forward to the thaw, Mrs Shelley," Lizzie says.

I catch her staring at the mass of papers littering the table.

"Don't worry, Lizzie. You can leave those. I haven't finished with them yet."

Her hand lingers on the volume of poetry we were reading yesterday.

"Will we be reading again, Mrs Shelley?" she asks.

"Of course…"

"Only if there's time," she adds tentatively.

"There is always time, Lizzie," I tell her, even though I know it is not true.

It runs like sand through the hour-glass for me and for Lizzie. And even as I think these thoughts, I see before me the silent figures of my little William and baby Clara, Shelley and Byron, and my poor sister Fanny – all of whom are lost to me.

Then I hear the faint drip drip drip of a river-swollen corpse and I know that she is here again.

The one I never speak of.

Don't turn around, I whisper, but Lizzie does not hear me.

Why should she?

Young and innocent as she is, she has no need to fear the corpse of a woman who is not even there.